Life's Work

By the same author

THE LIME PIT
FINAL NOTICE
DEAD LETTER
DAY OF WRATH
NATURAL CAUSES

JONATHAN VALIN

Life's Work

DELACORTE PRESS/NEW YORK

Published by Delacorte Press
1 Dag Hammarskjold Plaza
New York, N.Y. 10017

Manufactured in the United States of America
First printing

Library of Congress Cataloging in Publication Data

Valin, Jonathan.
Life's work.

I. Title.
PS3572.A4125L5   1986   813'.54
ISBN 0-385-29503-0
Library of Congress Catalog Card Number: 86-2055

To Katherine, as always,
and to Kim

Life's Work

I

Hugh Petrie didn't have the sort of office that an executive of the Cincinnati Cougars should have had. There was a regulation NFL football sitting on the couch like a big brown button, but the couch was covered in satin and the rug beneath it was a genuine kilim in pale rose. There were framed eight-by-tens on the wall, autographed portraits of famous athletes. But there was also a small photo of Jonathan Winters dressed as Maud Frickert on the corner of a chrome and glass desk, and a tryptich of the Three Stooges by the louvered windows. None of this would have been unusual in a different office; only the men who ran this business weren't noted for their sense of fun or style. They were dour La Jolla Republicans, at home at Pebble Beach, playing skins with oil money, insurance company executives, and other NFL owners. That wasn't a Three Stooges foursome. At least, it wasn't supposed to be. Sitting on the couch in the soft yellow glow of a baby spot, listening to a grandfather clock smack its lips in the corner, and staring at Curly's mad grin on one wall and Dick Butkus's even madder one on another, I could see a pattern. It just wasn't the pattern I'd expected.

I contemplated the meaning of the room for a few minutes, then the door opened and Hugh Petrie stepped in.

"Thanks for coming, Stoner," he said, without giving me much of a look. He walked over to the desk, sat down in a high-backed leather chair, and swiped at a paper clip as if he were swatting a fly.

Like the office, Petrie wasn't what I'd expected in football management fashion. He should have been going to fat, potbellied, and bearded with extra chins like a middle-aged high school gym coach. But under the sports coat he was bigger, more muscular, and in better shape than some of his players. Bald on top, gray as flannel on the sides, his skull curved like a helmet above his deep-set blue eyes. His lower face fit into that helmet like a hardwood dowel driven in by a hammer. He looked to be about forty-five, square-jawed, steely-eyed, tough.

"Tell me all you know about football," Petrie said, peering out at me from beneath his helmetlike brow.

"I like to watch it," I said. "I used to like to play it."

"You used to play?"

"In college. I had a dream about being drafted by the pros. But the war came along. After that, playing football didn't seem that important to me."

Petrie nodded mechanically, as if my opinion wasn't all that important to him. "You know anybody on the squad?"

"No."

He sighed. "It would be better if you were closer to the game. The men you'll be dealing with are a tight-knit bunch."

"I can make my own way," I said.

He looked unimpressed. "These guys aren't ordinary people."

"They've got more muscle," I said, trying to sound unimpressed myself. "And better reflexes."

"They're genetic freaks," Petrie said flatly.

"That's one way of putting it."

"Don't kid yourself," he said. "It's the only way of putting it. They're winners in a genetic crapshoot, pure and simple. Somewhere in the past there was another freak in the family, a man who was bigger and stronger and quicker than other men. He didn't earn that distinction any more than they have. He was blessed with it. Don't forget that, Stoner. No matter what you hear about how unfairly we treat them, these guys are the lucky ones. They were lucky from the start."

He sounded bitter about their chemistry, but then I guessed he hadn't figured that those select strands of DNA would also be programmed to hire agents or to demand the renegotiation of contracts. Or to snort cocaine and get caught doing it, like Carl Monroe, Nate Calhoun, and Jack Greene had done. Several months before the start of training camp, Monroe, Calhoun, and Greene had been caught in a DEA sting operation. In exchange for immunity against prosecution, they'd testified before a grand jury. All three admitted to purchasing cocaine from a Bellevue fireman named Tate. Tate got twenty years in Mansfield, and the football players got slapped on their wrists. They'd drawn the usual stiff sentences meted out to athletes—the grand jury had ordered them to spend six months counseling "troubled youths." And it had looked like it was going to end there, until the league put its foot down and suspended all three for the remainder of training camp and the first five games of the regular season. I thought perhaps that was why I'd been called in—to keep an eye on them for the

Cougars until the suspensions were lifted. But I thought wrong.

"I guess you know who Billy Parks is," Petrie said.

I nodded. "Who doesn't? He's the nose guard on your football team."

"Nose guard," Petrie said dully and laughed, way back in his throat.

"If you think you've got another cocaine problem here," I said warily, "I'm the wrong guy for the job. You'd be better off contacting the league or the DEA."

"We're not sure what Bill's problem is," Petrie said.

"Have you tried asking him?"

"We can't ask him. He left camp three days ago, and nobody knows where he's gone. Or at least nobody's saying. Not his family. Not his neighbors. Not his friends. Of course, we've tried contacting him at home. And at his parents' home. But we've had no luck at all. Even his so-called agent isn't talking."

"Has he done this sort of thing before?" I asked.

"He wouldn't be on the team if he had."

"Then why do you want him back?"

"I *don't* want him back," Petrie said bluntly. "But the general feeling among the coaches is, with Carl, Nate, and Jack suspended until the sixth week of the season, we can't afford to lose another veteran player."

"You could probably save yourself my fee by just sitting tight," I said. "He'll come home eventually. It seems like they always do."

Petrie shook his head. "I can't run a business by 'sitting tight.' And there are only four more weeks of training camp left before it starts."

"The season?" I said.

Petrie nodded and stared past me, with a fierce, vigilant look on his face, as if he could already see it formulating itself in some recess of that odd showpiece of a room—the season, the cloud banks, the unpredictable weather of the next sixteen weeks. For just a moment, he almost looked frightened. Then he sloughed off his mood and refocused his eyes on me.

"We've had a contract dispute with Bill," he said in a businesslike voice, "which may be the reason for the walkout. But we can't find out unless we talk to him. And we can't talk to him unless we know where he is. He also has some personal problems that may have a bearing on this situation."

"What kind of problems?" I said.

Petrie fished through the top drawer of his desk and pulled out a manila folder. He eyed it with distaste and tossed it over to me. "Take a look," he said.

I picked the folder up and glanced through the Xeroxes inside. They were copies of arrest reports filed against Billy Parks, all-pro. There were four different cases, the earliest dating back to 1978, the latest in January of this year. All four arrests were made for assault and battery. All four victims had been young women. Photostatic snapshots of the ladies were attached to the report. It was difficult to tell from the snapshots, but the women looked badly beaten up, especially the last one, a pretty girl with blond hair. Both of her eyes had been blackened, her lower lip was split, and there were wads of stained cotton in her nostrils. She stared indignantly into the camera, as if the cops were taking a mug shot rather than an evidentiary photo. I searched through the report and found her name. Candy Kane. Her profession was listed as "dancer." Probably a stripper, judging from the stage name. Her address was the Caesar Apartments in Clifton.

I put the folder back on the desk and looked up at Petrie. He was trying to force a smile, only it didn't wash as a smile. It was a grimace, a look of utter embarrassment, as if he held himself responsible for what I'd seen under this particular rock.

"On average, they make about a million and a half dollars over their careers," he said, with that sick, incredulous smile on his face. "Enough to buy a house, to take care of their parents, to start a family, to prepare for their life's work . . ." His voice died off and his mouth shut abruptly, like a puppet's.

"There are good and bad in any profession," I said.

"I'm not *in* any profession," Petrie said with so much indignation that he impressed me.

Of course, I reminded myself, his indignation wasn't completely righteous. It was just good business to expect his players to plan for a life ahead. It made it easier to justify cutting them when they grew old and tired. And it was good business to become outraged when they did something like what Parks had done. It confirmed the somewhat convenient belief that if it weren't for a genetic accident they wouldn't have deserved a break in the first place. But practical considerations aside, there was a part of me that had been struck just as speechless as he had by those photographs—a part that was just as indignant as he seemed to be. I didn't own a football team, but I held a rooting interest. And while I'd never bought the crap about football players being models for youth— pillars of a society, that would be pretty damn strange, if you thought about it—I didn't believe that they should beat up young women and get away with it, either.

"Didn't any of these ladies file charges against Parks?" I asked.

Petrie shook his head. "The first three cases were settled out of court or dropped outright. In the most recent one, the girl didn't want to prosecute, but the cops filed for her." He laughed grimly. "I guess even the police have had their fill of Billy at this point."

I flipped the folder open and took another look at the rap sheet. It was pretty skeletal, even by a beat cop's standards. In fact, all that was indicated was that the arresting officer, a Sergeant Phil Clayton, had been summoned to the girl's apartment on the evening of December 31 of this past year. Parks had been arrested there on an assault charge, booked, and released on bond the same night. There was no indication of who had filed the complaint or who had pressed the assault charge against Parks. I studied the girl's battered face. That was why she'd looked so disgusted. She'd wanted to take her beating and forget about it, but the cops wouldn't let her do it. They must have talked her into cooperating. Either that or they had an eyewitness to the beating. Otherwise, I couldn't see how they could prosecute the case.

"When is Parks supposed to go on trial?" I asked.

"At the end of training camp. The police gave Billy that much leeway."

"There are four weeks of training camp left. If the trial is the reason he skipped camp, why would he do it now?"

"We just don't know," Petrie said.

I closed the folder and told him, "I'll take the case."

"Good. Find Parks and get back in touch. We'll handle it from there."

"I'll want to talk to some of the players."

"We'll take care of it," he said. "But do it quietly. They're still in training, and we want to maintain a semblance of order, if that's still possible after what we've been through."

"Is there any one player Parks was particularly close to?"

"He's roomed with Otto Bluerock for the last four years."

"Could you arrange a meeting with him? Today, if possible."

Petrie nodded. "You ought to know that Otto isn't the most easygoing guy in the world."

"Tough?"

Petrie smiled as if I'd named one of his children. "As

store-bought nails. Plus he's got a little something extra to be steamed about."

"What's that?"

"We're going to cut him tomorrow," Petrie said mildly. "And he knows it."

II

Petrie let me take the folder with me when I left, along
with an autographed portrait of everybody's hero—Bill
Parks. He'd been a rock during the Super Bowl year, an
all-pro who'd deserved the honor. He'd been off his form
in 1984 and 1985, but so had the team. At twenty-nine,
with a new season coming up, he should have been at the
top of his game, peaking as an athlete and a player.

I studied his picture when I got out to the Stadium lot.
I wasn't used to seeing him without the gridwork of a
face mask, and he looked older than I'd expected. Pros
are funny that way. Some of them always look like brood-
ing Pillsbury Doughboys and some of them look wizened
from the start—middle-aged and beaten down, as if
they'd never known what it was like to be young. Thinking back, I didn't remember Parks as one of the young–
old man types. He'd been one of the Doughboys, the
kind with huge arms and a huge chest and a face so fat
and featureless that he didn't seem to have a pair of eyes
—just a black crease between nose and brow. Eight years

of pro football had changed that. He still had a brow like a rolled roast, and his arms, neck, and chest were enormous. But the crease had opened up, the jaw had sagged, the chin looked misshapen, and the fat had hardened and cracked, leaving a netting of wrinkles around the mouth and eyes. His curly red hair had begun to thin at the temples, receding on either side of a V-shaped forelock. In the photograph, he looked ten years older than twenty-nine. He also looked crazy.

He may have looked that way all along. It was hard for me to tell, because I'd never been able to see his eyes before. But there were hospital corridors in these baby blues—the zapped, deadened stare of psychopathy. Of course, he was wearing his game face, like they all do for those pictures, and that contributed to his look of smoldering madness. And I did have those four Xeroxes in hand. But even if I hadn't seen the arrest reports, I knew at once that this was not the sort of man I wanted to tangle with. This was not the sort of man I wanted to know at all. And yet I'd volunteered to find him in a momentary dudgeon.

I took another look at Billy Parks's mad eyes and slapped myself on the back. Good going, Harry.

At four o'clock that afternoon, I drove out to Bloomington, Ohio—the little college town northeast of the city where the Cougars hold their annual training camps. The story went that Carl Lovelle, the patriarch of the Cougars and Hugh Petrie's boss, had played basketball in Bloomington when he was a kid and had been so impressed with the town that he'd made a point of coming back yearly and of bringing his football team with him. For six weeks every summer, the Cougars' players and coaches roomed in the Bloomington College dorms and practiced on the college's football field.

I'd never seen the place before, but after I'd spent an

hour driving through sun-stricken cornfields and desert turnip patches, it came as a welcome sight. The state road I was on turned to trees and white slat porches about a mile outside the city and continued to run green and parklike through the suburbs, right up to the downtown blocks. Bloomington proper had the patchwork look of any small country town—circa nineteen-eighty-five—a crazy quilt of old-fashioned wooden storefronts, somber brick WPA projects, dusty brown grain elevators, and red-roofed McDonald's, all rubbing shoulders on the same street corners.

The college was located on the north side of the city, where the streets grew green again with oaks and sycamores. It was a tiny campus, a handful of Greek Revival buildings on a lawn. I followed road signs to the dormitories, which were situated on a rise overlooking the football field, and parked in one of the dorm lots. There were plenty of other cars around, but no other people on the tarmac or the sidewalks leading to the big concrete dorms. The people were down at the stadium, a sizeable crowd of them, sitting in the skeletal aluminum stands watching the Cougars run through their afternoon workout.

From the rise, I could see the players assembled in rows in the center of the field. They were doing calisthenics—squats, thrusts, head rolls. They barked out their counts in unison and applauded wildly at the end of each exercise. Considering the fact that over half of them weren't going to make it through the next few weeks and that fifty more had already been cut, and that it was better than a hundred degrees on the grass, that applause sounded as thin as forced laughter from where I was standing. The coaches posted like guards in the tall aluminum watchtowers flanking either goalpost made the scene seem even more like a pep rally in a prison yard.

I watched for another minute then walked up to the deserted dorm complex. Bluerock had been told to skip practice in order to talk to me. He was supposed to be waiting in one of the basement rooms that the coaches used for offices. I found the right room fairly quickly, but I didn't find Bluerock inside—just a desk and a chair and a little piece of sunlight that had fallen through an open window and flattened itself on the concrete floor.

I thought I might have gotten the room numbers mixed up, so I rattled a few other doorknobs on the basement floor. When no one answered, I walked upstairs, looking for someone who could tell me what had become of Otto. A transistor radio had been left on in one of the rooms on the ground floor. I followed its tinny voice down the hall to an open door by the fire exit.

A man was lying on a single bed inside the room. He was wearing khaki shorts, sneakers, and a gray sweatshirt that had ridden up his fat belly. I couldn't see his face because he was holding a comic book in front of it. On a nightstand by the bed the transistor radio was playing "Stand by Your Man." The man tapped his sneakered foot against the air in time to the music, and when Tammy broke into the refrain, he joined in loudly in a froggy bass. I let him finish the song then knocked on the doorframe.

"What can I do for you?" he said, without lowering the comic book.

"I'm trying to find Otto Bluerock. Know where he is?"

The man on the bed dropped the comic to his chest and lunged forward, pulling himself upright with a jerk. It was a little like having a bulldog lunge at me. He had that kind of face—fierce, square-jawed, with a scowling, jowly mouth, heavy-lidded gray eyes, and a knobby, puckered brow. His brown hair was cut very short, dipping down his forehead in a broad U. His upper body was enormous—duckpin arms, barrel chest, neck like a steel truss. Only the gut betrayed his lack of conditioning. It gathered above his thighs like a loose undershirt.

"Otto Bluerock?" he said in a deep suspicious voice. "Who's looking for him?"

"Harry Stoner."

The man swung his legs onto the floor. His knees were heavily scarred. Keloid zippers, the kind that come from reconstructive surgery. He pressed his palms on top of them, as if he were testing the seams, and slowly got to his feet. He was a good six three. My height, but fifty pounds of fat and muscle heavier.

"I'm Bluerock," he said, holding out a hand.

I shook with him and winced. Bluerock had a grip like a trash compactor.

"Take it easy!" I said.

He dropped my hand as if it were infected and gave me a contemptuous look. "If I were you, sport, I'd work on that handshake some. Do some curls, for chrissake. You don't want people thinking you're a fag, do you?"

"I didn't know it was a contest," I said, although I wanted to punch him in the mouth. I was better than forty years old, in reasonable shape, and fairly mature about most matters; but for some stupid reason, getting beaten to the draw by this ox made me feel like I was sixteen again.

"Didn't know it was a contest?" Bluerock said with a dismissive sneer. "Now how the hell could a man not know that?"

Staring at Bluerock's surly face, I suddenly realized why he'd made me feel like I was back in high school. I'd met him before—in every gym class I'd ever been in. He was the joker who liked to snap towels at your ass in the locker room and to beat up the Jews and niggers on the playing field. I used to wonder what happened to assholes like him once they got out into the real world. Now I knew. They grew up to become pro football players.

For a guy with a very cold future staring him in the face come Friday, Otto Bluerock seemed pretty goddamn loose.

"So you're the one they're sending after Billy?" he said, giving me another cold sizing up. "Jeez, I hope you've got your Blue Cross paid up, fella."

"You figure there's going to be trouble, huh?"

"Naw. Billy likes fags in sports coats." He sat back down on the mattress, which sang out in distress under his weight. "Pull up a chair, sport."

There were no chairs in the room. I leaned against the doorjamb.

"Shoot away," Bluerock said. "All I got is time."

"The rest of your life, from what I hear." I said it to pay him back for the handshake and the ragging. And to my surprise, it got to him. Just a little, just for a second. His eyes went wide, then closed to slits.

"Funny man," he said under his breath.

My business sense got the better of my adolescent streak. After all, I had to talk to the man, or get him to talk to me. "Forget I said that," I told him.

He grunted. "Why? Everybody's got to quit some day. Tomorrow's my day. That's all. Time to get on with my life's work." He said the last part mockingly, as if the phrase "life's work" were a familiar cliché in his world. "I had eleven good seasons. That's more than most."

"I guess so."

"What do you know? You're a fucking civilian."

He had a point. He hadn't gotten those scars on his knees snapping towels at people's asses. Or the scar that ran through his right brow. Or the flabby, flattened nose that comes when they take the cartilage out when the nose has been broken too many times to repair. He'd paid his dues, all right. So had I. But now wasn't the time to say so.

A big cheer went up from somewhere down on the football field. Bluerock flinched.

"Sounds like they're done," he said. He looked around the barren room and stood up. "What say we get out of here, sport? I feel like hoisting a few."

He didn't wait for an answer. Just clicked off the radio and brushed past me out the door.

III

We went to a bar in a bowling alley on the north side of town. Bluerock told me how to get there, and that was all he had to say until we'd gotten inside the building, past the inevitable glass case with the register on top and the bowling ball and tinned plastic trophies on display, and settled in a "lounge" with a commanding view of alleys 1 through 10. The fact that I knew that he was going to be cut had apparently nicked Bluerock's pride more deeply than I'd thought. Or maybe he'd suddenly realized that a lot of other people were bound to find out.

I didn't feel particularly sorry for him. He was a bully, and like all bullies he was easy to hurt and quick to pity himself. But I could appreciate how strange it had to feel, after eleven seasons, to come to the end of the road. A road that had ended not because he'd wanted it to, but because someone else had decided that he couldn't hack it anymore, that it was time for him to get on with his "life's work."

We were sitting in the lounge, drinking beer. Below us

the bowlers made a thick, explosive racket. Bluerock's bulldog face grew grimmer with each pitcher. He began to look like a man aching for a fight. Like Parks had looked in that picture. He also got more sentimental, more self-righteous, and oddly, more articulate with each beer. I knew that he was going to explode before the night was out, possibly in my direction. A smart man would have left him to his booze and his furies. But I wanted to hear about Parks. And some kindred part of me didn't think he should be drinking alone—perhaps the same part that had wanted to punch him out twenty minutes before.

"You know why they hired you, don't you?" he said, after he'd downed the first four glasses of beer very quickly.

"To find Parks."

"Bullshit," Bluerock said. "They hired you to get rid of him, man. To nail his ass to the wall. They've been dying to unload him for a long time."

"Why?"

"His agent. They don't like his agent. Plus Bill's had some problems."

"Like what?"

He laughed. "Like you don't already know, huh?"

"I know about the girls he beat up, yeah."

Bluerock stared somberly into his beer glass. "Some of those bimbos were looking to get hurt."

"Like Candy Kane?" I asked.

He didn't answer me right away.

"What do you know about football players?" Bluerock finally said. "All you see are those media whores on TV. The ones who make careers out of proving how deep and sensitive they really are. Football's war, for chrissake! What else could you call it, when the object is to go out there and beat the other guy into the ground, to bury him under the turf? Before he sold out on TV, Dick

Butkus was a vicious, violent son-of-a-bitch. Now he gets dressed up in a monkey suit and acts cute and dopey and everybody thinks that's what he was like all along—that he really was this sweet, funny guy underneath. Well, let me tell you something. You're not one guy on the football field and another fucking thing off it, no matter how it looks on TV. Guys like Butkus and guys like Bill Parks aren't putting on an act out there, sport. They're not playing the game for your entertainment. It isn't a game to them at all. You're seeing who they really are when they belt some guy so hard that he has to be carried off the field on a stretcher. And I'll tell you something else— you're loving it. You're screaming your goddamn head off. 'Kill him! Kill the fucker!' But when Bill knocks some faggot on his ass in a bar or punches out some whore who tries to stiff him, suddenly it isn't such a terrific thing. Right? Suddenly, he's a sick guy."

"So if you're tough, it's okay to beat up women," I said.

Bluerock glared at me. "You're not fucking listening to me, pal. I'm wasting my breath on you. Nobody I know gives a shit whether you think what they do is okay or not. I'm telling you about a game that doesn't stop when you step off the field or when they tell you not to bother to show up at practice anymore. I'm talking about what it's like to be a player, man. You know? A player."

"I'm listening," I told him, although I could see that it was too late for conciliation. The beer had caught up with him and he was ready to explode.

"The hell you are," he said, throwing his right hand dangerously close to my jaw. "Nobody's listening. Nobody ever does. All they do is tell you things, and all they've got to say, from the moment you first suit up to the moment it's over, is bullshit. Bullshit!"

"Take it easy," I said.

"You take it easy, motherfucker." He poured another

glass of beer and gave me a look that was nothing less than a threat—a naked dare to open my mouth again. I used common sense and clammed up.

"Bullshit!" he said again, and gave me another red-eyed, ferocious look. "You want to hear about Bill Parks?" he said, swallowing the beer in one gulp. "I'll tell you about Bill Parks. I'll explain it so even an asshole like you can understand." He slammed the beer glass down, leaned across the table, and stared fiercely into my eyes. "Between the white lines, they tell him, 'Be an animal. Be hard. Be tough. Don't give any quarter. If you got your foot on somebody's neck, don't let up. Keep the pressure on until you hear the bones break. 'Cause in this world you're either a heel or a neck. And heel is better.' Coach drums it into him, Dad drums it into him—his mom, his girl. They all expect him to be a killer on the field. Now, they don't think about where all that violence is coming from—what it has to do with him as a person. Or with them. They just like to see it happen. They like to watch it come out in the open and run around loose for a couple of hours. But off the field it's a different story. Christ, is it different!

"Off the field, they say, 'Be Mr. all-American. Be the gentle giant. Don't get mad, don't use your edge, because after all, you're bigger than other people, and somebody might get hurt.' " Bluerock snorted with disgust. "You hear what I'm saying? You're supposed to be able to turn it on and off at will—to be a killer and a well-rounded individual at the same time. To be a warrior and a wimp. *Like it's all make-believe, for chrissake! Like it has nothing to do with real life!*" He threw himself back in his chair so violently that he almost tipped it over. "It's a fucking impossible lie! And that's Bill Parks's problem, sport. That's all there is to it. Not the bimbos. He just couldn't turn the game off like he was supposed to do. He couldn't stop being a player. Understand?" He didn't wait for an answer. "No, you don't understand. You can't. You're not one of us."

We sat in silence, drinking beer, for another half hour or so. By then several more Cougars had come into the lounge, to down a few quick ones before lights out. A couple of players looked as if they wanted to talk to Bluerock, but Otto ignored them. He was in a world of his own now, and I guessed he was trying to get used to it.

Around seven, a tall kid with the physique of a body-builder walked into the bar, spotted Bluerock, and came over to the table. He had the kind of face that Parks had had when he was his age—big brow, nose like a gherkin, a crevice for eyes, and a baby's thick, flared, crimson lips. He was wearing a muscle shirt with "Property of Cougars" printed on it, and he sauntered as if he figured that everyone in the world would be watching him. He did have quite a set of arms—big-veined, massive, with huge squared-off biceps and forearms so hard and well-defined that the skin looked as if it had been flayed away, like drawings in an anatomy book. Bluerock was as big as this kid, but in no where near the same kind of condition.

"Missed you at practice, Blue," the kid said, in a needling voice.

Bluerock looked up from his glass balefully. "You know," he said to me, "it's not often in life that you get to meet your own doom. But there he is, in the flesh. Number Double Zero. My replacement." He waved a hand in the kid's direction. "The funny thing is that the *putz* looks just like I used to look."

"You didn't call me a *putz*," the kid said lazily. He looked at me. "He didn't call me a *putz*, did he?"

I stared back at the kid. He was enjoying himself at Bluerock's expense, which was pretty stupid under the circumstances. I fully expected Otto to punch his lights out.

"Careful," the kid said when Bluerock lifted his beer glass to his lips. "You'll get some in your mouth."

Bluerock put the beer glass down on the table daintily and sighed. "Did Professor Walt send you over to check up on us, Fred? Is that the deal? Or did you do a little too much juice tonight? You feeling studdy, Fred?" Bluerock blew him a kiss.

Fred grinned at me. "You shouldn't believe everything he says, mister. He's a terrible liar. He was a shitty football player too. All mouth."

"Get lost, Freddy," Bluerock said dully.

"Sure, Blue," Fred said. "You have a nice life, hear?" He laughed loudly and walked away.

I watched the kid saunter out of the bar, then turned to Bluerock. "What's his problem?"

Bluerock smiled icily. "His problem is that he's twenty-three years old and he thinks he's going to stay that way forever." The smile disappeared. "I hit him a little harder than I should have the other day in practice. Knocked him on his can. It's one thing to get beat, another to get knocked off your feet. Especially to a guy like him."

"What's so special about him?"

Bluerock stirred in his chair. "Maybe I'll tell you about it on the way downtown."

"We're going downtown?"

Bluerock got up and headed toward the exit.

"I guess we are," I said to myself.

IV

Halfway back to Cincinnati I stopped at a roadside bar to let Bluerock buy a quart of Scotch. As soon as he got back in the car, he cracked the bottle open and took a long drink. I started the Pinto up and eased back onto the highway. I wasn't sure where we were headed. I hoped we'd end up somewhere near Bill Parks, but that was up to Bluerock. It was his night to howl, even though I'd become part of it. Hell, I'd made myself part of it, boosting him to beers and encouraging him to talk about his career. Now I felt obliged to live the rest of the night out with him—no matter where he led me. Such is the vanity of a drunken, middle-aged fan.

"It's been a long time since I got really loaded," Bluerock said, handing the bottle to me.

I took a drink and gave it back to him.

"I used to like booze," he said, as he polished the spout on the palm of his hand. "But you give up a lot of things along the way." He tipped the bottle to his lips and took another swallow. "Last good fight I got into was in a bar. A bar in Madison, Wisconsin."

"What was it about?"

He looked at me blankly. "Huh?"

"The fight," I said. "What was it about?"

"It wasn't *about* anything," Bluerock said, as if the question made no sense. "There were just a bunch of us in a bar and somebody started throwing furniture around. Before it was over, we'd torn the place apart. Broken chairs, broken tables, broken glasses. Everybody lying on the floor groaning. Just like in a western. I mean, we leveled the joint. You know what the best part was?"

He straightened up in the seat and rocked forward, as if recalling the story had made him feel alive again. "The guy who owns the place comes out from behind the bar, looks at the mess, and starts to whoop. 'Boys,' he says, 'I've been waiting all my life for a fight like this to break out in my place. And I want to thank you for it. Tonight, you've made an old man's dream come true.' The son-of-a-bitch was genuinely grateful! I'm not kidding, sport. He was beside himself. He even bought us all one for the road!"

I started to laugh. So did Bluerock. We were both pretty drunk, so we laughed for a while. The laughter died out all at once, as it will when you're loaded, and we spent a few minutes mourning it—and the passing of all fellow feeling—in silence.

"Liquor's been a part of every good time I've ever had," Bluerock said suddenly. "Now what the hell does that mean?"

"I don't know," I said.

"Let me give you a f'rinstance. I spent two seasons in Canada, before they called me down to the NFL. Things were a lot looser up there. First day of practice, we get out on the field, and we're running wind sprints or something. And I happen to notice this big cooler sitting by the bench. So I ask one of the veterans what it's for. He just smiles and says, 'You'll see when we're through.' I don't think much of it. We work out—hard. And when we're done, we gather around the bench, and I'm waiting for the lecture on slipping a block or the team prayer or whatever the fuck they do in Canada. Then I realize that everybody's lined up in front of this cooler. I wait my turn, not knowing what to expect. Get to the head of the line. You know what they're handing out?"

"Nope."

"Beer!" Bluerock said with enormous satisfaction. "Not Coke or Gatorade, but beer! Do you know how that felt, sport? I was just a kid, twenty-one years old. And up till then, nobody'd done anything but tell me what *not* to do. I get to Canada, run through my first workout, and there's a cold bottle of beer waiting for me when it's over —just like I'd done a day's work! 'Blue,' I said to myself, 'you finally made it. You're finally a man.' And that's the way it felt, too."

Bluerock leaned back in the seat, shutting his eyes and hugging the bottle to his chest. "Good story, huh?" he said.

"Great story," I said.

He laughed. "Where are we? Are we in town yet?"

"Not quite."

"Well, wake me when we get there. I want to go to the Waterhole. See if I can find Wild Bill."

For a second I couldn't place the name. "You mean Parks?" I said.

"Yeah," he said. "Let's go talk to Wild Bill. I miss the son-of-a-bitch."

The Waterhole was one of a number of nightclubs located on Front Street, near the Stadium. Like the others, it catered to blue-collar money. Plumbers, carpenters, hard hats. Guys who didn't mind spending the extra dollar for a drink or a toot if they got their vanities patted down by good-looking women in leotards and got to rub shoulders with jocks. A lot of the players hung out there during the season. After all, they were blue-collar workers too. They were suckers for the same thin mix of class and cleavage. Plus, they got their backs slapped, got their drinks taken care of, and got their choice of the girls who worked there. It didn't seem like Otto Bluerock's kind of place. It certainly wasn't mine. But Bill Parks apparently liked it there, so that's where we went.

I parked the Pinto in a little lot underneath the L&N bridge, and Bluerock and I stumbled out of the car and up to the club. From the outside the Waterhole looked like a collision between a family restaurant and a riverboat. Half of it was quaint white brick house, with trellises and vines snaking up its sides. The other half was scuppered, portholed, streamlined metal.

"It's like a theme park without a theme," I said.

Bluerock laughed and said, "Oh, it's got a theme, all right. Wait till you get inside."

There was a canopied entryway in front of the brick part, with a doorman standing beneath it. He had on red livery and a black billycock hat, but inside the uniform he was the same sleazy guy who stands beside the sandwich sign yelling, "Girls, girls, girls!"

"Where's Bill?" Bluerock roared at him.

The doorman laughed nervously. "Bill who?"

" 'Bill who?' " Bluerock mocked. "Bill Parks, you weasel-faced bastard."

"I haven't seen him, sir," the doorman said. "He hasn't been around in several months."

"Balls!" Bluerock said, and pushed past him through a metalized swinging door into the club.

The doorman, who'd been intimidated by Bluerock's size and bulldog face, wasn't so intimidated by me. "We don't like noisy drunks around here," he said.

"Tell *him,*" I said.

"You tell him," the doorman said in a nasty voice. "We run a nice clean place."

"Sure, you do," I said.

I followed Bluerock through the door into the night-club. It was so dark inside that I had to stand still for a moment, eyes shut, in order to dark-adapt, and at that, the only things I could make out clearly were the burnished hardwood dance floor and the bar, which was glowing like an aquarium on the far side of the room. I walked toward it, feeling my way with my hands and brushing into a few startled customers sitting at the tables scattered around the dance floor. As soon as I got close enough, I grabbed for the bar, sat down on a chrome stool, and looked around for Otto. It was hard to believe, considering his size, but Bluerock had vanished. I started to get up again when they turned the music on —a blast of Prince that hit me like a feather boa with a length of lead pipe in it and knocked me right back onto the stool. As soon as the noise started, couples began to file onto the dance floor. Someone turned on the strobes and lasers. Within a few seconds, all I could see was a tangle of flashlit limbs and leering faces. I turned back to the bar, where a big bartender in a black bow tie, diamond vest, and white shirt with garters on the puffed-up sleeves leaned over to get my order. I couldn't quite figure out how the western outfit fit in with the hi-tech look of the rest of the club. I thought maybe it was the Waterhole's bow to tradition, like that first dollar bill framed above the bar. The music was so loud that the bartender couldn't hear me when I said, "Scotch." He moved his mouth again and made a questioning face.

"He wants to know what you want to drink," someone said close to my ear.

I looked around. A pretty blond in a black tube top,

designer jeans, and red pumps had seated herself on the stool beside me.

"I know what he wants," I yelled at her. "I just can't make him understand."

"Tell me!" she shouted back, pointing to her chest.

I laughed. "Scotch up."

"Scotch up," she shouted at the bartender, who nodded serenely and walked away.

"I'll be damned," I said.

The girl grinned. She was very pretty and very young —no more than twenty-one or twenty-two—with short, shaggy ash-blond hair cut in a punk style, and a gamine's angular hollow-cheeked face. She'd made up heavily, mouth as red as cut strawberries and eyes blackened with mascara. Two spots of rouge glowed on either cheek, giving her a pert and vaguely doll-like look. It was hard to tell over the roar, but her voice had sounded Kentuckian.

"Thanks for the help," I said to her.

She gestured casually. "No big deal."

"What are you drinking?"

She picked up a glass of what looked like a gin and tonic and swirled it around.

"You want another?" I said.

She smiled like a belle. "Thank you, sir," she said, and almost curtsied.

I yelled at the bartender, and we went through the same ridiculous charade, until the girl stepped in and translated for us again.

"They should hire you to do this for a living," I shouted at her when the bartender had gone.

"They do," she said with a wink.

"So it's like that, is it?" I said.

"Sometimes. Not always." She gave me a coy look. "What's your name?"

"Harry," I said. "Yours?"

"Laurel."

I raised my glass. "Here's to free enterprise, Laurel."

The girl studied me over the rim of her glass. I wanted to believe that it was my looks that were dazzling her, but I had the gut feeling that she was wondering whether I was Vice.

"I haven't seen you here before, Harry," she said, almost on cue. "You new in town?"

"It just looks that way," I said.

"Are you married?" she said in a cute little voice that was designed to tickle.

I shook my head, but she acted like she didn't believe me.

"It's okay. I think married men are neat." Laurel frowned suddenly and said, "Damn," under her breath.

"What's the matter?"

"Oh, it's nothing." She gave me an embarrassed look. "I just made a bet with myself, that's all. I swore off using those dumb kids' words like *neat* and *cool*. It was kind of a New Year's resolution—you know, like when you give up drinking or smoking."

I smiled at her. "How old are you, Laurel?"

"Twenty-four?" she said, as if she were guessing my weight.

I didn't believe that. I wasn't sure I believed anything about the girl, including the little scene about giving up "kids' words" and the racket she had going with the bartender. Her whole act was too practiced, too cute— like that sweet, ticklish voice of hers. But practiced or not, it was an amusing play, and a far cry from the hard sell of the B-girls of my era. She wasn't the first whore I'd met who was bent on improving herself, but she was the first one who'd incorporated it into her patter.

"At twenty-four you're allowed to use words like *neat* and *cool.*"

"Yeah?" she said, looking pleased.

I turned toward the dance floor and stared into the tangle of bodies, hoping to catch sight of Otto. But it was hopeless.

"Christ, it's loaded in here tonight," I said.

"Oh, this is nothing," Laurel said. "Wait till the season starts. Once training camp is over this place really swings."

"You like football players, do you?"

"Oh, yes," she said. "I think they're totally bosco."

I heard her say, "Damn," again, and I laughed. "You got a favorite?"

"I like Chris."

I suddenly remembered I was a detective and asked: "How about Billy Parks?"

Laurel grimaced. "He's taken. Besides, he's weird."

"How's that?"

"Just weird," she said with a shudder. "Believe me."

"Who took him?"

She frowned as if she didn't like the question. It *was* a little blunt, so I put an edge on it by grinning like a tourist. "Just curious," I said.

"It's no big deal," Laurel said. "She's a friend. She used to work here. I guess she got what she wanted, all right. I guess."

I wanted to ask her the girl's name, but I couldn't think of an innocent way to do it. Before I could say anything at all, the bartender reappeared, leaned over the bar, and whispered something into Laurel's ear. She gave me an alarmed look.

"Did you come in here with another guy? A real big dude?"

I nodded.

"Clay says he's causing some trouble."

"Now, there's a surprise," I said. I got off the stool. "Where is he?"

"Follow me," the girl said.

Laurel plucked a lace shawl off one of the stools, took my hand, and headed into the crowd. She guided me to the other side of the room in about a quarter of the time it had taken me to get to the bar.

When we got to the metal door, Laurel put a cautioning hand to my chest. "Are you a cop?" she asked gravely.

"No."

She bit her lip. "All right. But don't get me in any trouble with the cops."

She pushed the door open and we stepped outside.

It was quite a scene. Two patrol cars were parked beneath us on the apron of pavement at the foot of the canopied stairs. Their blue flashers were on and their radios were squawking loudly in the hot night air. The sleazy doorman was sitting on the bottom stair, head bent, hat gone, hands between his legs. Another man, who looked just as sleazy, was sitting opposite him, one stair up, leaning against a canopy strut. His nose looked broken, and his left eye was black and swollen completely shut. A dozen bystanders were gathered in a semicircle in front of the patrol cars, staring at the main attraction —Otto Bluerock, who was lying on the pavement, wrestling with the cops. The cops—all four of them—were trying to keep Bluerock pinned to the concrete, but he kept bucking them off, like so many kids playing roughhouse with Dad.

"Jesus," Laurel said softly. "Who is he?"

"Otto fucking Bluerock," I said with disgust.

I walked quickly down the stairs to where the cops were struggling with Otto. Two of them were holding his legs down, the third was sitting on his left arm, and the fourth was trying to get a pair of cuffs around his right wrist. Bluerock thrashed mightily beneath them.

"Why don't you arrest them?" he bellowed. "They're the goddamn lowlifes."

"Shut up!" one of the cops shouted.

The cop who was trying to cuff Bluerock looked up, white-faced. "They won't fit," he said, with something like awe in his voice. "His wrists are too damn big for the cuffs."

At that moment, Bluerock managed to work his left arm loose again. He swung it up and toppled the cop who was holding it, then punched the cop who was sitting on his right leg and threw the one on his left onto the ground.

The cop with the cuffs jerked his nightstick out of his Sam Browne. "All right, motherfucker," he said. "You asked for it. You're going to get it."

Bluerock snarled at him and lunged at his pants leg. The cop brought the stick down hard on top of Bluerock's head. The stick made a *pock* like a mallet hitting a croquet ball. Otto groaned and fell backward, his fingers still grasping the cop's trouser cuff. The cop jerked his leg loose and raised the stick again.

I yelled, "Hold it!" at the top of my lungs.

The cop with the stick whirled around, his face livid with anger.

"Hit that man again," I said, "and I'll see to it that you serve time for aggravated assault."

"And just who the fuck are you?" he shouted, jabbing me with the stick.

I reached into my jacket with my left hand and pulled out my old badge—the one I'd worn as a deputy with the DA's office. "I'm a sworn officer of the court," I said, flashing the badge at him. "Just like you."

The cop stared furiously at the badge in its leather case. I could tell that he thought it was a phony. I could also tell that he was no killer—just a tough man who'd lost his cool. Which wasn't to say that he'd liked me telling him his job. No cop likes that, and I knew that I'd pay for it later on, when he found out that his instinct had been right. But at that moment, the badge was enough of a distraction to calm him down. He glared at Otto, who was groaning on the pavement, and back at my badge. Then he slipped the nightstick slowly into his belt.

"Put that asshole in the car," he said to the other cops. "As for you"—he turned to me—"you're coming with us. And if you aren't who you say you are, I'm going to charge you with obstructing justice."

I looked back at Laurel, who was still standing at the top of the entryway.

"Do me a favor?" I called to her.

She stamped her foot. "You lied to me. You said you weren't a cop."

A couple of the cops laughed.

"Call Hugh Petrie," I said. I spelled his name for her and gave her his number. "Tell him to meet Harry Stoner at Station X."

"I don't like this," she said.

"Just do it, Laurel. Please."

The cop with the billy club grabbed me by the arm and pulled me to the patrol car. "Who the hell is that monster?" he said as he stuffed me into the back seat alongside Otto.

"Just a guy who's had a bad day," I said.

V

Around two o'clock that morning, Hugh Petrie visited me in the Station X lockup in the basement of City Hall. I'd been there for some time, sitting in a holding tank with assorted other drunks and sad cases. They'd taken Otto to University Hospital to have his head patched. Me, they'd thrown in jail—after the cop I'd tangled with discovered that the badge I'd shown him was a ringer.

I'd been talking to a drunk for better than an hour when Petrie finally showed up. The drunk, whose name was Elmer, had been telling me his philosophy of life, which mostly consisted of the single admonition, Don't forget to eat.

"It's when you forget to eat that they start slipping by."

"What?" I asked him.

He looked at me piteously. "Why the days, man," he said. "The days."

"Oh, them," I said. The days.

Of late, Elmer had had to remind himself to eat, because his wife had gotten fed up and left him, and his children wouldn't speak to him, either. He lived off his sister, a good Catholic woman who prayed constantly for his redemption and turned the other cheek when he filched beer money from her purse. Elmer thought she was a hypocrite because of the priests.

"I say to her, 'Those priests of yours, they have a pick-me-up of a morning. What the hell d'you think they got in those cups? Pepsi-Cola?' That shuts her down."

He was a card, Elmer.

He had just begun to explain the virtues of buying eyeglasses at Walgreen's rather than at K mart, when Petrie walked up to the cage. Elmer glanced at Petrie's iron-jawed face and paled. "Don't forget to eat, Harry," he said in a stricken voice, and retreated a discreet distance. I was still a little loaded, so I laughed.

"Howdy, Hugh."

Petrie stared at me for a moment. His shirt was misbuttoned at the collar and his cheeks were dark with a day's growth of beard, but he still looked tough and businesslike in a sleepy, disheveled way. He wore a felt hat over his forehead, shading it sharply the way his brow shaded the rest of his face.

"What happened?" he said softly.

"I don't think Otto liked being cut. He went a little nuts in a downtown bar."

Petrie nodded, as if he'd heard the story before. "What was he doing in the bar?"

"Looking for Parks. Or so he said."

"Does he know where Bill is?"

I shrugged. "Apparently he thought he was at the Waterhole. He was pretty drunk, and feeling sorry for every football player who ever butted heads with management. I'll tell you one thing—he isn't too crazy about you guys at the moment."

"The feeling is mutual," Petrie said. He peered

through the bars at Thursday night's collection of losers. "How'd you end up in here?"

"A cop was using Otto's head for batting practice. I stepped in."

"From what I've been told, Otto did a little practicing of his own."

"He got in his licks," I said.

"Maybe we shouldn't have cut him, after all," Petrie said dryly. "My lawyer's arranging for your release. You should be out of here shortly." He wrinkled his brow and the brim of his hat kissed the bridge of his nose. "By the way, who is Laurel Jones?"

"A girl I met at the Waterhole."

He gawked at me in disbelief. "You gave a girl you met at that bar my private number?"

"I didn't know how long it would be before I could get to a phone," I said. "And I thought you'd want to know that one of your players was in trouble."

"He's not one of my players anymore," Petrie said. "Not after tonight. We're going to get him released from custody. But he's not welcome back at camp. When you get out of here, take him home, Stoner."

"Why me?"

"You brought him to this dance. You dance with him."

I stared at him for a moment. "Where's home?"

"Somewhere in Clifton. Ask him."

Petrie turned to go.

"Can I ask *you* something?" I said.

He nodded at me over his shoulder.

"Why'd you cut him?"

"Because he's twenty pounds overweight, he's had three knee operations, and he's got a bad attitude," Petrie said bluntly. "The man's almost thirty-five years old, Stoner. If he plays another year, he's going to get hurt and he's going to hurt the team. The plain fact is, he's through."

* * *

Petrie's lawyer—a fat, pompous man with cheeks like dewlaps and the black, bulging eyes of a Chihuahua—sprung me at seven in the morning. I caught a cab to the Waterhole, picked up the Pinto, and drove to the hospital on Goodman Street. The lawyer had said that Bluerock would be released from custody at eight. I was waiting in the downstairs lobby when he stepped off the elevator. He had a white bandage on his head and his shirt was a little worse for wear, but on the whole he looked as if he'd been enjoying himself.

"Hey, sport!" he said in his croaking bass. "Where'd you spend the night?"

"In Station X," I said sourly.

Bluerock slapped me on the shoulder so hard he almost knocked me over. "You could be all right, Stoner."

We walked out to the Burnet Avenue lot. The sun was early-morning bright, a flat, blazing disc in the eastern sky. Bluerock glared at it as if he wanted to punch it out.

"My fucking head hurts," he growled.

"You probably have a concussion."

"That's what they tell me." He touched the bandage on his head and winced. "What did that son-of-a-bitch hit me with? Lead pipe?"

"Billy club," I said. "What happened, anyway?"

"Some guy gave me some lip, so I popped him one," he said.

"Lip about what?"

Bluerock grunted. "You ask a lot of questions, you know that?"

"And I get damn few answers," I said. "Are you planning to talk to me about Parks or do we have to get drunk again first?"

He ducked his head and sucked some breath in through his front teeth. "Look, I know I owe you something, sport. But this is a funny situation. You spend four years in the trenches with a guy, four years rooming with him, it's kind of like a partnership. You don't piss on something like that without thinking it over." He gave me an abashed grin. "What were you planning to do if you did find Bill?"

"Tell Petrie," I said.

"That asshole," Bluerock said.

"That asshole got you out of a lot of trouble last night."

"He got me *in* a lot of trouble, too."

I didn't say anything.

"I don't know," Bluerock said, squinting up at the morning sky. "Maybe it *is* time to get on with my life's work." He looked down at the pavement, as if the thought weren't a bit comforting.

"You want to get some coffee?" I said.

He nodded. "Then I got to get some sleep. I feel like I could sleep for a week." He laughed grimly. "Maybe I will."

We drove to Newport to the Anchor Café and had eggs, goetta, and coffee in one of the spare wooden booths in the back room. Bluerock scarcely fit into the seat. With the bandage on his head and a day's growth of beard on his fierce, bulldog face, he awed the teenage waitress who'd brought us our menus. She eyed him closely as we gave her our orders and kept staring at him after we were done, as if she were afraid to turn her back on him.

"Quit looking at me, will you?" Bluerock said testily. "You're making me nervous."

The girl laughed giddily and practically ran out of the room.

"Women," Bluerock said with disgust. "You can't find one decent one in a thousand. And even if you do, she'll change. Everything fucking changes for the worse."

"You're a cheerful guy, aren't you, Otto?"

He frowned at the old-fashioned jukebox on the wall. "Fuck you, too," he said.

A few minutes later the teenager came back with the food and arranged it carefully on the table. She smiled shyly at Bluerock when she was through.

"You're Otto Bluerock, aren't you?" she said in a tiny voice.

"I used to be," Bluerock said, picking up his fork.

"Man, you're good," she said.

Bluerock put down the fork and smiled at her. "I was good, wasn't I?"

"The best," the girl said. She held out a piece of paper and a pencil. "Do you mind?"

"I guess not," he said.

He gave the girl his autograph. She tucked it in her breast pocket, patted it, and walked away.

"Nice kid," Bluerock said, bending to his plate.

I laughed.

Bluerock looked up, egg hanging from his mouth. "Do I contradict myself?" he intoned. "Okay. I contradict myself. Or however the hell it goes."

After breakfast, Bluerock ran out of steam. The concussion was catching up with him, along with everything else that had happened in the last twenty-four hours. He was a tough guy, but he wasn't Superman.

"I've had it," he said, as we walked out to the car. "Better take me back to camp. It's a helluva way to spend my last day as a Cougar—sleeping."

There was no easy way to put it, so I said it outright. "They told me not to take you back to camp. They told me to take you home."

Bluerock's jaw knotted up and his face went gray, but he didn't say a word. When we got in the car, he huddled by the door and stared darkly at the bleak Newport streets.

I started the Pinto and pulled out into the sparse morning traffic. Bluerock sat silently by the door. I took the suspension bridge over the Ohio and headed north toward Vine and the downtown blocks.

When we got to Fountain Square—or what passes for it nowadays—I asked Otto where he lived.

"Wheeler Street," he said sullenly, and gave me an address in Clifton.

I drove up Vine to the parkway, past the red brick facade of Music Hall and through the Over-the-Rhine wasteland to Ravine Street and then east on Warner. He was almost asleep when we got to Wheeler, head drooping against the car window, eyelids squeezed shut like a sleeping dog's. I coasted up Wheeler until I came to the address he'd given me. It wasn't much of a house for a football player—a two-story frame Victorian with a porch like a sprung cushion and two narrow strips of burned-out grass for a yard. It was the house of a man who didn't really think of it as home.

"We're here," I said.

He opened one eye and squinted at the dilapidated building.

"Jesus," he said mournfully.

Bluerock pulled himself upright with a groan, opened the door and got out.

"I'll be in touch, Stoner," he said over his shoulder, and trudged wearily up to the door.

VI

I went home.

The day's heat had already filled the apartment, and I began to sweat as soon as I stepped through the door. I stripped off my shirt, got a beer out of the refrigerator, flipped on the Globemaster, and collapsed on the couch. Appropriately enough, the man being interviewed on NPR was talking sports. I pressed the cold beer can to my forehead and listened sleepily to his familiar spiel. Athletes, he said, were in the entertainment business. They were show folk, like actors and singers, and because their careers onstage were so short and risky, they deserved to make as much money as they could get, even if that meant the renegotiation of contracts.

I had the gut feeling that no actor would last very long if he constantly demanded the renegotiations of his contracts in the middle of films. In fact, I wasn't sure I bought the show-business analogy at anything but the most superficial level. Otto Bluerock certainly wouldn't have. According to him, neither would Bill Parks. Otto didn't think of himself as an entertainer. True, he demonstrated his talents before a crowd, but that was because that was where the game was played on Sunday afternoons. During the rest of the week it went on outside the white lines. According to Otto, it never stopped.

Bluerock's philosophy may or may not have been so much macho bullshit, although I'd seen him live some of it out in the Waterhole parking lot. But even if it was bullshit, it was appealing bullshit. It was principled bullshit. It was a couple of steps above the greedy, self-serving crap that the man on the radio was handing out. Of course, it hadn't done much to prepare Otto for that long, lonely walk up to his front porch. What fact or fiction would have? But it could pull him through later on, I thought—if there was a later on for Otto. If he didn't turn his machismo inside out and destroy himself with it.

And that could happen, too. I'd seen it happen to other hard men—to cops and soldiers, tough guys who'd suddenly found themselves on the outside, armed with a code and a sense of loyalty that only worked for them on the beat. Nights like the one we'd just gone through might even end up being Bluerock's life's work, and that fierce, combative pride of his might degenerate into ordinary paranoia, into a ceaseless conjuring up of enemies to fight. It all depended on him—for the first time, really. Up until then, it had depended on men like Petrie, men who had their own macho fantasies to live out, their own tough philosophies to preach. In a way they were the same guy, Bluerock and Petrie. The guy that Otto said Parks was—the one who played the game for keeps, on the field and off.

Bill Parks was the last thing on my mind as I wandered off to bed. But that was because he didn't exist for me yet. He was just a name and a picture. But I knew instinctively that he wasn't the kind of man that Otto had made him into. And I also knew that somewhere down the road I'd find out who he really was, and that I wouldn't like what I found.

The telephone woke me around eleven, two hours after I'd gone to sleep. I opened one eye and stared bitterly at the black box gabbling on the nightstand. When it didn't shut up, I snatched the receiver from the cradle and gave it a good hard squeeze before putting it to my ear.

"Who the hell is it?" I barked.

"Glad I caught you in a good mood," a man with a deep voice replied amiably. "This is Harry Stoner, isn't it?"

"Yeah. So what?"

The man laughed tunelessly, as if he were practicing laughing before a mirror. "My name's Walt Kaplan, Mr. Stoner. Perhaps you've heard of me?"

"Can't say that I have, Walt."

"I'm calling because I understand that you're looking for a client of mine."

"And who would that be?"

"Bill, of course. Bill Parks."

That woke me up a little. "You're Parks's agent?"

"Not exactly his agent," Kaplan said in his deep, pally voice. "I'm his advisor and his friend."

"And just who told you I was looking for your advisee?"

He went on as if he hadn't heard the question. "I'd like to have a little chat with you, Harry, if you've got the time."

"You going to tell me where Billy-boy is?"

"I'm going to explain his situation," he said demurely. "After all, you've only heard one side of it. Then perhaps we can talk about the right thing to do—for everyone involved."

Walt Kaplan sounded very much like a lawyer, and a smooth one, at that. But then some agents *were* lawyers. And some were second cousins. It was a weird business. I picked a pencil up off the nightstand and dug a scrap of paper out of the drawer. With all-pros for clients, I figured Walt for a suite in the DuBois Tower.

"When do we meet?" I said.

"Well, you sound as if you could use a few more hours of sleep. And I have a doctor's appointment at one. I've got this bowel problem."

Tell me about it, I said to myself.

"Let's say three thirty," Kaplan said. "Is that all right with you?"

"Where?"

"My place, I guess. It would be more convenient for me. I've got another appointment at five."

I scratched an *X* through the square I'd drawn on the scrap sheet. "What's the address?"

"Eighty-eight hundred Winton Road. Kaplan's Club. Right across from the Sohio station."

"You run a bar?" I said with surprise.

"A gym, Mr. Stoner," Kaplan said. "You have a nice day."

I went back to sleep after Kaplan called and didn't wake up again until the alarm went off at two thirty. The afternoon sun had made kindling out of the bedroom furniture, and as soon as I got my ground sense back, I bolted for the bathroom and took a quick shower.

I plunged back into the bedroom and guided a handful of clothes out safely. As soon as I'd dressed, I sat down at the rolltop desk by the living room window, picked up the phone, dialed Information, and got Otto Bluerock's number. I hated to be the one to call him to reveille—he had a bad day ahead. But I wanted some information about Walt Kaplan before I met with him. It was either

Otto or Petrie, and I was pretty sure that the Cougar management wouldn't approve of me conferring with Parks's agent. I went ahead and made the call to Otto.

He answered on the seventh ring, in the same mood that I'd been in earlier that day.

"What?" he bellowed into the phone.

"Hi, Otto," I said. "How's the head?"

"Who is this?" he said darkly. "No. Don't tell me. I'd recognize that limp-wristed voice anywhere. I already told you, Stoner—don't call us, we'll call you. Got it?"

"I got it," I said. "I just thought you'd like to know that Walt Kaplan called me."

"Did he, now?" Bluerock said with interest. "And what did the cocksucker want?"

"He knows I'm looking for Bill."

"That's my fault," Bluerock said. "When Petrie told me you'd be coming out to Bloomington, I mentioned your name to a couple of guys. And there isn't much around camp that Walt doesn't pick up on."

"He claims he's Parks's agent," I said.

Bluerock grunted. "He's a fucking subculture, that's what Professor Walt is."

"You don't like him, do you?"

"No, I don't like him," Bluerock said coldly.

"Can I ask why?"

"I don't fit into his game plan, sport," Bluerock said. "We're not on the same mailing lists."

"What's his angle?"

"Professor Walt? He's into what you might call health, the whole person game. Walt's guru to a bunch of local bodybuilders and football players. The guys worship at his feet—work out together, eat right, sleep right, do each other's hair. Kind of like Moonies with muscles. Fred is one of the Professor's boys. Remember Fred?"

I remembered Fred from the Bloomington bar. Bluerock had implied that Fred's guru, the Professor, had sent him to spy on us. At the time, I thought nothing of it, since I didn't know who the Professor was. Now that I'd gotten that phone call and knew that "Professor Walt" was also Parks's agent, Bluerock's accusation didn't seem quite so far-fetched.

"Why do you call him 'Professor' Walt?" I asked Otto.

"He's got a Ph.D. in exercise physiology," Bluerock said. "Or so he claims. He got the nickname when he won the Nationals in power lifting a couple of years ago. The muscle mags dubbed him the 'Professor of Press.' "

"He's a power lifter?" I said. "Over the phone, the son-of-a-bitch sounded like a corporate lawyer."

"Oh, Walt's a class act, all right. If *you're* impressed, just think how he comes across to guys like Fred—guys whose entire life's reading consists of back issues of Joe Weider magazines."

"Fred's a protégé?"

"A star pupil."

"What about Parks?"

"It's different with Bill," he said, without explanation.

I started to ask him what he meant, but I knew I wouldn't get an answer. The sense of loyalty that had kept him from talking to me the night before hadn't evaporated overnight. And nagging him about Parks wasn't going to change that. Instead, I asked him how Kaplan had gotten involved in the agency business.

"How do you think?" Bluerock said. "You tell somebody how to spend his time, pretty soon you're telling him how to spend his money. And how much money he should make. It's a very sweet racket."

"Okay, Otto," I said. "Thanks for the help."

"Stoner," Bluerock said. "Give me a call after you get done with the Prof."

"All right."

"And Stoner?"

"Yes."

"Quit calling me Otto. I hate that fucking name."

"What do you want me to call you?" I said.

"Mr. Bluerock would be nice. But friends call me Blue." He laughed. "You know, I'm setting a precedent here."

"You afraid you're going to regret it?"

"I think I already do," he said, and hung up.

VII

As holy shrines go, Kaplan's Health and Fitness Club was no Taj Mahal—just a long, low concrete building with a plate glass door and window and a flat asphalt roof. It was located right where Kaplan had said it would be, across from the Sohio station on Winton Road, in one of those little shopping plazas that used to be the rage before the big malls were built. The club was on the south side of the plaza, across from a bakery and a drugstore. I couldn't see into the gym from where I'd parked in the lot out front—the window was blinded and the plate glass door to its right had been painted over—but it looked identical to the bakery and the drugstore, except for the parade of men and boys who kept trailing in and out.

Not all of Kaplan's clients were bodybuilder types. Some of them were chunky teenagers—high school football players with bull necks, crew cuts, and peach basket rear ends. A few were middle-aged businessmen, carrying canvas bags with "Adidas" and "Pony" stitched on the sides. But a goodly number of them were muscle-bound jocks in tank tops and shorts, with the rapt, tanned, hyper faces of professional bodybuilders. I spent a couple of minutes watching two of them standing on the narrow concrete curb in front of the club. They were talking to each other, but I didn't see them make eye contact once. In fact, they didn't seem to be looking at anything at all. It was as if they were still standing in front of a mirror, practicing curls, as if that circuit had never been broken. They flexed their biceps, shifted their weight from foot to foot, rolled their heads on their necks, and wiggled their fingers like they were practicing the scales on a piano. But they never looked at each other and they never stopped fidgeting.

I waited until the bodybuilders had gone. Then I got out of the Pinto, walked up to the window of the club, and peered through the blinds. There was a small desk inside, manned by a burly beachboy in T-shirt and cut-offs. He had his feet on the desktop, and he was smiling at something that was going on in the gym. I couldn't see what he was laughing at because there was a drywall partition behind him, which cordoned off everything but the desk and a small waiting area to its right. I checked my watch—I was on time—and opened the door.

The place was filled with noise—the creaking of chain pulleys on the Universal machines, the thud of barbells being dropped to mats, the whizzing of flye pulls and exercise bikes, and behind it all, like the night sounds of crickets and distant traffic, the groans of the bodybuilders themselves. I stood in front of the kid at the desk, waiting for him to acknowledge my presence. But he was listening to a ball game on a transistor radio—one of those ghetto blasters that look like assorted pie plates glued to a masonry block—and couldn't be bothered. He was an ugly kid, with a nest of curly red hair and a red, lumpy face, acne-scarred along the chin and neck.

After a minute or two, I got tired of waiting, and started for the opening that led to the gym.

"Hold on there, cowboy," the kid behind the desk said.

He looked up from the radio, glanced at my face, then studied my arms and chest, as if my muscles were the windows to my soul. "What can I do for you?"

"I've got an appointment to see Kaplan. The name is Stoner."

"Stoner," the kid repeated slowly, as if he were sounding out syllables in a book. "Just a second."

The kid reached out and jabbed at an intercom sitting on his desk.

A voice crackled over the intercom speaker. "Yeah?"

"Walt, a guy named Stoner is here to see you," the kid said.

"Show him in," the voice said.

The kid swung his feet off the desk, stood up, and led me through the entryway into the gym. The place was surprisingly old-fashioned on the inside: mirrored wall to the right, with benches and Universal machines lined up in front of it; dumbbell racks, flye pulls, and more benches on the left; squat racks and curling stands at the rear; and a half dozen exercise bikes set up on gray mats by the door. Overhead, big-bladed ceiling fans stirred the boiling air.

We picked our way among the machines and the men working out on them. Most of the bodybuilders were young—college-age jocks. But there were a few grown-ups in the crowd, including three guys in short-sleeve Cougar sweatshirts, working out on a squat rack at the back of the room. I recognized one of them—Fred, Kaplan's protégé. He didn't see me. He was too busy trying to lift four hundred pounds of weights draped across his back. Eyes squeezed shut, jaw set, lips quivering, his face beet red and pouring sweat, he trembled and groaned beneath an oversize Olympic bar so loaded down with plates that it drooped at either end. The other two Cougars stood beside him, arms outstretched, ready to lift the bar off his back if Fred failed. They shouted at him savagely, urging him on as if he were a horse caught hoof-deep in mud.

The beachboy stopped to watch Fred for a moment, then looked at me as if to say, *"That's* what it means to be a real man!" He shouted, "Work!" at Fred, then walked up to a shuttered door by the racks and knocked. Someone said, "Come in."

"You heard the man," the kid said and wandered back to where Fred was squatting.

I went in. The door opened on a small white-walled office, decorated with posters of bodybuilders and with newspaper clippings. There was an air conditioner chugging in a window by a door in the far wall. The blast of cold air hit me so hard it made me shudder.

Two men were sitting inside the room. One of them— a huge kid with ringlets of brown hair all over his head and a fat, dimpled, stupid face—sat on a chair next to the door. His head was tilted back so that it was resting against the wall. Eyes half shut, chin pointing upward, arms folded across his chest, he peered down his nose at me, as if he could just barely make me out. The other man was sitting behind the desk. If anything he was a little bigger than Baby Huey. He was also a good twenty years older, and on the surface, at least, a lot more intelligent-looking. He had a ruddy, pockmarked face, fringed with a bushy black beard, muttonchops, and a thick mustache. His hair had been combed forward from beneath the crown, presumably to cover a bald spot. It made a little curtain of curls across his forehead. He was wearing a blue T-shirt with "Kaplan's Health and Fitness Club" silk-screened on the front. Maybe it was the beard or maybe it was the fact that the T-shirt rode so high up his chest, but the guy didn't seem to have any neck at all. His head rested on his shoulders like a bowling ball on a shelf.

"Glad to meet you, Harry," he said, holding out an enormous hand. "I'm Walt Kaplan."

I shook with him. He didn't squeeze down, the way Otto had. But I could tell from the size of his biceps that if he'd wanted to, he could have crushed my hand like an empty beer can. His upper arms were enormous and so thick with black hair that they almost looked simian. The only part of him that appeared even remotely weak were his eyes, and that might have been an illusion caused by the black horn-rim glasses he was wearing. One of the screws had fallen out of the right hinge, and he'd stuck a paper clip through the hole in its stead. But the clip didn't hold the glasses together tightly, and they drooped across his right eye, giving him the pained, fidgety look of a man stuck behind a pillar at the ballpark.

"I'm glad you could make it out, Harry," Kaplan said in his deep, friendly voice. "Please, have a seat."

I sat down in a desk chair across from him.

"Would you like something to drink?" he said. "Juice? Gatorade?"

When I said no, he turned to Baby Huey.

"This is my friend and associate, Mickey," he said, addressing the kid directly, as if Mickey periodically needed to be reminded of who he was. "Mickey works for me here at the club."

Mickey indicated by the slightest movement of his head that he recognized that I had entered the room.

"Mickey," Kaplan said, with that undue courtesy that bosses use with their hirelings around strangers, "would you mind leaving us alone for a few minutes? Harry and I have some business to discuss."

Mickey grunted, got to his feet, and walked out the door to the gym.

As soon as Mickey had left, Kaplan picked up a roll of antacid tablets lying on his desk, pried one of them off, and popped it into his mouth. He chewed on it ruminatively and smiled sadly. "I'll tell you, my friend," he said. "It's no fun getting old." He rubbed his forehead vigorously, and the loose skin bunched up in pleats beneath his fingers. "I just had a bowel movement that looked like Chicken and Stars soup. Now my head hurts. Doctor told me there's a virus going around. You heard about that? A virus or something?"

"Hell if I know," I said.

"I guess it's a virus," Kaplan said.

For a guru, he certainly wore his foibles nakedly. He pried another antacid tablet off the roll and stuck it in his mouth. "You've got to listen to your body, Harry," he said. "It'll tell you everything you need to know, if you can just interpret the messages correctly. This mind-body duality crap is the bane of our civilization. Some day people are going to wise up and realize that the two are one—the unconscious mind *is* the body." He adjusted the glasses on his nose. "I guess it's a virus."

"Probably."

Kaplan leaned forward, bending so close to me I caught a chalky whiff of Tums. "I want to talk to you, my friend," he said with great earnestness. "I want to let you know what Bill Parks is really like."

"Why?" I said.

Kaplan laughed unhappily, as if I'd made a rude noise. "Because I think you've been fed some misinformation. Or should I say, disinformation? It's Mr. Petrie's specialty."

"Exactly how have I been misinformed?"

"You've been led to believe that Bill is a 'missing person.' Let me assure you that he is not missing. He had good reasons for leaving training camp in the way that he did, and Mr. Petrie knows this."

"You mean the contract dispute?"

"Exactly." Kaplan popped another antacid tablet into his kisser and crushed it noisily between his teeth. "I approached Mr. Petrie on three different occasions earlier this year, in an attempt to settle our differences fairly. And on each of these occasions he made it clear that he wasn't interested in being fair. As a result, Bill felt that he had no other choice but to leave camp without further notice."

"Parks *is* under contract, isn't he?"

"Yes," Kaplan said. "A contract that he signed better than three years ago. Things have changed in his life since then. Dramatically. For one thing, his skills are more valuable now. And then he has new responsibilities to meet, a wife and family to support. All of this costs money."

"Parks is married?" I said.

"He plans to be," Kaplan said. "He's very much in love, I can tell you that. With a wonderful girl, who's had a terrifically positive influence on his life."

"May I ask her name?"

Kaplan didn't answer me. "Mr. Petrie knows that Bill will return to camp as soon as Petrie starts bargaining with us in good faith. Excuse me for being so blunt, but hiring someone like you is nothing less than a slap in Bill's face. Just one more instance of bad-faith bargaining, and an insidious way of pressuring my friend into making a bad—a fatally bad—decision about his future."

"All I've been hired to do is find him," I said.

"You can't be that naive," Kaplan said, leaning back in his chair. "If Bill wanted Mr. Petrie to know where he was, he would have told him."

"Do you know where he is?"

"We have been in contact, of course." Kaplan stared at me for a moment. "Bill has authorized me to ask you to leave him alone. I'm asking you, too, as Bill's friend.

Continuing this . . . inquisition will only cause him trouble, and will ultimately undermine any chance we may have of securing a fair settlement of the issue."

"And how will it do that?"

Kaplan shook his head and sighed. "I thought you were an adult, Harry," he said long-sufferingly. "I thought we didn't have to play this kind of game. But since you insist, let me put it to you bluntly. How would you like to have your life picked over by a stranger? A stranger who is working for a man who does not have your best interests at heart? We all have things in our pasts that we're not particularly proud of, and I'm not going to insult your intelligence by pretending that Bill Parks is any different. He's a troubled man who's had many problems, some of which he's just now beginning to resolve. But those problems are nobody's business but his own. He has a right to privacy, even if it's merely the privacy to contemplate his own follies. Whether you realize it or not, you are violating that right. And I am asking you again, on Bill's behalf, to let us settle this dispute in our own way."

"Mr. Kaplan," I said, getting to my feet, "you can make my job much easier by simply telling Parks to get in touch with the Cougars. As far as I'm concerned, that will close the case. Until then, I'm obligated to keep looking for him."

"Obligated?" Kaplan said with outrage. "What about your obligation to your fellow man? Your obligation to be fair? Does that go by the way simply because you took money to do someone else's dirty work?"

"I agreed to do a job," I said. "I intend to do it."

I turned to go. Kaplan came out from behind the desk. He was a hair over six feet tall, but all those muscles made him look enormous.

"I've asked you politely," he said in a very tough voice. "Stay out of Bill's life." The glasses had slipped down his nose, and he pinned them to his forehead with a forefinger. "Bill works for the Cougars. They don't own him."

"And you don't own me," I said.

He took a deep breath, and his stomach rumbled. "You're upsetting my stomach," he said. "You're making me angry. Don't make me angry, Mr. Stoner. Believe me, you won't like it."

"I'll have to take that chance," I said, and walked out the door.

VIII

I wasn't in a particularly good mood as I drove back to town. I didn't like being threatened by a dyspeptic bully, and more than that, I didn't like what the bully had said. Kaplan was the second person in two days who had told me that I was being used by the Cougars as a weapon against Parks. Of course, Otto had been drunk and angry when he made his accusation. And Walt wasn't exactly a disinterested party. He stood to benefit directly from the renegotiation of Parks's contract. But the two stories were enough alike to make me feel vaguely uneasy about Petrie's motives—and about my own. I'd taken the case because I hadn't liked what Parks had done to those four girls. I still didn't like that. But they weren't the reason I'd been hired. I'd been hired, I reminded myself, to find the son-of-a-bitch. And if Petrie saw it differently, we'd have to have a little renegotiation of our own.

And yet even as I was telling myself that Parks's past sins were his own business, I couldn't help wondering which one of them had Kaplan so worked up. The three

assault arrests and the Candy Kane trial weren't secrets
to Cougar management. Kaplan had to know that, seeing
that he seemed to know everything else about the Cougars. Which meant that something else was bothering
him—something he was afraid I'd uncover in the course
of the investigation. Since drug scandals were rife that
summer, I wondered if Bill had run afoul of the same
DEA sting that had netted Monroe, Calhoun, and
Greene. If he had, the Feds hadn't gone public with it yet.
But that would be a career-buster, all right—something
that could really throw a wrench into contract negotiations.

As soon as I got back to the apartment, I called Hugh
Petrie at his office in the Stadium. The girl from his
answering service said that he was gone for the day, but
that she would relay my message. About ten minutes
later, Petrie himself called back.

"What's the problem, Harry?" he said.

"I need to meet with you about Parks."

"Fine," he said. "Come in on Monday morning."

"It can't wait until Monday morning," I said.

Petrie sighed. "Okay. If it's that urgent, you better
come out here. I can spare a half hour this evening. No
more." He gave me an address in Indian Hill and rang
off.

It took me about twenty minutes to drive out to Indian
Hill and another fifteen minutes to find Petrie's home,
which was hidden away in a maple grove at the end of a
winding, tree-shaded lane. I'd half figured Petrie for one
of the flashy white Colonials along the Camargo drag—
the kind with the two-mower lawn and the flagpole set in
concrete and the carriage house as big as a four-family
apartment in Reading. But the bungalow at the end of
the shady lane *was* a carriage house, and a relatively small
one, at that. It had been spruced up with white trim, red

siding, and Pennsylvania Dutch shutters on the upper-story windows, but it was still recognizably a barn—loaf-shaped, mansard-roofed. In fact, between the siding and the shutters, it looked like a child's painted lunch box. There was a car parked in a gravel lot to the left of the house—a puke green Toyota Tercel with muddy tires. Without advancing any genetic theorems of my own, I'd expected something more patrician from a man like Petrie. But he'd fooled me again—first with the office and now with the house and the car.

I parked my heap behind the Toyota, got out into the afternoon sun, and followed a gravel path around a late-blooming magnolia to the front door. The magnolia had perfumed the whole yard, as if someone had spilled cologne in the grass. I waded through the stink, stepped onto a slate stoop, and knocked at a Dutch door. After a time, the top half swung open and Petrie appeared, clad in a sweat-soaked T-shirt and khaki shorts. His bald head was gleaming with perspiration, and he was breathing hard through his mouth.

"I've been working out," he said. "C'mon in."

He opened the bottom half of the door and waved me through it into a small tiled kitchen as neat and modest as the outside of the house. A cellar door was stopped open on the left-hand wall. Petrie started for it.

"We might as well go downstairs," he said. "I can finish my workout and you can give me the scoop."

I followed him down a wooden staircase into the cellar. The basement had been converted into a full-scale gym. There was springy green Astroturf on the floor, a wet bar on the short wall, and on each of the long walls rows of Nautilus machines—spare black skeletal structures of heavy steel and chain, like oddly twisted jungle gyms or the cabs of heavy lifters.

Petrie watched me as I took it all in, with a look that mingled pride and embarrassment, as if I'd caught him in an excess that he couldn't quite justify but wasn't prepared to give up. I had the feeling that I'd gotten a peek at his diary. And apparently, so did he.

"I like to keep in shape," he said, by way of apology, I supposed.

"Hey, I'm impressed," I said.

Petrie walked up to a pair of parallel bars protruding from one of the Nautilus machines and began to do dips —his feet tucked behind him, his legs bent, his arms doing all the work of raising and lowering his body.

"So," he said, "what's so important?"

"I'm getting some mixed signals about Bill Parks," I said.

"Mixed how?"

"Some people seem to think that you guys hired me to finish his career."

"Which people?"

"Walt Kaplan, for one."

Petrie stopped exercising and lowered himself to the floor. He stood there for a moment, his arms resting on the parallel bars, his red face pouring sweat. It took me a moment to realize that he was angry. So angry that he couldn't find his voice.

"Who gave you the authority to talk to Walt Kaplan?" he finally said with barely controlled fury.

"Nobody."

Petrie gave me an astonished look. "He's the enemy, for chrissake!"

"To me, he was a lead."

"I don't know about you, Stoner," Petrie said, tugging at the skin on top of his head as if there were still hair there to be pulled out. "Why do you think we hired you? Who the hell's side are you on?"

"I thought you hired me to find Bill Parks as quickly as I could."

"That did *not* mean you were to negotiate with his fucking agent!"

"I didn't do any negotiating, Hugh. He called me up, and I went to see him."

"How the hell did he know you were on the case!" Petrie almost shouted. He took a deep breath. "Don't answer that. I don't think I want to know."

"Kaplan claims that Parks left camp over the contract dispute. That you know that, and that you hired me to pressure Bill into signing."

"Pressure him how?" Petrie said.

"Presumably by employing me to dig into his past, possibly into a drug problem, and then by using what I get on him to bring him back to the bargaining table." I stared at him. "Is that your strategy, Hugh?"

Petrie didn't answer the question. "What the hell do you care what Kaplan said? Just find Bill, okay?"

I shook my head. "Not okay. I told you before, if you think that Parks has a drug problem, you go to the league or the DEA. I'm not interested in blindly involving myself in a cocaine case."

"Did Kaplan say that Parks had a nose problem?" Petrie said with curiosity.

"No. But he gave me the impression that Bill's career could be ruined by my investigation. Given the current atmosphere, I assumed that meant drugs."

Petrie eyed me for a moment. "That's probably a safe assumption," he said dryly, and walked over to the bar on the far side of the room. He poured himself a beer out of an open can on the bar and sat down on a wooden stool. "You want something to drink?"

I shook my head.

"I don't know why I should be surprised by this crap anymore," he said.

He seemed genuinely aggrieved, although I had trouble believing that he hadn't speculated in the same way that I had about Parks—and probably about some of his other players too.

He must have guessed what I was thinking, because he drew himself up on the chair and gave me a cold look. "You know, Stoner, I don't owe you an explanation of why we hired you. The team doesn't owe you anything but your salary."

"I don't have to keep working for the team, either," I said.

Petrie laughed. "A cop with principles—there's a change." He took a sip of beer and put the glass down on the bar. "As far as I know at this time, Bill Parks is clean. We have heard rumors about a second grand jury investigation, following up on another DEA sting. Several sealed indictments are to be handed down in the near future. Whether Bill is part of that package I don't know."

"But it wouldn't surprise you," I said.

"Like I said, nothing should, anymore." Petrie turned on the stool so that he was facing me, one foot cocked in the rungs, the other leg stretched to the floor. "Five, six years ago I would've gotten really worked up over this kind of thing. Kicked in a TV set or broken somebody's jaw. Now I just don't care." He cribbed his hands around his knee. "The human race sucks. Let's face it. So fuck them all. I run my business. I make a good profit. I'm fair to the players. I give them a chance to make a lot of money. And when things go wrong, I look for a reasonable solution. But I'll be goddamned if I'm going to beat myself over the head because of somebody else's hard luck, or greed, or stupidity. If it turns out Bill has a drug problem, we'll trade him. Or maybe we'll let him play out his contract and then trade him. You wanted to hear the truth. That's the truth. We'll know in time, won't we?"

"So why bother to look for him?" I said. "Why not let

nature take its course and wait for the grand jury to release its findings?"

"Who knows exactly when that's going to happen?" he said. "Besides, given what I now know, I have to presume that he's after more money, that he—or Walt—is planning to take advantage of the fact that we've lost three starters, and is going to try to blackmail us into renegotiating."

I eyed him suspiciously.

"You don't believe me?" he said with a laugh.

"I don't know what to believe," I said.

"Look, you want to know what this contract dispute with Bill is really about?" Petrie said.

"It would ease my mind some, yeah."

"All right," he said. "I'll tell you. Why not? Three years ago, Parks came into my office and told me that he wanted a raise. Now it just so happened that I liked Bill. He's a good football player—you can't take that away from him. When he came up as a rookie eight years ago, he was a late-round pick with nothing but the game on his mind. He signed for peanuts, played hard, and worked his way into a starting spot in two years. Off the field he was a maniac. A lot of them are, including your friend, Otto. But he did his job—kept himself in hard muscular condition the year round, hunkered down in training camp, and never gave less than a hundred percent on the field. He deserved a raise. Not as much as he was hoping for, but a decent chunk. Anyway, we negotiated for a couple of weeks. And then Kaplan got into the picture. Don't ask me how, because I don't know. One week Bill was training with him—the next, Kaplan was his agent. As soon as Kaplan stepped in, the whole process changed. You met the man, so you must know that his whole act is intimidation, physical and intellectual intimidation. He's a strong-arm thug with a shrewd line of patter. And when the patter doesn't work, he's been said to take more drastic measures."

"What kind of measures?" I said curiously.

Petrie shrugged. "It's just scuttlebutt, but two guys from Youngstown who tried to set up a rival health club turned up mysteriously dead in a Little Miami culvert a couple of years ago. It was an unsigned picture, but Walt was generally given the credit."

"He killed them?" I said.

"That's how the story goes," Petrie said without batting an eye. "I know for a fact that he's worked over several guys who got on his bad side. He's got a couple of goons on his payroll who are built like refrigerators."

"I think I met one of them," I said, thinking of Mickey. "He's never threatened you guys, has he?"

"Not with violence," Petrie said. "Walt's too clever for that. Plus he's made friends in the media. You know, it used to be that your average fan dreamed of being a football star. But the yuppie of today has set his sights higher than that. He doesn't want to be a player, he wants to be an owner. He wants to buy and sell flesh, he wants to run a team. Most of your media men understand that, and so does Walt. In fact, the first thing he did during the last negotiation was get himself on the Trumpy show, where he could wail about the incompetence of ownership. He called us names in the *Enquirer*. He got interviewed by Dennis Jansen on the tube. There was nothing unusual about his tactics—negotiating through the press, fueling fan resentment. He was just a little better at it than most of them are, a little smoother and a little smarter and a little more reasonable-seeming. And then he got lucky. Somehow, the national media got hold of the story, and *SI* had an article using Bill as an example of the inequity of the player-management setup. The whole thing snowballed, and we ended up with a public relations nightmare, while this dumbbell with three assault arrests and his smooth-talking thug of an agent played the put-upon innocents. Eventually Bill got most of what he wanted—a raise, a bonus, incentives, the works. Of course, we got a piece of what we wanted too—a long-term agreement to protect our investment."

Petrie picked up the beer again and drained the glass. "Three weeks after we'd signed the deal and all the publicity had died down—three weeks, mind you—Parks came in to talk to me. He told me he was broke, and asked if I could arrange an interest-free loan for him. Now, I'd just got done signing a bonus check with his name on it for over one hunded fifty thousand dollars. I said to him, 'How the hell could you be broke, Bill?' You know what he told me? He'd signed the entire bonus over to Kaplan. Not only that, but Kaplan got a healthy bite out of his first year's salary to boot. And that, my friend, is why Bill Parks wants to tear up the deal his agent blackmailed us into and renegotiate now. To get back to even." Petrie laughed with disgust. "The hilarious part is that Kaplan will probably do the negotiating again. And I'm not about to sit around and get raped by that son-of-a-bitch a second time. This time we're going to talk directly to Bill. And if Kaplan tries to pressure us through the media again, we'll pressure back. This is one we're not going to lose. A man's word has got to mean something, even if he is a fucking football hero."

"Kaplan gets that big a bite of Parks's contract?" I said.

"Fifteen percent, right off the top. But even if Kaplan hadn't soaked him for a couple hundred grand, somebody else would have. Somebody is always ready to spend a man like Bill Parks's money."

"Couldn't you do something about that?"

"Like what?" Petrie said. "Talk him out of it? Who are you going to listen to? The guy that tells you to plan ahead because someday the money's going to dry up? Or the guy who tells you that they can't pay you enough? That management is just sitting back and raking in the dough?"

I looked around the room. "Seems like you're doing all right."

"I make a good living," he said. "I don't apologize for that. *But so do they.* Answer me this, Stoner—how much is enough? How much do you have to pay in order to pay someone what he's worth? Can you put a dollar figure on it?"

"Whatever the market will bear, I guess."

"We offered Parks three hundred thousand dollars a year, plus incentives, for five years. Is that enough? A million and a half dollars for playing a fucking game that he'd play even if nobody paid him a dime? Should I be penalized because he doesn't have sense enough to think for himself? Because he can't run his own life? Or because he has 'personal' problems, and a thief for an agent?"

"I suppose not," I said.

Petrie got off the stool and walked back over to the machines. "Look, I got things to do tonight," he said, as he boosted himself onto a chinning bar. "I gave you the facts. Are you going to stay on the case, or what?"

"I'll stick," I told him. "But I'm still not going to involve myself in a drug case. If I find out that Bill *does* have a nose problem, I'm going to throw him back to you."

"Fair enough," Petrie said and went on with his dips.

I walked back upstairs and showed myself out.

IX

I had dinner at In The Wood in Clifton and spent a couple of hours listening to Katie Laur sing jazz at Arnold's on Eighth Street. Around nine, I drove down to the Waterhole to find Laurel Jones and try to weasel the name of Parks's girlfriend out of her.

There was a new doorman standing beneath the canopied entryway of the club. Which was probably a break for me. He didn't look any different from the other one, right down to the red suit and the billycock hat. As I walked up to him, I caught a whiff of cheap cologne coming off his mottled face, a smell like rotten bananas in a straw basket. I must have winced a little, because he smiled the way people do when they think they've embarrassed themselves but aren't sure how they've done it.

"You waiting for valet parking?" he said, as if he thought that that was why I'd given him the funny look.

I shook my head.

" 'Cause we don't have valet service."

"Then it's a good thing I'm not waiting for it."

He nodded uncertainly.

"Actually," I said, "I'm looking for a friend, a girl named Laurel Jones. Do you know her?"

"They're a lot of girls in there, mister," he said without interest.

I dug a ten-dollar bill out of my wallet and slapped it into his palm. I must have pressed the right button, because his mangy little face lit up like a store window going on for the night.

"Laurel Jones?" he said, as if he were scratching his head. "Blond? Early twenties? Nice build?"

"That's the one."

"Yeah. Come to think of it, I think she might be here tonight." He grinned at me. We were pals now. We'd broken bread together. "Tell you what, you ask Clay the bartender. Tell him Willie says you're okay."

"There's a recommendation," I said.

He smiled feebly, as if he didn't quite catch the joke. I pushed past him into the club.

The place was even more crowded than it had been on Thursday night. I worked my way through the maze of tables surrounding the dance floor over to the neon bar with its chrome stools. Clay, the impassive bartender, gave me a small smile. I crooked a finger at him, and he leaned toward me.

"Is your friend Laurel here?" I shouted over the din.

He nodded. "Upstairs with Stacey, in the game room." He pointed to a spiral staircase at the far end of the bar. "How's that friend of yours doing?" he asked with a grin.

"He's all right. I still don't know what got him so pissed off last night."

"I heard he was looking for Bill Parks, and just wouldn't take no for an answer."

"Could be," I said. "You haven't seen Parks in here tonight, have you?"

"Nope. Haven't seen him in weeks."

He flashed me the peace sign and turned back to the bar. I couldn't figure out why he'd been so agreeable, until it occurred to me that Laurel must have told him I was a cop.

I walked down to the end of the bar and climbed the spiral staircase. The second floor of the Waterhole was little more than a railed, four-sided balcony overlooking the dance floor. Pinball machines and video games were stacked against each wall. Most of the machines were occupied, and the noise was incredible—an electronic farrago of beeps, buzzes, sirens, and bells. Every now and then a computerized voice would issue a command or utter a threat in a robotic monotone.

It took me a while, but I finally located Laurel Jones standing with a girlfriend in front of a Galaga machine. She was dressed in a pink short-sleeve sweater and skin-tight blue jeans, and with her shaggy blond head bobbing over the video screen and her cute little butt swinging in time to the music drifting up from the first floor, she looked very young, very sexy, and very easy. Her friend was a redhead, dressed in a black leotard and black satin pants. She had affected a punk look, but it didn't go very deep, judging by the expert makeup job on her face and the manicured gleam of her long red fingernails.

I stepped up to blond, beamish Laurel and tapped her on the arm.

"Watch it!" she squealed, without looking up. "You're going to make me lose this rocket."

She'd apparently forsaken her vow of maturity, for the time being at least. I stepped back and let her finish the game. Her red-haired friend smiled at me in a speculative way.

"Damn!" Laurel said, when the last rocket had exploded. "Just once I'd like to beat this sumbitch!"

She looked up at her friend with a grin, realized that her friend was looking at me, and turned around.

"You!" she said with surprise. She put on a stern, toe-tapping face. "I don't think I want to talk to you, Harry. You lied to me."

Her friend arched an eyebrow at me from behind Laurel's back, as if to say that she'd be happy to talk to me if Laurel wouldn't.

"You told me you weren't a cop," Laurel said, wagging a finger under my nose.

The girlfriend's eyebrow collapsed, and her face went as blank as a chalkboard.

"I didn't lie to you," I said. "I'm not a cop. I just told the police that to keep them from killing Otto. Do you think they would have arrested me if they thought I was a cop?"

"And there's another thing," she said. "I don't like your friends, either."

"There doesn't seem to be much about me that you *do* like."

She squinted at me, and her friend squinted too. "I didn't say I didn't like you," she said. "I just don't want to get in any trouble."

"Well, at least let me buy you and your friend a drink, to make up for last night."

Laurel pretended to think it over. She turned to her girlfriend and said, "What do you think, Stacey?"

Stacey grinned. "I think he's neat."

Laurel jabbed her with an elbow. "Don't you know anything, girl," she said with disgust. "All right." She turned back to me. "We'll have a drink with you. But I'm still mad."

We went back downstairs, the three of us, and found an empty table in a dark corner of the barroom. I got drinks from Clay, who for some reason didn't need a translator on this evening, and brought them over to the girls.

They'd apparently been talking about me while I was gone, because Stacey giggled wildly when she saw me come up to the table, and Laurel jabbed her again—hard —with her elbow.

"Don't pay any attention to her," she said when I sat down. "She's just a kid and she doesn't know any better."

"While you're all grown up," I said.

Stacey giggled again and Laurel glared at her.

"I'm as grown-up as they come around this joint," she said defiantly. She stuck out her chest. "If you've got a hundred dollars, I'll prove it to you."

"If I *was* a cop, I could bust you for saying that."

"Go ahead," she said. "Arrest me."

I grinned at her and Stacey laughed.

"What's so damn funny?" Laurel said to her.

Stacey shrugged. "I dunno."

"That's your whole problem, girl—you don't know nothing. Why don't you just go over to the bar and find some company of your own?"

Stacey gave me a disappointed look, picked up her drink, and got to her feet. "Pleased to make your acquaintance, I'm sure," she said to me. She stared daggers at Laurel and walked away.

"She's such a child," Laurel said.

"Not too neat, huh?"

Laurel sneered at me. "I still think you're a cop, you know."

"I'm not a cop. I'm a private detective."

"Bullshit!" Laurel said with a giddy laugh.

"Want to see my ID?" I pulled my wallet out and flipped it open to the Photostatic copy of my license.

She studied it for a moment. "Is this a joke or something?" she said, tapping the license with her thumbnail.

"No. That's me, all right. Harry Stoner, Private Investigator."

"Well, who the hell are you investigating? Me?"

I shook my head. "I'm trying to find Bill Parks."

"Why?" she said. "What did he do?"

"He didn't do anything. He's a missing person."

"Bill?" She screwed up her face, as if she thought I was putting her on. "This *is* a joke, isn't it?"

"Uh-uh. He really has disappeared, and I've been hired to find him."

"Hired by who?" she said suspiciously.

I'd already given her Petrie's home phone number, so I saw no reason not to tell her the rest of it. "By the Cougars. By the guy you called up last night."

"Oh, yeah? I thought I recognized the name." She laughed her ticklish little laugh. "All the guys think he's a bastard, but I thought he sounded kind of sweet."

"He's a lollipop, all right," I said to her, although I was thinking that Laurel Jones was far too young to be in the trade she was in. "You can be a big help to me, Laurel. Last night you told me that Parks was seeing one of your friends. How about telling me her name and where I can find her?"

"I don't know," Laurel said with a frown. "I don't want to get anyone in trouble."

"There won't be any trouble. All I've been hired to do is find Parks and put him in touch with Cougar management."

"Yeah, but what if he doesn't want them to know where he is?"

I didn't have a particularly good answer to that one—no better than I'd had when Kaplan had asked me the same question.

"He probably doesn't," I admitted. "But I'm not going to arrest him, just talk to him."

She combed her curly blond hair back from her forehead with her right hand and sighed. "Christ, why couldn't you be someone simple, like a plumber or a bricklayer or something?"

"I thought you liked football players."

"I'm not too crazy about the one you're looking for." She let her hair drop back down, although a couple of strands continued to stand up at odd angles, giving her a rumpled, electrified look. "Let me think about it, okay?"

I nodded.

"How about we go someplace else?" she said suddenly.

"Like where?"

She grinned and her cheeks dimpled up. "I'm still not convinced you aren't a cop."

"What'll it take to prove it to you?"

"I've got a test in mind," she said with a twinkle in her blue eyes. "If you've got the cash."

I studied her sweet little grin and wondered if she really was as ingenuous as she pretended to be. She looked so damn appealing that I wasn't sure that it mattered. But for just a second I had the terrible feeling that around Laurel Jones, *I* was the one who wasn't old enough for the trade.

X

We went uptown to a hotel room and completed the transaction. Laurel had a firm, athletic body, and she was expert at using it. A little too expert, I thought when we were done. The lovemaking wasn't exactly by the numbers, but she did order everything on the menu, like a teenage kid trying to impress his date. She'd impressed me, all right. She'd also worn me out a little too soon to do my ego any good, although she seemed to take my lack of staying power as a compliment. Seeing me tangled in the sheets, spent, sweating, and out of breath, she'd grinned with satisfaction, as if in her world wearing her partner to a nub was as close as she ever got to expressing affection.

Only that wasn't quite fair. Afterward she sat at the top of the bed, her legs and hips covered with the sheets, her small round breasts and flat tummy exposed, and watched me with what I took to be genuine pleasure as I dressed.

"What are you grinning at?" I said to her as I put on my shirt.

"I had a good time," she said, "so I'm smiling. That's okay, isn't it?"

I smiled back at her. "Sure, it's okay."

I got my wallet off the dresser and plucked two fifties from it.

"You don't have to pay me right now," she said. She blushed a little. "It kind of spoils the fun, you know?"

I sat down beside her on the bed. "You're a weird chippy, you know that?" She giggled. "If it means anything, I had a good time too."

She put her arms around my neck and pulled me toward her. "Good," she said, kissing me on the mouth. "Now how about taking me out to dinner? I'm starved."

"Okay. What do you want to eat?"

"Pizza!" Laurel said. "I just love good pizza."

"Pizza it is, then," I told her.

We went to Papa Dino's, a little restaurant on Calhoun Street. Somehow the girl looked more at home sitting across from me in a pizza parlor booth than she had in the hotel room, although I was probably kidding myself about that. She really wasn't very old, and once we got to the restaurant she started to act her age, ordering Coke upon Coke while we waited, and oohing and aahing when the pizza finally arrived on its beaten tin platter. She pulled a stringy piece of cheese off the top and dangled it above her mouth.

"I just love pizza," she said, and swallowed the cheese like a strand of spaghetti.

I think I had more fun watching her eat than eating it myself.

About halfway through the meal, I asked her how a nice girl like her had found her way to a place like the Waterhole.

"You make it sound like the end of the line," she said with an embarrassed laugh. "It's a big step up for me." She blotted her lips with a paper napkin and folded her hands under her chin. "I used to work in Newport when I was younger, but nude dancing gets old pretty fast. And things aren't what they used to be in Newport, anyway. There's more class on this side of the river. Better opportunities."

"More football players?" I said.

She shook her head. "Not really. They hang out at the strip joints, too. Only over there they just automatically think of you as a piece of meat. Over here, you got a chance to be treated like a lady, if you dress nice and talk nice." She beamed at me like a girl in a promotional brochure. "Hey, it can happen! And even if you don't land a football player, there are other advantages."

"Such as?"

Laurel gave me a suspicious look. "You sure you're not a cop?"

"Would a cop treat you to pizza?"

"That's practically all they eat," she said dismally. "I know. I used to go out with one in Highland Heights for a couple of years."

"What happened?"

"Oh, he was too serious about things," Laurel said. "He wanted to settle down right away, start a family. But I'm not ready for marriage yet. I want to have a little fun first. Try to make a big score, you know? Shit, ol' Dicky would die if he knew some of the things I'm into now." She looked down gloomily at her plate, but the gloom didn't last very long. "It's my life, isn't it? And I'm only going to have this one chance, right? I'll be goddamned if I'm going to waste it by getting married right away, like my momma did. Or her momma did before her." She lifted a piece of bacon off the pizza and tossed it in her mouth. "You ever been to Corbin, Kentucky?"

I shook my head. "Why?"

"That's where my family is from is all. Corbin's like that scene from *Deliverance*, the one with the idiot boy on the porch. Most depressing spot I ever lived in. Only thing it had going for it was sulphurated apples. Boy, I used to love those things, sliced up and fried in butter." She licked her lips as if she could still taste them. Then her expression changed, as if that memory had led her to other, less pleasant ones. "You know, they say down-home folks are straighter than other people, more righteous. Don't you believe it. The only thing they worship down in Corbin is money."

Laurel threw her hand at me in disgust. "Don't tell me about down-home folks being more righteous! They tell me I'm bound for hell. I tell them right back, 'Then, I'll meet you in perdition.'"

She reached down and picked up another slice of pizza. "The way I live may not go down so good in Corbin, but I'm using what God gave me the best way I know how. And I'm improving myself all the time. Like right now I'm taking ballet classes at CDT. And twice a week I take this night course at Xavier on short stories. I'm not just . . . Well, what they say I am."

I smiled at her. "No, you're not."

She smiled back and bit into her pizza. "That's what I like about football players," she said as she chewed. "I can identify with them. I mean, they're in the same situation as me. They've got to sell their bodies for money too."

It was a novel way to look at it. "Have you had any luck with them?"

"Not really. But C.W.—" Laurel clapped a hand over her mouth and threw the piece of pizza back onto the pan. "*Damn,*" she said with disgust. "Look what you made me say."

"I take it C.W. is Parks's girlfriend?"

She nodded hesitantly.

"What's C.W. stand for?" I asked.

"It doesn't stand for anything," Laurel said. "We gave her that nickname 'cause of the movie *Bonnie and Clyde*. Because she always wore a cap like C. W. Moss. Her real name is Carol. I'm not going to tell you her last name."

"She used to work with you at the Waterhole?" I said.

Laurel nodded and made an unhappy face. "I guess we're bound to talk about this. I guess I knew that all along. But if we do, Harry, you gotta promise me that you'll never let anyone know where you heard it. 'Cause C.W. would never speak to me again if I got her man in trouble. God knows, she has enough to worry about as it is. And then there's Bill." She shivered a little. "He just isn't like other people. I've known a lot of guys, so you can believe what I'm telling you."

"How is he different?" I asked.

Laurel shook her head. "You gotta promise me, first."

I promised.

"And this is going to cost you something, too," she said, as if it had just occurred to her.

"More than a pizza?"

She laughed. "The Cougars can afford a few dollars, can't they? I mean if it's so damn important?"

"I'll work something out," I said.

"All right. But I'm not going to tell you where C.W. lives. You can ask me anything but that."

"That's what I need to know."

"Take it or leave it," Laurel said firmly.

"Okay," I said. "I'll take it. Now tell me about Bill."

She leaned back against the booth seat and hunkered down, as if she were bracing herself for an ordeal. "Bill's a real tormented guy. I'd feel sorry for him if he wasn't so damn mean. I don't know exactly what his problem is, but he acts like somewhere along the line someone made him feel so bad about himself that he never got over it. I mean, he's always on the muscle. Always. He's got to be the toughest, the baddest, the strongest. And if anybody even looks at him funny, he'll take him apart. Believe me, I've seen him do it at the club. He's just not like the other guys. They act macho too. They go into the john at the Waterhole and do push-ups, so they can come out with their arms all pumped up and strut around like game-cocks. But once they start coming on to you, they're just like any other guys. But Bill . . . It's not an act with him, you know? Being strong, being tough. It's for real. I think the only thing Bill Parks really cares about is play-ing football, being the toughest player he can be. I mean, he's more hung up about it—about building his body up, making contact—than anyone I ever met. It's like he's got tough all mixed up with the rest of life. Like tough's the only answer in his head. It's scary to be around him."

Laurel ducked her chin. "I shouldn't tell you this, but I will. About a year and a half ago, I went to a party with Bill. This was six months before he met C.W. Anyway, I was kind of young and I wanted him to like me. So we ended up in a bedroom, upstairs in this house where the party was. I got undressed and lay down on the bed. But Bill . . . he just stood there staring at me, like I was painted on the bedspread. I remember thinking that he was looking at me the way a butcher must size up a carcass of beef, like I was one of those drawings with the parts of the cow on it, all the choice cuts and the waste. Like that was all he was seeing—just a diagram of parts."

She shuddered up and down her spine. "I've never been raped. I'm not even sure I believe in it. But I'll tell you this—I never felt more helpless in my life. He never got undressed. I don't think he even came. I mean, I could feel all these vibrations coming off him, all this heat. But they just never connected up with *me*. It was like he was still alone. When he was done, I practically jumped into my clothes and ran downstairs and went to the most crowded part of the room and stood there for a real long time, listening to people talk and joke and eat. And after a while I started to feel like a whole person again, like I was something more than this." She pinched the skin of her forearm between her right thumb and forefinger. "What I'm trying to say is that Bill Parks just isn't human."

"Your friend must think he is," I said.

She nodded. "C.W. loves him. Don't ask me why, but she does. He hurts her so much . . . and she just doesn't seem to care! You know what she told me once? She told me that she thought when he beat her up, it was the only way he knew of touching her! Like *that* was a kind of loving." Laurel shook her head. "C.W.'s crazy. First she went crazy for guys. Then she went crazy for God and got all fired up about Jesus. Then she just had to go out and find the most miserable sinner in the world and change his life too. Sometimes I think that's what she really loves about Bill—his badness. If he went over to Jesus, I bet she wouldn't know what to do.

"Oh, hell," Laurel said. "That's not fair. She has changed his life some. She's got him going to that Reverend What's-His-Name that all the players' wives like so well. And she got him off the drugs. Or so she says."

"What drugs?" I asked.

"I don't know for sure," Laurel said in a little voice. "But I think he did a lot of cocaine."

"This could be important, Laurel," I said. "Are you sure about the drug problem?"

"Pretty sure," she said. "I know he was snorting a whole bunch of stuff right before he met C.W. I think he may even have been shooting it up, 'cause I saw some works in his john. Then when they started living together last winter, she made him swear it off. And she claims he's been sticking to it ever since."

"She started living with Bill last winter?"

Laurel nodded. "At the end of December. I know it was December because that's when C.W. found out that she was preg—" Laurel covered her mouth, then dropped her hand. "Oh, hell, I guess it's okay to say that. Most everybody knows it, anyway. To tell the truth, I think that's how she got him to propose to her—telling him about the baby."

Something was rattling around in the back of my mind, some detail that didn't quite fit in with what Laurel was telling me. When I couldn't summon it up, I asked an obvious question. "I thought you said C.W. was born-again. Getting pregnant without getting married isn't part of that deal, is it?"

Laurel smiled. "She's real religious now. But she wasn't so faithful when she first met Bill. She didn't really get soulful until she had this car accident on New Year's Eve, and one of her friends got killed. Plus she's got this funny way of justifying things. She believes she can only save Bill by turning him toward Christ. And she thinks that anything she does to turn him in that direction is okay, 'cause Christ himself came bearing a sword to cleave sinners away from their sinful lives. She believes having a baby means Bill'll have to marry her. And once they're married, she thinks she'll be able to keep him away from all evil influences, like the drugs and the bad company he keeps."

"What bad company?"

"Oh, he used to be friends with this real hard-nosed football player that C.W. doesn't like. I don't know him, but I think she doesn't like him because he doesn't think much of all that Jesus stuff."

I thought of Bluerock and smiled.

"Then there's those guys at the gym."

"Kaplan's gym?" I asked.

She looked up at me with surprise. "You know about that place?"

I nodded. "I *am* a detective, Laurel. I did do a little poking around."

"Well, C.W. doesn't like them either, 'cause they're heathens and other stuff."

"What other stuff?"

She looked over her shoulder, to make sure nobody was listening in—then whispered, "I think that's where Billy got some of his drugs."

XI

Laurel had a downcast look on her face as we walked out of the restaurant. When we got inside the Pinto, she curled up on the seat, hugging her knees to her chest and propping her chin on her kneecaps.

"You know," she said mournfully. "This is the first time I ever felt like a whore. And I didn't even turn a trick."

I glanced over at the girl who was staring gloomily at the dash.

"You didn't do anything wrong, Laurel. I'm not a cop. I'm not even a bad guy."

She turned her head toward me and smiled tolerantly. "I know you're not a bad guy, Harry. I knew that when we first met. In my business, you learn to tell that sort of thing right away." She touched me on the shoulder to reassure me. "It's just that every once in a while I'd like to think that there's a part of me that's not for sale."

"Would it make you feel any better if I *didn't* pay you?"

"No," she said with a hollow laugh. "Then I'd feel like a fool *and* a whore."

"Laurel, I'm going to tell you something," I said and was damn glad there was nobody else around to hear me, because I'd sworn off giving fatherly advice too many times before, in too many public places. "You're not a whore until you start selling what's in here." I touched her breast, over her heart. "The rest of it doesn't matter."

"You think?" she asked with a halfhearted smile.

I patted her curly head and said, "I think."

She leaned back on the car seat and snuggled up against me. "Do that again, would you?"

"What?"

"Pat my head."

I rubbed her head again, gently, and she pulled my hand down to her cheek and nuzzled against it. "Thanks for saying that," she said. "Even if it isn't true."

She put her hand over mine, pulled it down beside her, and held on tightly as we drove back downtown.

I dropped Laurel off in front of the canopied entrance to the Waterhole around eleven thirty. She kissed me on the cheek before she got out.

"What about your pay?" I said.

"We'll discuss it later," she said. "I had a good time being with you. I want to be with you again."

I stared at her pretty, doll-like face, with its rouge spot on either cheek, red candy lips and shaggy blond bangs, and felt a surge of affection for the girl. The feeling embarrassed me a little, and surprised me too. I was too old to be feeling that way after a quickie with a twenty-four-year-old kid.

"Laurel," I said, "it's a trite thing to say, but I've got twenty years on you."

She gave me a hurt look. "What does that have to do

with it?" she asked in a wounded voice. "Don't you like me? You know I don't want to be with everybody I fuck."

It suddenly occurred to me that the girl was speaking my lines. She was speaking from the heart, while I was the one acting like a whore, making love to her and then kissing her off.

"Well we do still have some business to transact, don't we?" I said, smiling at her. "What say we get together later this week and . . . eat some more pizza?"

She grinned back at me. "I've got a little place in Newport on South York. Two twenty-five. Can you remember that?"

"I think so," I said.

"You come by around eight tomorrow night. I might even have a surprise for you."

She said the last part with a cunning little smile that made me nervous.

"Your surprise wouldn't have anything to do with your friend C.W., would it?" I asked.

"It might," she said cheerily. "I thought maybe I'd give her a call. Tell her what a good guy you are. Could be she could talk Bill into seeing you."

"Why don't you just give me her name and address, and let me handle it?"

Laurel shook her head. "No, I got to talk to her first. It wouldn't be right just to sic you on Bill without explaining things."

I admired the girl's sense of fair play, but acting as a go-between could put her at risk, especially if the drug rumors proved out. On the other hand, unless she was willing to give me C.W.'s name or I found it through another source, I didn't see where I had a choice. I temporized by telling her to wait until I gave her the okay before sounding C.W. out, and not to approach Parks himself under any circumstances. "Just leave Bill to me."

She nodded nonchalantly, as if she hadn't heard what

I'd said. I put my hand on her arm and squeezed it hard enough to get her attention.

"Ouch!" she said.

"Do you understand me, Laurel?" I said. "Leave Parks to me."

"Yeah, goddamn it!"

I let go of her arm.

"I don't like being treated like that," she said angrily. "I've had enough of that kind of shit in my life. My father used to put his hands on me all the time. And so did Dicky."

"I'm sorry," I said. "I just don't want you to get hurt."

"That makes a lot of sense, doesn't it? Hurting somebody so they won't get hurt?" She gave me a long-suffering look, as if that were the sort of logic she was used to hearing from her men. "The only way I'm going to get in trouble is if you let somebody know what I told you tonight. I mean, about the drugs." She looked me over carefully. "You wouldn't do that, would you, Harry?"

"I told you I wouldn't."

"Good." She got out of the car. "See you tomorrow?"

"I'll try," I said.

"You better show up, mister," she said, putting a tough look on her face. "You owe me something." She turned to go, then glanced back coyly over her shoulder. "Get my drift?" she said with a wink, and walked off, hips swaying, into the club.

I hadn't been surprised by what Laurel had told me about Parks. It was merely the dark side of the picture that Otto had painted the night before, a picture of a man who couldn't love without inflicting pain, who couldn't compete without punishing, who probably drove himself hardest of all, like the narcissistic bodybuilders I'd seen in Kaplan's club. A man who had mistaken physical strength for all of manhood, like the boys for whom the muscle magazines were designed. I didn't for a moment doubt the fierceness of his heart, the competitiveness that Bluerock admired. And maybe it was also true that Parks had been made the way he was by other people—parents, lovers, coaches, club owners—who had bred him to violence like a pit bullterrier. Maybe that's what it took to be a great football player, but I didn't have to like it.

I didn't have to like the probability of drug abuse, either, although I certainly wasn't surprised by it. I guess it would have been more surprising if a man like Parks didn't take something to dull the pains and feed the fires inside him. I wasn't even surprised to hear that he might have gotten his goods from Walt Kaplan, the guru of health and fitness. It certainly helped to explain why Walt had such a devoted following. You hear that sort of thing all the time, anyway—agents supplying their athletes with drugs to get them to sign, to keep them happy, to keep them indebted. It's a way of life in the eighties, and not just for football players. However, it did shock me that the rumor was so current that a girl like Laurel had heard it. If Laurel had heard it, I figured the DEA couldn't be far behind. Or the grand jury that Petrie had mentioned. All of which put an entirely different complexion on what Kaplan had told me, and on the case itself. I hadn't bargained on butting heads with drug dealers, especially drug dealers who were as outsize and dangerous as Professor Walt. His warning to lay off Bill seemed a lot more persuasive, now that I knew the reasons behind it. I wasn't about to risk my life or anyone else's to help the Cougars to a winning season.

If I confirmed what Laurel had told me, I figured I'd give Hugh Petrie one more day of my time. I'd locate Bill's fiancée for him, even if I had to use Laurel to do it. And if Bill was with C.W., fine. If not, I'd leave a message in her mailbox, report back to the Cougars, and let *them* negotiate with Walt Kaplan.

XII

I decided to drop in on Otto Bluerock before I called it a night, to see if he could confirm the drug rumors or help me out with C.W.'s name and address. I wasn't sure if he was going to tell me anything. There was a code of silence among athletes, especially when it came to the drug problems of their peers. And even if there weren't an unwritten law on the subject, Otto had already proved that he was old-fashioned enough to value things like friendship and loyalty. What I was hoping was that he'd see the peril of my position and throw a little of that friendship and loyalty my way. Without his help, I'd have to rely on Laurel exclusively to locate C.W. And I didn't want to do that if I didn't have to.

At half past twelve I pulled up in front of Bluerock's dispirited-looking Victorian house on Wheeler Street. It was a hot moonlit night, and there were still a few college kids sitting on their front porches, listening to WEBN on the radio and getting high—or higher. I couldn't see their faces in the dark, but I could hear their chatter and their music and see the flare of a joint dancing like a firefly from hand to hand. I walked up to Otto's sagging porch, which creaked ominously underfoot, and knocked on the door several times.

A moment or two passed. Then I heard a stomping in the hallway behind the door, as of an elk or a bear or a giant in snowshoes. The door opened a crack and Bluerock peered out malevolently. When he saw that it was only me, he opened the door a little wider. His bulldog face was grizzled with two day's growth of beard. His eyes were swollen with sleeplessness and suspicion, and there was a purple bruise above his left brow, shaped like the business end of a nightstick.

"What the fuck do you want!" he bellowed.

"Glad to see you, too, Blue," I said with a smile.

Bluerock ran a hand through his short brown hair and stared past me toward the street and the late-night camp fires burning on the distant porches.

"I've only been here a day," he said, "and already I want to move. Listen to that shit!"

A few riffs of electric guitar drifted across Wheeler and settled with the bang of a drum kit at Bluerock's feet. Otto winced.

"It's like my worst nightmare," he said, with real pain in his voice. "I'm out of work and surrounded by phonies." He stepped further out on the porch, cupped his hands at his mouth, and shouted, "Shut the fuck up over there!"

The music went off abruptly and was replaced by the sound of high-pitched nervous laughter.

"They're laughing at me!" Bluerock said with astonishment. "I ought to go over there and twist their legs off."

"Go ahead," I said. "I won't stop you."

He gave me a wry look. "What's troubling you, sport?

You're supposed to be the cool head around here. Talk me out of this shit."

"Tonight you'll have to fend for yourself."

"Had a bad day, huh?" he said dryly. "Try to imagine what mine was like."

"Hey, you brought some of it on yourself."

"I didn't bring this crap on," he said, sweeping one huge hand across the porch. "This is God's handiwork, my friend. It's his way of clueing us in to the fact that the end of time is near. We're in the latter days." He laughed hoarsely. "I heard some cocksucker say so on the radio tonight. Sounded just like Reverend Jimmy."

"Who's he?"

"Rev Jim? He's the dildo who says the team prayer."

Bluerock opened the door and went back inside. I followed him in. The downstairs was dark and swelteringly hot. Bluerock walked into the darkness and clicked on a lamp, lighting up a small, surprisingly neat living room. The furniture wasn't fancy, but it wasn't the hodgepodge I'd half expected. There were even drapes on the windows and two teak bookshelves on either side of the mantel. If I hadn't noticed the stack of comics by one of the couch legs and the chrome snout of a barbell peeking out from behind an upholstered chair, I would have thought I was in a rented room.

"Who did the decorating in here?" I asked him.

"My old lady," he said.

"You're married?" I said with surprise.

"I used to be," Bluerock said in a voice that indicated that that was all he had to say on the subject. But from the condition of the house, it was pretty clear that he'd lost interest in the place once his wife had left him. I tried to picture the woman who would have tried to domesticate Otto and drew a blank.

Bluerock dropped heavily onto the couch and propped his feet on a walnut coffee table. He was wearing a sleeveless sweatshirt, and in the lamplight I could see that the armholes were stained with sweat. Sweat covered his forehead too. Otto propped his hands behind his head and stared at me.

"Do me a favor, Stoner," he said. "Next time, call before you show up. This isn't a fraternity house."

"You told me to get in touch after I'd talked to Professor Walt."

"I said to call, not invite yourself over. What did that douche bag have to say, anyway?"

"According to Walt, your boy Billy has turned over a new leaf. He's settled down, made peace with his past, and plans to get married to a wonderful girl named C. W. Something. I don't know her last name."

"O'Hara," Bluerock said dully. "C. W. O'Hara. And, believe me, the *W* doesn't stand for Wonderful."

"C. W. O'Hara—that's a help," I said, and eyed him balefully. "You might have told me about her last night, Blue."

"C.W. and I aren't exactly what you'd call pals," he said.

"Well, she's pals with Parks. And according to Kaplan, the only reason Bill left camp was over a contract dispute."

"That's bullshit," Bluerock said with a sneer.

"The contract dispute?"

"Yeah, the contract dispute," he said, giving me a long-suffering look. "What the hell did you think I was talking about?"

To be honest, I was happy—and a little perplexed by the fact—that he was talking at all. "How do you know that he didn't leave because of his contract?" I asked. "That's what Petrie gave as the reason. Bill's apparently got some money problems to go along with his legal hassles."

"Petrie!" Bluerock snorted. "What does that *putz*

know about what's going on in the locker room? The night before Bill ducked out of camp we went out drinking together, and he didn't say a word about contracts, money, or the law."

"What *did* he talk about?"

"His mother, Jewel. A Mormon bitch who lives out in Missoula, Montana. I met her once, when she came through here with Bill's old man. The only things she had on her mind were the end of time and who was going to hell and who was going to be a saint. It was pretty goddamn depressing."

"What did Parks say about her?"

"Not much really," Bluerock said. "Talking to Bill is like opening a new bottle of ketchup—you gotta wait a while before anything comes out. Sometimes you wait and nothing happens. That's the way it was on Monday. Of course, he was stewed to the gills and so was I, so that might have had a bearing on it. I think maybe Jewel had been lecturing him about C.W. again. C.W.'s a Baptist, and they're goddamn heathens to the Mormons. Bill doesn't usually talk about Jewel unless she's giving him some kind of grief. She made him pay a lot of dues when he was a kid."

I thought about what Laurel had said about C.W.'s attempts to "convert" Bill. Apparently that was part of an old and somewhat surprising pattern in Parks's life, although I could have guessed that his past had been pretty damn strange. It just turned out to be strange in an unexpected way. It occurred to me that marrying a pregnant girlfriend—and a Baptist, at that—probably wouldn't sit too well with his strict Mormon mother. Though it seemed absurd in a tough cookie like Parks, it was just possible that he'd left camp in order to run home and explain things to Mom.

"Did Parks's mother know that he was going to marry C.W.? Or that she was seven months pregnant?"

"*I* didn't know that they were going to get married or that she was pregnant," Bluerock said. "But then, like I said, C.W. and I didn't get along, and Bill knew that. I haven't seen her since last December. In fact, I didn't see Billy until the minicamp in May."

"What is it you don't like about C.W.?" I said, out of curiosity.

"She's another version of Bill's batty mother," Bluerock said grimly, "full of the same crooked crap. An amen sister with a streak of self-righteousness a mile wide and the morals of a whore. I knew she'd sunk her hooks into Bill last fall. I guess I just didn't know how deep. I always thought he put up with her Christian bullshit to score some steady ass. But if she reminded me of Jewel, I guess she must have reminded Bill of her too. A lot of football players end up marrying their mothers. Hell, did you ever take a good look at the wives' section? It's like staring at a shelf of bread."

I laughed. "Well, this loaf has some bruises on it. From what I hear, Bill beats her up pretty regularly."

"Yeah, and she loves it," Bluerock said with contempt. "It gives her an excuse to tattle with the other players' girlfriends. C.W.'s a shrewd little bitch. The way she looks at it getting slapped around gets her to heaven faster. Not to mention giving her a leg up on the other football wives. C.W. is always looking for an edge, a way to boost herself into the main ring. Self-pity and Jesus are her stepladder to glory. She's just another cunt, looking to score a football player and to get respectable all at once. I used to think Bill had enough on the ball not to get caught up in her game. But maybe I was wrong."

"Do you think C.W. was why Parks left camp?" I asked. "Do you think he went back to Missoula, to settle things with Jewel?"

Bluerock chewed on his lower lip. "I don't know,

sport. I'm beginning to wonder about why he left, myself."

Chewing his lip was about as close as I'd seen Bluerock
get to expressing a doubt. And I was certain that his
doubts went a lot deeper than he was letting on. I had the
feeling that that was why he'd suddenly decided to talk to
me about Bill. Of course, he hadn't really said anything
that could get Bill in hot water—nothing about the drugs
that Laurel said Parks had been abusing. And nothing
about Kaplan's part in supplying them. While Parks
might have left camp to visit home, I couldn't see Bluerock getting worked up about it. But if he thought his
friend was in some cocaine trouble, that would be a
damn good reason to get worried. And he *had* shown a
special interest in my conversation with Walt Kaplan. I
had nothing to lose by bringing the subject up.

"Bill didn't mention Kaplan on Monday night, did
he?"

Bluerock shook his head. "Just Jewel."

"That kind of surprises me," I said. "Kaplan implied
that he'd been in constant contact with Bill. And from
what I hear, Bill had good reasons to stay in touch with
him."

"What did you hear?" Bluerock asked ominously.

"That Bill had a nose problem—at least, before he met
C.W. And that Kaplan or somebody at the gym was his
supplier."

Bluerock pulled himself up on the couch with a jerk
and stared at me for a long, unsettling moment. "You
know, sport, guys can get killed for spreading rumors
like that."

"I know that," I said. "Is it true?"

"I'm not one of Walt's disciples. How the hell should I
know if it's true?" he said defensively.

I took that as a probable yes. "You know, I'm not going
to arrest Parks, Blue. I'm just trying to find him."

"Then what do you care whether Bill has a nose problem or not?"

"Because if he does, Kaplan's going to care—a lot. Walt has already made it pretty clear that he doesn't want me on this case. Of course, he didn't tell me why. He just said I was butting in where I didn't belong."

"You are, sport," Bluerock said. "You really are. Look, Harry, I don't think you have any idea of what you're getting into. Three of my teammates have already been busted for possession of cocaine, and a lot of other people are getting mighty goddamn paranoid. You're not dealing with school kids, sport, snotty college punks who do a line or two on the weekends. The guys you're talking about are big, dangerous cats. Believe me when I tell you that you would not stand a chance against either one of them. Kaplan would eat you alive and spit out the parts he didn't like. And Bill—Bill is the toughest son-of-a-bitch *I've* ever met."

"I'm thin, but I'm wiry," I said meekly.

Bluerock laughed at me. "I'm going to do you a favor, Harry. I guess I owe you one. You go ahead and find Bill, if you can. Maybe he did go to Missoula. Or maybe he's shacked up with C.W. You're better positioned to find out than I am. But when you do find him, you call me. Understand? You don't try to talk things over with Bill, you don't call Petrie, and you sure as hell don't call Walt. You call me. Maybe I can keep you from getting killed."

"You think it's that serious, then?"

"I don't know for sure," he said, shaking his head. "But the way people are worked up, it fucking well could be."

XIII

It was a little past two thirty when I got back to the Delores. By then, I was too damned tired to care about the summer heat, which had moved into my apartment for the month of July, or about C. W. O'Hara, Bill Parks, and Walt Kaplan. I sat down on the couch, thinking that I would make the trip to the bedroom in easy stages, unbuttoned my shirt, and fell asleep where I was sitting. At three A.M. the ringing of the telephone woke me with a start.

Even hard-boiled detectives associate late-night phone calls with catastrophic news, and I could feel my heart pounding as I walked over to the desk and picked up the receiver. In the back of my mind, I was wondering who had died.

I didn't even have a chance to say hello. The woman on the other end was too perturbed to exchange courtesies. In fact, she was close to hysteria. It took me almost a minute to realize that the voice belonged to Laurel

Jones. A minute later, I was out the door and on my way to Newport.

She hadn't been collected enough to make good sense. It had to do with Parks and with C.W. and with our conversation earlier that night. The gist of it was that Laurel had talked to C.W. that evening. She'd paid her a visit, in spite of the fact that I'd asked her to wait. And on that visit, something had gone very badly wrong, so wrong that it had virtually unhinged Laurel. I was afraid that Parks or Kaplan had beat her up or threatened to beat her up, and that that was what had terrified her. I cursed myself for giving the girl any encouragement to act as a go-between.

I was so furious with myself, that I was a hazard behind the wheel, making it over the river and into Newport in less than six minutes. I caromed through Newport's maze of decrepit, one-way streets to the red-light district on York. At that hour the legitimate shops were locked and lit for the night. The rest of them—the strip-and-clip joints—were wide open. I shot down York, and eventually the neon storefronts gave way to gaslights and maple-shaded tenements. Two twenty-five was just one more brick apartment house in a long row of apartments, three blocks south of the unmarked dividing line that ran like a part in Newport's hair, separating the respectable side of town from the unkempt one. I double-parked on the street and ran up a short flight of steps to a courtyard with a mass of hollyhocks in its center. A U-shaped building rather like the Delores surrounded the court, with a lobby door in each of the wings. I tried the wing on the right and got lucky. *Laurel Jones/Number Six* was written in neat script on a card in one of the brass mailboxes. There were two apartments per floor and two flights to each landing, which meant that it was six flights to Laurel Jones. By the time I finished bounding to the top landing, my lungs were on fire and my face was pouring sweat.

I pounded on Laurel's shiny mahogany door. A frightened little voice that sounded like Laurel with all the gumption let out asked, "Who's there?"

"Harry!" I shouted. "For chrissake, open the door!" I heard chains sliding in locks, then the door opened and Laurel ran out—straight into my arms.

She came flying toward me so quickly that I didn't get a chance to examine her face. And then she wouldn't let go for a minute—head buried in my chest, arms wrapped around my neck.

I held her for a long moment then gently pushed her away and tilted her face up to the light. I'd been sure that she'd been worked over by Parks or by Kaplan, but there were no marks on her face or her forearms.

I thanked God for big favors and asked her what had happened.

"I couldn't . . ." Her voice failed, and she took a couple of deep breaths. "I couldn't get hold of you." She stared at me, her blue eyes wet with tears. "I tried calling, at one and one thirty and two and two thirty. Where *were* you?"

Her voice was so plaintive, her pretty doll-like face so full of disappointment, that I felt as if I'd truly let her down—as if I *should* have been around to look after her. As if I'd contracted to do so earlier that night.

"I'm sorry, Laurel," I said guiltily. "I was looking for Parks."

Her face shook when I mentioned his name. "Oh, God," she said. "Oh, God. I don't know what to do."

I wiped the tears from her eyes with my fingertips.

"It's going to be all right," I said. "Whatever happened, I'll take care of it." I glanced over her shoulder at the open apartment door. "Do you want to go inside?"

She gasped. "God, no. I've been sitting in there for two hours."

"Then let's go out."

Laurel stared fearfully down the stairwell.

"My car's right in front. Everything will be fine."

She nodded weakly. "Okay," she said in a tiny voice.

We got to the car without any trouble, although from the way Laurel was acting I thought we might be attacked at any moment. She was so distraught that I had to remind myself that this was no teenager, scared of her own shadow. This was a tough, streetwise hooker, who'd been making her own way in a very hard world. Whatever had her so frightened must have been pretty goddamn unpleasant. And to be honest, the prospect of finding out what it was chilled me, too.

I put Laurel in the front seat of the car, got in myself, and started back up York toward the red lights. The bustle and glare of the clubs seemed to calm Laurel down a bit. By the time we got to Fifth Street, the color had returned to her cheeks and she'd stopped shaking so violently.

I turned west on Fifth toward the suspension bridge.

"Where are we going?" Laurel said in a faraway voice.

"To my apartment," I said. "You'll be all right there."

She took a deep breath and let it out slowly. "I guess we better go to C.W.'s place first," she whispered.

"Why?"

"I guess there's something you'd better see."

"What?" I said. "What happened tonight, for chrissake?"

Laurel held up a hand, as if she couldn't bring herself to talk about it yet. "Just don't ask me any more questions for a while. Okay?"

I looked over at her. She was wearing her version of a game face. She was living it out—whatever *it* was.

I did as she asked and let her alone.

Once we'd crossed the bridge into Cincinnati, Laurel told me to turn west onto River Road. I followed her directions, taking Sixth Street to the underpass and then dipping down toward the Ohio. To the south I could see the city lights, guttering like windblown candles in the deep black river current. Then the row houses started up on either side of the road, dark and boarded up, most of them, with spaces between the rows where the river lights made the only light on the street.

We kept heading west, through Riverview to Anderson Ferry. By then we'd gone better than five miles out of the city, and Laurel had had a chance to calm down.

"How much farther?" I said to her.

"Just outside Harrison—about fifteen more miles."

"And what are we going to find there?"

"I don't know," Laurel said. "I mean, I don't know what we're going to find. I didn't stay long enough to see."

"You went out there tonight?"

She nodded. "After you let me off." She gave me an apologetic look. "I *had* to talk to her, Harry. She's my friend. And I felt guilty for telling you all that stuff without explaining it to her first."

"You could have waited, Laurel," I said wearily, "like I asked you to do. You could have gotten yourself killed tonight."

"I think somebody already did," she whispered.

I tightened my grip on the steering wheel and stared grimly at the dark road unfolding before us.

"I guess you better explain this," I said after a moment. "I don't want to walk into a murder with my eyes shut."

Laurel sat back on the seat, stretching her legs to the floorboards as if she wanted to push herself right through the cushion into another life. "I thought you could help them," she said in a tiny voice. "I didn't know Bill had left camp until you told me. C.W. never said anything about it. I thought maybe if you could put Bill back on track with the team, he might ease up on C.W. about the other things."

"What other things?" I asked.

"They'd been fighting all week. About the baby, mostly. It wasn't growing right or something. And that pissed the shit out of Bill. I guess 'cause he never wanted a kid in the first place. And then Bill's mom started jumping all over C.W.'s case. And Bill's agent started telling him all sorts of bad things about C.W."

"What things?"

"I don't know. Just bad-mouthing her, I guess. Saying that she was bringing him down, sapping his strength. It got to the point on Monday where C.W. said that Bill wouldn't even stay in the same room with her. He'd just sit up all night, alone, doing exercises in the mirror and popping pills. The last thing she needed was to have Bill blame her for his troubles with the Cougars too."

"Did you talk to C.W. tonight?" I asked.

She shook her head. "She didn't answer the door. I went around back to make sure nobody was home, 'cause sometimes they can't hear you knock if they're in the kitchen. The back door was open, so I went in."

Laurel began to tremble. "Something terrible'd happened, Harry. I mean, there was stuff all over the floor . . . everything broken . . . and there was this knife. And there was blood," she said, with a thrill of horror in her voice. "Christ, so much blood! I—I just ran. I drove home and called you."

I pulled her toward me.

"I think she's dead," Laurel said, leaning heavily against my side. "I think the bastard flipped out and killed her."

"We'll take a look," I told her.

* * *

We hit a patch of river fog somewhere south of Saylor Park, and for a few minutes I had to concentrate completely on the road, on the reflectors and signs glittering in the headlights. In a way it was a relief to turn my mind to something other than the ugly mayhem that was waiting for us at the end of the trip. Whatever we found at C. W. O'Hara's house, I figured that Bill Parks was probably going to be out of my hands by dawn and back where I supposed he had always belonged—with the cops. That part was all right with me. I didn't know how it was going to sit with Otto or with Hugh Petrie. But, frankly, I didn't want to confront the son-of-a-bitch. In fact, the thing that worried me was the possibility that Parks might still be waiting in C.W.'s home, sitting all alone in the dark, practicing curls in front of a mirror.

The fog lifted about three miles south of the I-275 turnoff. Laurel directed me onto the expressway and then off again onto a jagged state route, and from there to a two-lane highway running north above the Little Miami River. A tree-covered hillside rose up on the left of the roadbed and fell away, in a talus of roadside rubble, toward the river on the right. We passed a couple of deserted shacks, then Laurel put her hand on my arm and whispered, "Slow down."

I slowed to a crawl and glanced nervously from side to side, searching for the next turn-off.

"There's a gravel driveway about a hundred yards up the road on your left," Laurel said.

Almost at once, my lights caught on the gravel, as if someone had tossed a handful of it at the car. I turned left off the road onto a hillside drive. There was a rusted mailbox on a post at the foot of the driveway, with a name painted on the flag—*O'Hara.* I stopped beside it, putting the transmission in Park, and stared up the gravel lane. It climbed the hill at a steep angle for about two hundred feet, then disappeared into a thick dark woods.

"How far does this go before we get to the house?" I said to Laurel.

"A couple hundred feet," she said.

I could tell from her voice that she was very frightened.

"Is there any other way up or down?"

"No."

"Can you turn around up there? Or do you have to back out?"

"There's a turnaround by the garage," Laurel said.

I took a deep breath and glanced at the girl, who was staring intently through the windshield at the gravel driveway. "It would be much better if you weren't here, Laurel. In fact, you could go to the cops right now if you're convinced a murder has been committed."

"I don't know," she said nervously. "I didn't see a body. Just the blood."

"You could still go to the cops with that."

"But what if he just beat her up or something?" she said. "He's done that plenty of times before. C.W.'d kill my ass if I called the cops on Bill."

"All right," I said. "Are you sure you want to go up there with me? You sure you don't want to wait somewhere else while I take a look?"

"I guess I've got to know for sure," she said. "Anyway, I don't want to be anywhere by myself."

I reached over to the glove compartment and pressed the button. The door fell open above Laurel's knee. I groped around inside and pulled out the Colt Gold Cup.

Laurel gave me a terrified look, as if she were afraid I was going to turn the weapon on her.

"He might still be in there, Laurel," I said, cocking the piece, putting on the safety, and sticking the pistol in my belt. "You sure about the cops?"

She nodded. "I don't want to get involved with cops."

She laughed, a little hysterically. "I don't want to be involved in this, at all. It's a terrible thing to say, but I don't. If she *is* dead in there, Harry, you've got to promise to keep my name out of it. You gotta promise me, Harry."

"She's your friend, Laurel," I said, giving her a look.

She stared back at me defiantly. "Yeah, and I'm here, trying to help. Which is the last place on earth I want to be, believe me. But if C.W. is dead, it's not going to make a bit of difference to her what I do." She looked scared to death and fiercely belligerent at the same time. "I've still got plans. I've still got my dreams and my life. If the wrong people find out I was connected to this . . ."

I felt like lecturing her on the bloody idiocy that her friend had probably brought down on her own head by trying to realize the same dreams. But I didn't do it. There wasn't enough time, and she didn't want to hear it anyway. "Okay, Laurel. I'll try to keep you clean. Just one thing, though. When we get up there, you do *exactly* what I say. You hear me?"

"Yes," she whispered. "I promise."

I clicked off the headlights, flipped on the parking lights, and started up the gravel drive.

XIV

There was a ranch house at the top of the drive, surrounded by the thick woods of the hillside. I stopped the car on the gravel about twenty yards away from it and backed around so that the Pinto was facing down the driveway. After dousing the lights, I turned the engine off and got out. Laurel got out on her side, and for a moment we stood there, staring silently at the house.

There was enough of a moon beaming down to light up the shingled roof of the ranch and the unpainted pine-board garage to its right. There was no other light coming from the building or from the woods. Once I shut the car off, there was very little noise either, just the woodland sounds of the crickets and of the hot summer wind in the pines. Somewhere off in the trees a branch creaked suddenly, like someone turning over in bed. Both Laurel and I jumped.

I pulled the pistol from my belt, unlocked the safety, and got a good firm grip on the butt.

"How do we get in there?" I said in a whisper.

Laurel pointed to her left, where a gravel path made its way between the ranch house and the garage.

"That goes to the kitchen," she whispered.

"All right. Stay behind me. Keep your arms at your sides. And try to be quiet. If anything happens to me, go straight to the car and drive away. I've left the keys in the ignition. Don't look back. Don't think about it. Just get the hell out of here and call the cops as fast as you can."

"Harry," she said shakily. "I'm really scared."

I said, "It's going to be all right."

I started walking across the yard and Laurel fell in behind me, so closely that I could feel her press against my back as if we were riding double on a motorcycle. When we got to the path between the outbuilding and the ranch, I stopped, and Laurel bumped up against me.

"Where's the kitchen door?" I whispered.

"About twenty feet up ahead," she whispered back. "On your right."

With my back to the ranch house wall, I worked my way slowly down the path, both hands on the pistol. A bit of dawn light was beginning to spread through the woods— enough of a glow so that I could see a white frame screen door in front of me. The screen door was hanging open above a one-step concrete stoop. The kitchen door looked as if it was open, too. Just the way, I assumed, that Laurel had left them.

"There's a light switch to the left of the door," Laurel whispered.

"Stay where you are," I whispered back. "I'm going inside."

I crept up onto the stoop, knelt down, and eased around the doorjamb, holding the pistol close to my body. Inside, I could see the silhouette of an overturned kitchen table, its aluminum legs sticking up like the stiff, splayed legs of a dead horse. There was a lot of broken crockery on the floor—shards of porcelain and glass. The room looked as if it were tiled with glass.

It wasn't until I was actually through the door— hunched on my heels, back against the doorjamb, gun arm extended—that I got my first whiff of blood. That stale, coppery smell, like the taste of pennies on the tongue.

I crept across the doorway to the left-hand wall and crouched in front of a cabinet. From that angle, I could see farther into the house, past the wrecked kitchen table into the hall. There was a gelid pool of something glistening on the floor and the shocking silver reflection of a knife blade, shining so brightly in the dawn light that it looked like a white hole in the carpet. Without standing up, I reached above my head, feeling along the wall for a light switch. It took me a while, but I found it and flipped it on.

The room filled with light from an overhead fixture. I had to shut my eyes for a second to adjust to the brightness. When I opened them, I took another look at the kitchen, then called Laurel into the room. She came around the doorjamb slowly, clinging to the wall as if she were walking on a ledge.

Laurel stared dully at the broken plates. Her eyes swept across the floor to the hall, where the knife lay in its pool of coagulating blood. She jerked her head away and put a hand over her mouth.

"Oh, Christ!" she said with terror.

"Are you going to be all right?" I said.

She nodded, her head still turned away.

"Stay put," I said.

Laurel nodded again.

I walked across the kitchen—across all those broken dishes—to the hallway. The crockery crunched like rock salt underfoot. There was a trail of blood leading away from the pool with the knife in it toward a closed door at the far end of the corridor. I stood there for a moment, listening so intently to the silence of the house that I could hear the blood pulsing in my ears. There was no sound anywhere in the place.

I held the pistol in front of me and followed the bloodstains down the hall to the closed door. I hesitated for a second in front of it, then put my free hand to the knob. It felt like a lump of ice in my palm. I turned it and pushed. The door fell open noiselessly, and the smell of death hit me full in the face. I covered my mouth with my free hand and felt along the wall with my gun hand for a light switch. I found one and clicked it on.

She was lying on the bed—spread-eagled. Her legs had been tied to the bedposts with wire coat hangers, her arms to the headboards. The hands dangled lifelessly above the wrists. There was a swatch of white tape across her mouth, stained reddish-brown at either end. Her eyes were wide open, still staring up at the ceiling in agonized horror.

I didn't look at her for long. I couldn't. What had been done to her lower body with the knife, to her belly and to what had been growing inside it, was almost too awful to believe. So awful it was like an atrocity picture or one of Foxe's lives of the martyrs, a horror so sneaking and gruesome that it sickened, then numbed me.

I gazed around the room, at her dresser with its combs and brushes, at the vials of makeup standing in a glass tray, at a framed photograph of her and Parks propped in front of the dresser mirror. Unlike the kitchen, none of the furnishings in the bedroom had been broken. None of the dresser drawers had been ransacked. The folding closet door beyond the bed stood open, garments hanging in eerie neatness from a long wooden rod. Except for the blood-soaked bed, everything seemed to be in its place. It made me think that she'd been unconscious when she'd been tied down—stabbed after a fight in the kitchen, then carried to the bedroom and butchered. There was nothing subtle about the killing. Nobody had taken a fine hand to her body. It was a messy, vicious murder, done by someone who'd wanted to make her suffer horribly. Done by someone who'd wanted to kill her, and the life inside her too.

Except for the Ripper killings, it was the most terrible murder I'd ever seen. And if it hadn't been so goddamn awful that it was almost unreal, and if I hadn't come across it so casually, I think I might have gone into shock. As it was my legs went rubbery and my throat dried up as if it were parched. I slapped at the light, and it went off—mercifully. Then I backed out of the room, closing the door behind me.

There was one other room off the hall, to the left and a little beyond the room with C. W. O'Hara's corpse in it. It would have to be checked. I knew it would have to be checked. But for a good half minute, I couldn't make my legs stop trembling. And even after a full minute, they still felt loosely connected to me, as if I were dangling them from a barstool.

I forced myself to open the door of the second room, and nearly fired my piece into a mirror that was sitting opposite the doorway—shooting at my own reflection in the glass. The shock of seeing someone standing in front of me when I opened the door sent a jolt of adrenaline through my body, raising gooseflesh on my arms and waking me up as if I'd been drenched with ice water. I clawed at the wall until I found a light switch and flipped it on.

Aside from the mirror, a chair, and a small desk, there was nothing in the room. No pictures on the walls. No drapes. No rug. The chair sat in front of the mirror. The floor between them was heavily scuffed, as if someone had been gouging it with a file. I knew at once that that was where he had sat—for the past week, according to

Laurel—practicing curls in the looking glass. In fact, I found the curling bar on the floor of a large walk-in closet at the back of the room. The only other thing in the closet was a short-sleeve shirt hanging from a wire clothes hanger. Maybe it was because her closet had been so full of clothes, but that single shirt, hanging all by itself in the huge closet, gave me the creeps. I examined it anyway. There were no visible bloodstains. I took a look inside the desk too.

In the top drawer I found a well-used pair of curling gloves, a jar of resin, several pamphlets announcing the end of the world, a dog-eared photograph of a middle-aged woman sitting on a porch swing, a muscle magazine with Sergio Oliva on the cover, a karate magazine, a survivalist handbook, and dozens of red and white capsules lying like loose change all over the bottom of the drawer. I slipped several of the capsules in my pocket, figuring the cops would never miss them. I wanted to take the photograph too. Instead, I spent a moment trying to memorize the woman's features—a plump, pretty, cheerful-looking face, ringed with curls. I closed the drawer, wiped my prints from the handle with a handkerchief, turned off the light, and walked back down the hall to the kitchen.

Laurel had righted a chair and propped it beside the door. She was sitting in it gravely, hands crossed in her lap, shoulders straight against the cushion, as if she were sitting in a pew.

"She's dead, isn't she?" Laurel said in a stricken voice.

"Yes," I said. "It's very ugly."

Tears spilled from her eyes and down her cheeks, but she didn't move to stop them. She didn't move at all. She *was* going into shock.

I took my jacket off and draped it over her shoulders. Then looked around the room for a phone. I found one above the sink. I picked it up and dialed the operator. "Give me the police," I said.

"County or city?" the operator asked.

"County."

She went off the line for a second, and I asked Laurel, "What's the address here?"

"Fifty-six Devil's Creek Road," she said mechanically.

"Devil's Creek," I said to myself.

When the sergeant came on, I told him where we were and what we'd found there. He said a team of detectives would be sent out immediately.

XV

I didn't have a chance to examine the rest of the house to see if Parks had left anything behind him other than his dead lover's torn body. But C.W.'s corpse was, in itself, a pretty unequivocal piece of evidence. Laurel had already told me that C.W. and Bill had been fighting violently about the baby and their impending marriage. It looked now as if Bill had probably left camp to finish the argument, spending that long hot week holed up in his room at the ranch house, high perhaps on those red and white capsules, meditating the bloody work that he'd finally committed himself to in a frenzy of hatred. The loathing he'd felt for his lover, and for the baby she was carrying, was evident in the crime.

Before the cops arrived, I found several notes taped to the refrigerator in the kitchen, little reminders that C.W. O'Hara had apparently written to herself in the kind of flowery hand that must have won the heart of her third-grade writing teacher. All the *i*'s had little hearts above them. You could have driven a truck through the loops of the *l*'s and the hoops of the *o*'s. It was a bold, grossly self-advertising hand—the script, I thought, of a shrewd, sugary, ambitious girl, a girl who had relied, even in notes to herself, on her sexual charm. A girl who certainly didn't seem to be aware of the disaster that was in store for her. One of the notes made reference to a Dr. A. *Get report from Dr. A.* A second note read *Get in touch with Dr. P.* And a third, *Meet with Reverend Dice at 4:00*, and was dated Saturday the 25th, which had just dawned in full through the kitchen window. The only note that smacked even remotely of family tensions was one that was printed, rather than written—one that was apparently meant for Parks himself. It said, in big block letters, BILL, CALL JEWEL. There was an out-of-state number written beneath it. Out of habit, I copied the number into my notebook, along with the texts of each of the other notes. I wanted to ask Laurel about them, about the doctors and Reverend Dice; but she was too far gone in grief and shock to answer questions.

The cops showed up around six A.M.—bubble-tops sprinkling blue light through the pines and breaking the dense, woody silence with the Klaxon wail of their sirens. They had an ambulance in tow. I had to move the Pinto to let all the police cruisers into the yard. And then the newspaper and television guys started trickling in. By seven the entire drive from Devil's Creek to the ranch house was lined with cars.

I managed to call Hugh Petrie before the newsmen showed up in force. When I told him what I had found in C.W.'s house, there was dead silence on the line. When he finally responded, he sounded thoroughly shaken up, as if Parks had finally pushed him past some limit of endurance, some nadir of cynicism, that he'd set in his own mind.

"I don't think I believe it," he said in a lifeless voice. "My God. Are you certain that it was Bill who did this?"

"Fairly certain, yes. He'd been fighting with the girl all week about the baby, and the way she was killed—well, it seems obvious that he was the one who murdered her."

"My God," Petrie said again. "He must have gone completely out of his mind."

"I think he's been out of his mind for a long time, Hugh."

"And am I responsible for that?" he said wildly, as if I'd accused him. "I just hire them, for chrissake. To play a fucking game! I run a business—that's all."

I didn't answer him. In half a minute, he'd recovered his cool.

"Are the newspapers there, yet?"

"Just a couple reporters, so far," I said. "But the cops are here."

He sighed heavily. "Okay. Better let me talk to whoever's in charge."

I handed the phone to the head honcho, a tall, pawky lieutenant named Larson, who had an Ichabod Crane face and a stinting, by-the-book manner. Larson was a bad, incompetent cop. He hadn't even had enough sense to cover the O'Hara girl's body with a sheet when Laurel made the identification. The result was that Laurel had gone into hysterics and had to be sedated by the coroner. Larson wrote the incident off as just one more instance of women's weakness, and proceeded with the main business at hand—trying to bully me into a confession. His conversation with Petrie seemed to straighten him out a little, and he did withhold Laurel's name when the TV guys showed up, although I could see that it cost him something to bite his tongue. TV shows were the whole reason he'd become a cop, and he felt a greater obligation to shape up in front of the cameras than he did in front of me, Laurel, and his own men.

At eight A.M. the coroner's team carried what was left of C. W. O'Hara out to the ambulance in a green rubber body bag. I was sitting on a plaid sofa in the living room, drinking cold coffee out of a styrofoam cup. Laurel, who had fallen asleep after the coroner sedated her, was stretched out beside me, covered from neck to toe with newspaper. I watched the paramedics work the body bag through the kitchen door and glanced at the girl beside me. I felt the urge to wake her—to make her rattle those newspapers like a businessman at breakfast. It was a childish urge and I restrained myself. I just wanted to make sure she was alive. I'd lost too many other women I'd felt affection for to my work. And that, I had promised myself, was never going to happen again, although I couldn't help suspecting that the only way to insure that it didn't was to keep from feeling anything for anyone. And if I followed that melancholy road, one day I'd wake up and find myself alone with my inexorable bachelorhood.

That was such a wearying prospect that it made me close my eyes. When I opened them again, a burly man was standing over me, smiling. He was a big guy, middle-aged and nicely dressed in a blue open-collared shirt, silk sports coat, and tan slacks. At first I thought he was one of the newspapermen. But as he sat down across from me in a wing chair, I realized that he was too neat and prosperous-looking to be with the press. What he really looked like was a dapper, small-time hood. His shiny brown hair was razor cut, wrapped like a scarf around his ears and plumped up at the nape in a little ducktail. His face was tanned and creased around the eyes with good-natured laugh lines. He wore an immaculately trimmed beard and mustache, and when he smiled, which he hadn't stopped doing since he'd sat down, he radiated some of the vain, little-boy charm of a Burt Reynolds. I had the feeling that I should have known who he was. He certainly acted like he knew me. He had that kind of grin

—like we went back years together, like it was time for me to return that mower I'd borrowed from his garage.

"Harry," he said in a pleasant baritone.

"That's what they call me," I said. "Do we know each other?"

"No," he said. "I got your name from Hugh Petrie. I'm Clayton. Phil Clayton."

The name rang a bell, but I was so tired and dispirited that it took me a few seconds to place it.

"Where is he, Harry?" Clayton said with infinite patience, as if he'd been asking me that same question for hours.

"Who?" I said dully.

"Bill Parks," Clayton said.

"I don't know." My mind cleared and I remembered where I'd seen his name. Sergeant Phil Clayton of District Two. He had been the arresting officer in the Candy Kane assault case. "I don't know where Parks is," I said again. "Why don't you tell me? You're the guy who arrested him, aren't you?"

I'd meant it as a wisecrack, but Clayton took it seriously.

"Why do you think I know where he is?" he said, tugging gently at his shirt cuffs to even them up beneath the sports coat.

I started to tell him that I'd been kidding, then decided I didn't owe him an explanation. In fact, I didn't owe him anything.

"Look, what is this?" I said irritably. "I just spent two hours getting grilled by the county cops, and I don't feel like doing it again. This case is out of your jurisdiction, anyway. What business do you have asking me about Parks?"

"Let's just say that Bill is important to me," he said with his unruffled smile.

"Let's just say that I don't give a fuck."

"Harry," Clayton said, scratching his earlobe. "You're not being very cooperative. Just answer a few questions and I'll leave you alone."

"What questions?" I asked suspiciously.

"Did you see Bill tonight?"

"No," I said.

"Did you follow him here?"

I said no again.

"Well, someone must have led you in this direction." He glanced almost tenderly at Laurel. "She tipped you off, didn't she?"

I didn't answer him.

"What did she tell you about Bill, Harry?" Clayton said, cupping his hands around his knee and leaning forward in the chair like the family doctor.

It suddenly dawned on me that this amiable thug thought I knew something I wasn't supposed to know. Since Clayton's only connection with Parks was the Candy Kane assault arrest, I began to wonder what it had to do with C. W. O'Hara's murder.

"Look, Harry," Clayton said. "I'm trying to be a reasonable guy, but you're still not cooperating. I asked you a question. What did that girl tell you about Parks?"

"I don't think I want to answer any more questions, Clayton," I said. "What the girl told me is confidential information."

He laughed. "Confidential? She's a whore. And you're working for the Cougars."

"So arrest me."

He shifted his legs, spotted a piece of fluff on the knee and flicked it off with his fingernail. "I'll tell you what I might do instead," he said, looking at Laurel. "I might arrest her. You know, we found some flake in her purse. Not a lot, but I can probably see to it that there's enough to get her on felony possession."

"You'd do that?" I said.

He laughed again. "Hell, yes, I'd do that. I'll take her downtown and use a stun gun on her tits, if you don't quit fucking with me."

He didn't stop smiling or change his tone of voice, but I took one look at his eyes and knew that he wasn't bluffing. I also knew that if I didn't tell him the truth he'd call me on it. Clayton already knew all about Bill Parks. He was trying to figure out how much I knew, though I'd be damned if I could figure out why. I said, "The girl told me earlier tonight that Parks was living here with C. W. O'Hara. Apparently O'Hara and Parks had spent the week fighting, and the girl was worried about them. She asked me if I'd come take a look. You know what we found."

"What did the girl tell you Parks and O'Hara were fighting about, Harry?" Clayton said.

"About getting married. About having a baby. About the troubles he was having with the Cougars."

"That's it?" he said.

"That's it."

Clayton glanced at the girl, looked at me for a second, then slowly got to his feet. "I hope you're telling me the truth, Harry. I hope it for *her* sake." He glanced at Laurel again. "If I find out different, you'll be hearing from me." He started to walk away, then turned back. "By the way, as of this moment, you're off the case."

"That's up to the Cougars," I said.

"I've already talked to the Cougars. Your number's been retired. So stay out of it. Otherwise . . ." He pointed his forefinger at the girl, then drew the same finger down to his chest. *"Bzzzzt!"* he said, making a raster noise. He laughed out loud and walked away.

XVI

Although I didn't understand the reason for his threats, talking to Sergeant Phil Clayton seemed an appropriate way to end an unforgettably ugly evening. Clayton went into conference with Larson after he'd finished with me. They spoke for about ten minutes, and I could tell that Laurel and I were part of the conversation from the way that Larson was eyeing us. As soon as they were through talking, Larson came over to the couch and told me that we were free to go.

I took Laurel back to my apartment and put her straight to bed. She was still drowsy with drugs and badly shaken by the ordeal that we'd gone through. I thought she'd drop off immediately, but as I tucked her in, she grabbed my hand and pulled me down beside her.

"Don't leave me alone," she whispered.

"I won't," I said.

I lay back on the bed and put my arm around her. After a time she fell asleep, but I didn't drift off for a while. Sitting there in the morning sun, feeling the heat settling over me like a blanket, I couldn't stop thinking about Parks—lifting his curling bar in front of that mirror, counting each good rep until he'd completed a set. Then doing another set, and another, late into the night. The sweat dripping down his ravaged, young–old man's face, down his huge, muscular arms. The summer heat, like the heat that was stealing through the bedroom, enveloping him in its fire. He'd sat there for three days. And on the fourth day, he'd gone violently insane.

I couldn't get him out of my mind. Or the image of what he had done to his lover and to their child. He hadn't just killed C. W. O'Hara. He'd killed a part of himself, too—his son, the coroner had said. Of course, men had killed their own before—in a rage, in a mad, infrangible moment. But there was an ancient ugliness about the crime. Sleeping with a woman like his mother. Fathering a child by her. And slaughtering both of them. It was like something awful painted in a cave, something conceived before the words to describe it, or for which the words wouldn't do.

And at the same time, it was horribly banal. He was a man who made his living acting out those violent rituals of hunt and sacrifice painted in the caves. He was a big, dumb, ferocious jock. A caveman in the flesh, who lived completely on the surface of life, completely through his muscles, who had no inwardness at all—unless his born-again lover's attempts to convert him counted toward a conscience, or his demons, the drives that kept him building muscles and knocking heads, constituted character. As for C.W., she was probably just what Bluerock had said she was—a gold digger looking to snare a real live football player of her own. Any way you looked at them, they weren't tragic types.

And yet something about the sheer brutality of the murder affected me as if it were true tragedy, shocked me and held onto me as if I'd shaken hands with a live wire.

It made the detective in me want to find out why it had happened. The rest of me, the sane part, was relieved to know that I probably never would find out—at least, not on my own. According to Clayton, the Cougars no longer needed my services. To be honest, I didn't see how they did, either. They no longer had a reason to find Parks. And although I resented having a cop threaten me and was damn curious about why Clayton was so interested in Bill, I figured he was right. Parks *did* belong to the police now. And I would have to learn what had driven him mad, through the civilian channels, second-hand, in newspapers and on TV.

I fell asleep beside Laurel and slept long into the afternoon. Around three, the phone woke me from a terrible dream about Parks. It took me a moment to recognize the bedroom and the girl lying next to me. I got up and went into the living room, with Parks still trailing me like a demon shadow. It was Petrie on the phone.

"I've got to talk to you this afternoon," he said, after he'd said hello.

He sounded oddly out of control for such a tightly controlled man.

"I thought you'd fired me," I said.

"Who told you that?"

"A guy named Clayton. He said you told him I was off the case, as of this morning."

"Well, things have changed since then," Petrie said grimly. "We very much need your help."

"Changed how?"

"I don't want to talk about it over the phone. I'll meet you at your place around six."

"What's wrong with meeting at your office?" I said.

"I'm not going near my goddamn office today!" Petrie said almost hysterically. "Look, do me a favor and don't ask any more questions. I'll explain everything tonight."

Only he didn't have to explain it. I figured it out for myself when I fetched the afternoon paper from the hall. One look at the headline and I knew at once why Petrie didn't want to go near his office and why he'd sounded so rattled. I also knew what he wanted to talk about. What I didn't know was how I was going to answer him.

With the newspaper in my hand, I sat down at the rolltop desk and read through the article a second time. FOOTBALL PLAYER WANTED IN BRUTAL MURDER, ran the headline, and underneath, "Cougars Implicated In Drug Scandal."

I skipped over the details of the murder, which were all too fresh in my mind, and perused the paragraph about Parks's alleged drug problems:

> A source close to the case has revealed that Parks was under federal indictment brought by the DEA task force looking into drug abuse in the NFL. Caught in a DEA sting operation last December, Parks agreed to testify before the grand jury in exchange for immunity on the drug-related charge. Although Cougar management has refused to comment on the case, the same source confirmed that team officials assisted in securing immunity for Parks.

The writer went on to speculate, in the next paragraph, that the ordeal of preparing to appear before a grand jury had contributed to Parks's apparent mental collapse. Although it wasn't spelled out, the implication was that the Cougars were indirectly to blame for the murder.

Although the evidence presented in the article was meager at best, my first reaction was to wonder whether the allegation leveled against the Cougar management was true. If the Cougars had helped Parks plea-bargain

his way out of a drug charge, then Petrie had flat out lied
to me on Friday afternoon when he'd assured me that the
Cougars weren't holding anything over Parks's head.

My second reaction was to wonder if Parks had in fact
testified, and if he had, whom he'd testified against. If
Walt Kaplan had been named in Parks's testimony, then
I'd be taking my life in my hands if I started poking
around in Parks's life again. Worse, I'd be jeopardizing
Laurel. As Bluerock had pointed out, people get mighty
paranoid when indictments are handed down. And if
Walt found out that Laurel knew about his drug dealing,
she'd be a threat to him. Something would have to be
done about that, whether I continued to work for the
Cougars or not. Getting the girl out of town for a time
would probably be the wisest move, although I had no
idea how Laurel would feel about it.

My third reaction to the article was to wonder who the
unnamed source was and why he'd waited until after the
murder to tell all. A drug bust involving a football player
was front-page news—good publicity for the DEA and
good gossip for the rest of the town and the league.
Although the feds hadn't shown any charity with
Monroe, Calhoun, and Greene, it was possible that
they'd been waiting to go public until after Parks testified
before the grand jury. There was no indication in the
newspaper article of whether Parks *had* actually testified.
But he might have left camp on Monday in order to do
so. He might have been sequestered for the week by the
feds, in advance of a trial. If so, the whole thing had
backfired horribly. If they'd been keeping him under
house arrest at C. W. O'Hara's home, they'd picked the
wrong damn place. Because it was pretty clear from what
Laurel had said, and from the grisly evidence of the
murder itself, that something else had been going on in
that house—something that had culminated in terrible
violence. Of course, if they had been sequestering him,

they would have needed a baby-sitter. Which made me think of smiling Phil Clayton, the man who shouldn't have been on the spot. He'd acted as if he were guarding a secret, although I'd assumed that it had something to do with the Candy Kane arrest. I didn't understand what that assault case had to do with a drug bust, any more than I'd understood what it had to do with a murder. But if I was going to have anything more to do with unraveling the Parks case, I figured I'd better find out.

I picked up the phone and dialed Mike Sabatto, a sportswriter I knew at the *Cincinnati Post*. A secretary put me on hold, and while I was waiting for Mike to pick up, my call-waiting line began to buzz. I stared at the phone in disgust for a moment. Ever since I'd had call-waiting installed, I'd gone through the same routine. The phone wouldn't ring all day, but as soon as I picked it up, I'd be deluged with calls.

It had happened too many times to be coincidental. It gave me the certain feeling that the phone company knew something I didn't. But then I'd had that feeling long before I'd ordered call-waiting. This time, I decided to forego my usual juggling act and let the second call go. It was lucky I did, because Mike picked up a moment after the call-waiting quit buzzing.

I knew Sabatto well enough to drink with him whenever we found ourselves in the same bar. Balding, ungainly, and acerbic, Mike was as Catholic as Elmer's sister, with a long-suffering spouse, six children, and that dour look of resignation that comes with the good Catholic life, like Continental Breakfast on the European Plan. Although he was barely thirty years old, he looked forty-five and acted it.

After asking him about his wife and his kids and his St. Louis in North College Hill, I turned the conversation to the day's headlines.

"We knew he'd skipped camp four days ago," Mike said when I mentioned Parks.

"How come it didn't make the papers?" I asked.

"You'd be surprised what doesn't make the papers," he said with glee. "The Cougar front office told us that he had 'personal problems,' and to hold off on the publicity until they'd had a chance to talk to him. We don't usually agree to that sort of thing, but in this case they made it clear that we'd be sorry if we didn't play ball." Sabatto laughed raucously. "Who's sorry now, I ask you? If they'd been up-front about the drug thing, they could have saved themselves a black eye."

"I'm surprised one of you guys didn't get wind of it anyway," I said. "You didn't have any trouble finding out about Monroe, Calhoun, and Greene."

"That's 'cause the DEA *wanted* us to know about them," he said.

"Why wouldn't they have wanted you to know about Parks?"

"They had their reasons," Sabatto said mysteriously. "You know they don't go public with everything. A lot of pretty nasty stuff is settled in closed chambers or out of court. We hear about it, but unless we can dig up sources willing to go on record, we can't print it."

"Where'd you manage to dig up the source on Parks?"

"A DEA guy phoned in the whole story right after the murder."

"You wouldn't know his name, would you?"

"I'm not supposed to," Mike said, "but for a friend . . . His name is Clayton. Phil Clayton. He's a local cop, a narc in the Second District who was detailed to help the DEA out with the Cougars. From what I hear, he was more or less in charge of Parks's case."

"Do you know what he got Parks on?" I asked him.

"Possession of controlled substances is what I hear. I guess that means cocaine."

It was a safe guess. "Do you know who Parks was scheduled to testify against?"

"Some local dealers."

"And did he testify?"

"That I don't know," Mike said.

XVII

After I finished with Sabatto, I tried calling George DeVries at the DA's office to see if he could tell me whether Parks had testified before the grand jury, and whom he'd testified against. But it was almost four thirty by the time I phoned, and George was never one to spend a long Saturday at the office. When I couldn't rouse George at home either, I called Lieutenant Al Foster at the CPD. Although Al hadn't heard anything about Parks and the grand jury—or claimed that he hadn't—he did confirm that Clayton was a narcotics agent.

"I don't know why you're asking about him, Harry," Al said in his achy, high-pitched voice. "But I'll tell you this —he's not a guy you want to fuck with. Believe me. He's built up quite a rep in the Second District."

"A hard case?"

"The hardest. He uses people up. Turns them, bleeds them, then hangs them out to dry. And Clayton always ends up getting a commendation." Al laughed mordantly. "It's a helluva world, isn't it?"

"A helluva world," I said to myself.

"Do yourself a favor," Al said. "Steer clear of him. At least, for the next couple of weeks."

"Why for the next couple of weeks?" I said.

"There's something in the works. An in-house thing. Clayton may get his ass fried. That's all I can tell you now. And if you tell anybody that I told you that much, it's the last help you'll get from me."

"It'll be our little secret," I told him.

I hung up and stared morosely at the desk. Apparently Clayton wasn't just a dangerous cop, he was a crooked one. At least, that's what I took Al's comments to mean. He'd compiled a hell of an arrest record in the Second District—good enough to get him a job with the DEA. And now his methods had landed him in some trouble. Thinking back, I realized that he'd acted like a man in trouble the night before. At the time I couldn't figure out what he had to be worried about. Hell, I couldn't figure out what he was doing at the ranch house, at all. But if Parks had been Clayton's case, then the O'Hara murder would have given him plenty to worry about. You don't get a star next to your name for cutting a deal with a psychopath. Maybe that was why Clayton had implicated the Cougars in the plea-bargaining process. Maybe he'd been trying to spread the blame for his mistake. On the other hand, he could have been telling the truth.

I took the Candy Kane rap sheet out of the desk and went through it again. According to the papers, the drug bust was made in December. So was the assault arrest. And both collars were made by Clayton. It was obvious that the two were connected, although I wasn't sure how. But I had the gut feeling that the Candy Kane arrest was a stalking-horse. God knew, that the case was flimsy enough. I'd thought that from the moment I'd seen the rap sheet. A charge pressed without a complainant, with a hostile party as the only witness. And one thing more—

something that had occurred to me as I was reading through the report again. I'd almost come up with it the day before, when I'd talked to Laurel in the pizza parlor. It was the date of the assault arrest—December 31. According to Laurel, Parks had moved in with C. W. O'Hara at the end of December, right after she'd told him about her pregnancy. By all rights, Parks should have been with the O'Hara girl on New Year's Eve, not with some stripper named Candy Kane.

The surest way to find out what was really going on was to talk to George DeVries, who would have access to the pretrial material in both cases. Since he wasn't available, my next best bet would be to talk to Candy Kane herself. I was about to call the Caesar Apartments to see if Candy was still living there, when Laurel wandered into the room.

Glassy-eyed, disheveled, and smelling of sleep, she made her way to the couch, sat down heavily on the cushions, and curled her legs up beneath her. She had put on one of my shirts over her panties, and she jerked the tail down over her bare knees as if she were straightening the hem of a skirt.

"What time is it?" she said groggily, kneading her cheeks with her fists.

"About five," I said.

"Five?" she repeated dully.

I stared at her for a moment. Un–made up, her electrified hair standing at all angles, her right cheek wrinkled like a sheet from where she'd slept on it, she looked, even to me, like a visiting relative—a niece or a cousin.

"Are you all right?" I said.

She shook her head. "No. My head hurts."

"It's the sedative they gave you."

She looked confused for a moment. Then it started to come back to her and her face went white. "Oh, my God," she said softly. "I almost forgot."

"Best to forget," I said.

I went over to the couch and sat down beside her.

"Oh, Harry," she said, giving me a forlorn look. "What am I going to do?"

"You can stay here with me," I said, pulling her against me, "until you feel better."

"But how will I live?" she said helplessly. "I gotta work. I got things to do."

"I think you better lay off work for a few days. If you don't want to stay with me, you could take a vacation. Visit your folks."

"In Corbin?" she said, making a tragic face. "I don't want to go there. I want to go home." She began to sob. "I didn't do anything wrong. I just wanted to help, for chrissake."

I thought she was going to break down again, as she had the night before. But this time the tears stopped almost as quickly as they'd begun. Laurel rubbed her eyes fiercely and straightened up on the couch, shaking my hand from her shoulder, as if she could do with a little less comforting. "Cut it out," she said to herself, like a coach in a locker room. "You're not a child anymore. You can take care of yourself."

She looked around my shabby living room, seeing it for the first time. "Where are we?" she asked.

"At my apartment."

Laurel sighed. "That's what I was afraid you'd say. It looks just like my place—cruddy."

She stood up with a jerk, as if she were coming to attention. "I've got to take a shower and a shampoo. I must look like hell. Then I've got some decisions to make."

"The bathroom's right through there," I said, pointing down the hall.

She glanced at me. "Is there any word about . . ."

"Not yet," I said.

"I hope they get him soon," she said fiercely. "I hope they get him and I hope they do to him what he did to her."

"They'll get him," I said. "There aren't a whole lot of places where a man like that can hide."

I didn't have any luck locating Candy Kane. Not that I thought that I would. It was an obvious stage name—just one more thing about the arrest report that made it suspect. I tried a few Newport strip joints after I phoned the Caesar, but nobody at the clubs was willing to talk over the phone. It occurred to me that Laurel would probably recognize the name, since she had danced in Newport. But I wasn't sure I wanted to ask her. Each time she helped me out she unwittingly got herself more deeply involved in the case. Each time she put herself in more jeopardy. It wasn't fair to use her like that—not without telling her about the risks she was facing. She didn't know about Clayton. And while she knew that Kaplan was a drug dealer, she didn't know that he might have been indicted by the grand jury.

I decided to wait until I'd talked to Petrie before I asked Laurel for any more favors or did any more detecting. I still wasn't sure I wanted to stay on the case, especially since there was no question that it was drug related and very dangerous. In fact, if I'd known the way things were going to fall out the day before, I would have quit on the spot. But the previous night had changed things. You can't witness a crime like that and not be changed by it.

At six sharp, Petrie knocked on my door. By then Laurel had showered and dressed and was lying on the bed, leafing through an old copy of *Popular Photography*. I'd told her that I was expecting company, and as soon as Petrie walked in she closed the bedroom door.

Petrie walked over to the rolltop desk and sat down in

the captain's chair. He looked thoroughly worn out—
eyes ringed with fatigue, his granite jaw peppered with a
day's growth of beard. He smelled through his suit of
sweat, bone-weariness, and alcohol.

"When's the last time you slept?" I said.

"Not since you got me up this morning." He rolled his
head back and the muscles in his neck bulged above his
shirt collar. "It has not been a good day."

"Not for any of us," I said.

"I suppose you saw the afternoon paper?"

"I saw it," I said. "Is it true?"

"Christ, no," he said in an outraged voice. "I told you
a couple of days ago that we had nothing on Parks. Hell, I
didn't have any proof that he had a drug problem until
this guy Clayton told me about it early this morning.
That's precisely why we need your help. We want you to
prove that we had nothing to do with helping that murderous moron out of whatever problems he was in."

"And how do you expect me to do that?"

"By finding out what really happened to Bill, writing it
up in a report, and submitting it to me. After that, I'll
take the appropriate legal action."

"You may have to sue Clayton. In case you didn't know
it, he was the one who told the newspapers that you
helped fix Parks's ticket."

"You're kidding!" Petrie said in a shocked voice and
his face turned an angry red. "Why that son-of-a-bitch!"

"He's a nasty son-of-a-bitch, Hugh," I said. "Last
night he warned me, in no uncertain terms, to stay out of
the case. And from what I understand he does not make
idle threats."

"I don't make idle threats either," Petrie said icily. "If
you can prove what you just said, I will sue his fucking ass
off. DEA or no DEA."

"What else did Clayton tell you this morning?" I
asked.

"He gave me the details of the case against Parks and he asked about the progress of your investigation."

"How did he know that I was on the case?" I said.

Petrie looked perplexed. "You know, it never occurred to me to ask. I suppose someone told him. Or he observed you. He was supposedly keeping an eye on Parks, wasn't he?"

"Did he give you a reason for asking about me?"

"Not really," Petrie said. "I had the feeling that he wanted to find out how much we knew about Bill's drug problems. I suppose he was worried that this plea-bargaining thing would find its way into the papers before the grand jury indictments came out. That's a guess, understand. After what you just told me, I don't know what the hell his motives are."

"*Did* Parks testify before the grand jury?"

"I assume he did," Petrie said.

"Did Clayton *tell* you he did?" I said.

"No. Not specifically. He wasn't very specific about anything, actually. Except for the murder."

"What about the murder?"

"I guess that didn't make the afternoon paper, did it?" Petrie said, massaging his huge brow. "It was about the girl. C. W. O'Hara. Clayton said that she'd cooperated in the investigation. She'd helped entrap Parks. Bill apparently found out about it this week. And that's why he killed her."

XVIII

I was so intrigued by what Petrie had said that I didn't answer him when he went on to ask me whether I was willing to continue to work for the Cougars.

"Are you sure Clayton said that C.W. played a part in turning Parks?" I said.

Petrie nodded.

"Did he give you a reason why she would do something like that?"

Petrie shrugged. "Your guess would be as good as mine. Bill wasn't the smartest man in the world, and it's probable that the girl stood to gain by betraying him. Maybe she thought she was doing him a service—getting him off drugs."

It was an interesting theory, seeing that it fit so neatly with some of the things that Laurel had told me about C.W.'s attempts to reform her man. On the other hand, it was a terribly risky way to go about doing it. And I said as much to Petrie.

"You don't know football players, Stoner," he answered superciliously. "Guys like Parks don't have any idea who they are off the field unless someone tells them. They're easy to dupe. Christ, I told you what Kaplan did to Bill. There's no reason to think that the girl acted any differently. Or that she thought she was taking an unjustifiable risk. She was probably expert at manipulating him."

"I have a little trouble seeing Parks as *her* victim."

Petrie furrowed his brow. "Something pissed him off at her."

That much was indisputable, although it didn't explain the way he had butchered her. It was the child *and* the mother he had tried to destroy. But then, according to Laurel, C.W. had used her pregnancy to manipulate Parks, too. Maybe he'd seen them as coequal, the drug arrest and the baby—two instances of a betrayal that C. W. O'Hara had visited on him. Just thinking about him like that, as capable of feeling betrayed, made him seem more complicated to me. More than the mindless caveman I'd imagined earlier in the day.

"Well?" Petrie said. "Are you going to help us out or not?"

I stared at his helmeted face and knew that he didn't give a damn what I found or what I hazarded, as long as the team came out of it without a blemish. And I didn't really care about cleansing the Cougars' stables. It was the crime itself that interested me, the savage puzzlement of it. I thought it over, weighing my curiosity against the undeniable risks I would be taking. I'd been warned off by two very dangerous men, Clayton and Kaplan. Three, if I counted Bluerock. Only I counted Bluerock on my side. And then there was Laurel to consider. She would have to be guaranteed safety.

"You'll agree to use your money and influence to help me out?" I said to him.

"Of course."

"And if there's trouble?"

"There's always that possibility," Petrie said with something like an appetite. "You'll have to use your own judgment. Remember, I don't want you to catch Bill. I don't give a damn about Bill anymore. I just want this Clayton mess cleared up and our reputation restored. In case you forgot, we still have a season coming up, a campaign to wage."

"I may need some help."

"What did you have in mind?"

"Bluerock," I said. "It would be good to have him in my corner."

"That's fine with me, if he's willing."

"There's got to be a payoff for him," I said. "If he agrees to help, you've got to promise that you'll give him another shot. Another year on the team, at top pay. That is, if he wants it."

Petrie's face darkened angrily. "I don't like to be blackmailed, Harry. I've told you that."

"It's not blackmail, Hugh. It's negotiation."

"Christ," he said dismally. "Another goddamn agent."

Around seven thirty we reached an agreement. I didn't even have to appear on the Trumpy show or talk to the papers. Petrie caved in like a sinkhole. Which was an indication of just how desperate he was to clean up the mess that Parks had left behind him. He promised to give Otto another year at top pay, although he didn't promise he'd start him. I said that that was agreeable. We shook on it, and Petrie left.

When she heard the front door shut, Laurel wandered in from the bedroom and sat down across from me on the couch.

"Is it okay if I stay in here?" she said. "I feel kind of like hired help in the bedroom."

I grinned at her. "It's okay."

I picked up the phone and called Otto.

He didn't sound his usual self when he answered the phone. He didn't bellow or curse. But then I realized that he must have seen the day's paper, that he knew what had happened at C.W.'s ranch house.

I presented him with the proposition. He heard me out in silence, without any of the usual heckling or jeers, and without showing any enthusiasm either. Then I gave him the hard part. Not the risk of crossing Kaplan or Clayton —he already knew about the one, and I explained about the other, about Clayton's reputation for corruption. It was his friend, Parks, who was the problem.

"He's a killer, Blue," I said. "We can't change that fact. And part of my job is going to involve proving his guilt."

Bluerock didn't answer right away. When he did, he sounded melancholy. "You don't know the whole story, sport," he said. "None of us do. Whatever Bill did, he did because he was driven to it. I'd stake my life on that. What you don't understand yet, Harry, was that Bill didn't play football, he *was* the football. So show a little mercy, for chrissake, until you've seen the big picture."

I started to tell him about the picture I'd seen in C. W. O'Hara's bedroom, but let it go.

"Are you interested in joining my team?" I said.

"I'm leaning that way," he replied. "Let me sleep on it."

"You do understand that it could get rough, Blue," I said.

Otto laughed. "Football's a contact sport."

"This isn't football," I said.

"Sure it is, Harry," he said. "It's all football. Haven't you figured that out, yet?"

I told Bluerock I'd call him in the morning to get his reply to my proposition, then turned my attention to Laurel, who had been sitting patiently on the couch, listening to the phone conversation with a rapt and vaguely calculating air. I didn't pull my punches with her either. I explained it all—about Clayton and his stun gun, about Kaplan and the grand jury. She already knew, firsthand, what Parks was capable of. I thought that hearing the truth might unnerve her, coming as it did so hard on the murder of her friend. While she paled visibly when I told her about smiling Phil Clayton, she heard the rest of it out with surprising cool.

When I'd finished, she stared at me so curiously that I didn't know what to make of her look.

"So what is it you expect me to say?" she finally said. "You expect me to freak out again? Well, I'm not going to do it. I'm not going to give you that satisfaction, Harry Stoner. I'll tell you this, though. I think you're fucked in the head. You, and your friend Bluerock too. You must be crazy to want to tangle with those guys."

"So I guess we can count you out," I said.

"I didn't say that," she said. "I don't understand how you could do that, anyway. Heck, everybody and his brother knows I've been hanging around with you. Clay and Stacey and the crowd at the Waterhole. I'm screwed no matter how you look at it. I can't go home and I can't leave here. I guess I gotta go along for the ride."

"You could go to Corbin."

"That ain't far enough," she said.

"Then maybe we could send you somewhere else. How'd you like to spend a month in Hawaii? All expenses paid, courtesy of the Cougars."

Her doll-like face, which had knotted up as if it were being squeezed in a vise, sprang back to its true proportions.

"You could do that?" she said, with a touch of awe in her voice.

I nodded.

She wrinkled her nose. "I don't know if I want to go that far—all alone."

"Then take someone with you. Take Stacey."

"She's such a child," Laurel said. But I could tell that the proposition pleased her. She spent a moment picnicking with the idea, then her face clouded over as if it had begun to rain on the sandwiches. "What's the catch? What's the trade-off?"

A couple of years of whoring had given Laurel a keen sense of commerce.

"You answer a few more questions," I said.

She thought it over for a moment with her rapt, deliberative air. I thought she was going to accept the deal. But when she finally spoke, what she said was, "What *else* is in it for me?"

I gawked at her, then started to laugh. "The Hawaiian vacation for two isn't enough?"

"Hawaii's a long way off," she said defensively. "I'm going to have to have some beach clothes to wear, and a little pocket change to live on. You know, I'd be giving up a lot, going away for a month. Do you know how much money I could make in a month at the Waterhole?"

"How much?" I said.

"A lot," she said.

"How much is a lot?"

She pursed her lips, closed her eyes, and silently totted up the blackmail. "Two thousand dollars," she said, and then corrected herself. "Two thousand two hundred fifty dollars. You owe me two hundred fifty dollars from last night—a hundred and fifty for telling you about Bill and C.W. in the first place," she explained.

I stared at her sweet face. The girl added a whole new meaning to the word *venal.*

"Okay," I said. "I'll arrange it."

"Then ask away," she said happily. "I'm all yours."

XIX

I opened the desk drawer, got out my notebook and the manila envelope containing the arrest reports, and brought them over to the couch.

"I want you to help me put together a picture of what led up to last night, what led up to the murder," I explained to Laurel. "We know that Parks left camp on Monday. I thought at first that it was because of the situation at home. But it looks now as if he may also have been preparing to testify before the grand jury in a drug investigation."

"That's news to me," Laurel said flatly.

It had been news to Bluerock too. But then, I supposed, it was not a situation that Parks or C.W. would have wanted to advertise—each for their own reasons.

"C.W. never mentioned a bust of any kind to you? Drug or otherwise?"

"Nope," Laurel said. "But she could be mighty close-mouthed about her personal affairs, especially if they didn't jibe with her plans for Bill and her. All she talked about the last time we spoke was the way Bill's mom was jacking him around. C.W. said Jewel'd been on Bill's case all week long."

"On his case about what?" I said.

"The baby, I think. Jewel's kind of a weirdo. I mean, she made C.W. look like a piker when it came to being self-righteous."

"You've met her?"

"Once, when she and Bill's dad came to visit."

"What did she look like?" I said.

"You know the little picture of Dolley Madison on those fried pies you get at the Stop-N-Go? That's what she looks like—a round, pretty face and big, dimpled cheeks and lots of curls."

That sounded like a fair description of the woman in the photograph I'd found in Parks's desk.

"She looks sweet as candy," Laurel went on. "But, good Lord, she's got a wicked tongue! She just about run everybody ragged trying to please her—Bill, and her own husband, and poor C.W. worst of all. Nothing was good enough for her. Nobody did things right. The food was lousy. The way C.W. kept house was lousy. The way she dressed was whorish. Jeez, you could kind of understand how Bill got to be the way he is just by watching her operate. I mean, you could never please somebody like her, no matter how hard you tried. And what made it even worse was that she kept reciting chapter and verse to prove her points. Like it wasn't enough for her to say that C.W. was a bad housekeeper. She said it was *sinful* to be a bad housekeeper. I mean Jewel saw everything as a sign of grace. And in her book, poor C.W. was as damned as they come."

"I guess C.W.'s pregnancy must have been hard for Jewel to swallow," I said.

"She didn't know about it until last week," Laurel said.

"They kept that a *deep* secret—them not being married yet."

"How did Jewel find out?"

"I think Bill must have told her. He and C.W.'d been fighting about it so much, he must've forgotten himself and blurted it out. It was certainly on his mind."

"Why?" I said.

"He never wanted her to have a baby, for one thing. And then C.W. went into Deaconess for this series of tests, and the doctors found out that something was wrong with the fetus."

"Do you know what was wrong?"

She didn't answer me directly. "C.W. acted like it was a shameful thing, like it was her fault that the baby wasn't right. And Bill—he acted the same way. He was furious with C.W. Like the whole thing was a judgment on her and on him. He got her so upset that she even thought of having an abortion. But Reverend Dice talked her out of it."

Dice was another name on my list. From what Laurel had said, I assumed that the two doctors, with the initials P and A, were C.W.'s obstetricians.

"You ought to talk to the Reverend," Laurel said, "if you want to know what was really going on with Bill. I mean, she told that man *everything.*"

"Who is he?"

"He's a lay minister," Laurel said. "A lot of the players' wives attend a prayer group that he runs. They just love him. He's so sweet and gossipy. He's got them doing all sorts of community projects. And they're building a special chapel for the team and stuff like that. I guess C.W. went to him at first 'cause it was kind of prestigious. But after she had her car accident, she said the Reverend was a real comfort. And it was a true fact that he changed her outlook. She got religious as all get-out once she started seeing him."

"She was supposed to see him today," I said. "You wouldn't know what about, would you?"

"The baby, I guess," Laurel said. "She goes to him with just about every problem she has."

I wondered if she had gone to him after the drug arrest. I wondered if that's what had sent her to him in the first place, the guilt she had felt over betraying her man. Even if it wasn't, it was clear that she had plenty of other reasons to seek comfort—the baby, Jewel, Bill himself. Judging by the picture that Laurel had painted, C.W. had spent her last week trying to shore up what must have seemed, even to her, like a hopeless situation. And once Bill found out that she'd betrayed him to the DEA, it had become a lethal situation.

I had one last thing to check out with Laurel before I called Petrie and arranged to pay her off. I opened the manila folder and took out the rap sheet on Candy Kane.

"Do you know her?" I said, handing her the photograph of Candy.

Laurel frowned. "Sure, I know her. It's Barb Melcher."

"The rap sheet says her name is Candy Kane."

"That was just her stage name," Laurel explained. "We all used them when we danced in the clubs. I called myself Misty Love." Laurel studied the bruises on Barb's face. "What happened to her?"

"She was beaten up. According to the rap sheet, she was worked over by Bill Parks, last New Year's Eve. Apparently she didn't want to press charges against him, but our friend Phil Clayton filed an assault count, anyway. Bill was scheduled to go to trial on the charge at the end of training camp."

"That's gotta be a mistake," Laurel said, and handed the picture back to me.

"Why is it a mistake?"

"Well, for one thing, C.W. and Barb were best friends. I mean, they were like sisters. They'd grown up together in Lexington. Moved to Newport together. Shared the same apartment at the Caesar, until C.W. moved into the ranch house with Bill. They'd do anything for each other. And for another thing, Barb and C.W. were together on New Year's Eve, 'cause that was the night that C.W. told Bill she was pregnant, and she wanted Barb around to lend her moral support. There's just no way that Bill would lay hands on that girl in front of C.W., especially right after C.W. told him about the baby."

"Maybe Barb made a move on him," I said, playing devil's advocate. "Maybe they both got a little smashed on New Year's Eve, and Bill and Barb got into a fight."

"No way," Laurel said, shaking her head. "Barb was just a little bit of a thing. She never would have fought with Bill."

"Even if Bill had attacked C.W. for some reason? Maybe he lost his temper after she told him she was pregnant."

Laurel chewed her lip. "If Bill attacked C.W., Barb might have tried to step in between them. It's all kind of beside the point, though."

"Why is that?" I said.

"The cops couldn't make the charge stick, that's why. Don't you remember the car accident I told you about? The one where C.W.'s friend got killed and C.W. got so soulful afterward?"

"I remember."

"That was Barb, Harry. She was the one who got killed. She's dead. She died that very night. They were out on Donaldson Road when they hit an ice slick." Laurel shook her head sadly. "I don't rightly see how they could press a charge against Bill with a dead person as the only witness."

I didn't rightly see how they could, either.

XX

I told Laurel that I was going out to get her a helping of her favorite food—pizza. And I did stop at Trotta's on Queen City to pick one up, but not before I'd stopped downtown to pay Al Foster a personal visit. I'd taken the Candy Kane rap sheet along to keep me company.

It was close to nine when I parked the Pinto in the WGUC lot. Even though the sun had set, it was still hot, and the cops were suffering, along with everyone else. The ones I saw in the brickyard wore their blue serge like coats of mail. So did the desk sergeant inside the door, a tough little Irishman named O'Malley whom I knew from my days on the DA's staff. He had an ancient rotating fan on the counter in front of him. The fan blade clanged against the protective metal cage each time the fan swiveled to the right. O'Malley stared at the contraption murderously. It clanged, and he grimaced.

"It's like a toothache," he said. "I'd like to stick my finger in to make the hurting stop."

"Why don't you turn it off?" I asked.

He eyed me darkly. "I had to pull rank to get the goddamn thing in the first place. It's an Underwood." He pointed to a sooty, rusted tag on the fan's base. "Underwood, for chrissake! They make deviled ham, don't they?"

I laughed. "That was after they got out of the fan business."

"Get lost, Stoner," O'Malley said. "Before I arrest you for loitering."

He tossed me a visitor's tag. I pinned it to my shirt, walked down the hall to the stairwell, and went up to the second floor. I found Al Foster sitting alone in his tiny office, staring morbidly at the lit end of one of his Tareytons. Another ancient rotating fan was spinning listlessly on his desk, and the single office window had been thrown open to the twilight. The thatch of black curls that was all that was left of Al's hairline was beaded with sweat. Sweat was rolling down his long, grooved cheeks. A drop of it hung like a Christmas tree ornament from the tip of his nose.

"Hot?" I said.

He rolled the cigarette between his thumb and forefinger and smiled. "No, Harry," he said softly. "But it was good of you to ask."

I pulled up a chair and sat down across from him. Al kept rolling the cigarette back and forth until the paper dissolved between his sweaty fingers and the livid ash fell sparking into the tin ashtray on his desk.

"You got it wet, Al," I said. "That happens when you get them wet."

"You think I should wear gloves, maybe?" he said, looking up at me.

"Or use a towel," I said.

"It's a thought."

He reached into his shirt pocket and pulled out another cigarette. "I don't hear from you in six months.

And now I get a call *and* a visit on the same day. So what's on your mind, Harry, this fine summer evening?"

I laid the folder on his desk. "Billy Parks."

Foster nodded judiciously and popped the cigarette between his lips. He flicked a lighter, and the tobacco flared and began to smoke. "What's your interest in him? You working for the Cougars now?"

"For Hugh Petrie."

"No kiddin'," he said. "Gee, that's swell for you."

"Parks skipped out of training camp last Monday, and I was hired to find him."

"I guess this one isn't going to go in your résumé then, huh, Harry?" Foster said dryly.

"We thought he might be running from a warrant, Al."

"He sure is—now," Foster said.

"This warrant was from last December."

"December?" Al said, plucking the cigarette from his mouth. "We had a warrant on Bill Parks from last year?"

"You've had four of them on Billy."

"No shit. What was he charged with?"

"Billy liked to beat up his women."

"If it was multiple choice, I think I could've guessed," Foster said.

"Parks has apparently got some pull down here at the plant. The first three charges were dropped before he got to court."

"And the last one?"

"He was scheduled to go to trial at the end of training camp."

"Well, four *is* the charm," Al said. "They'll give you two if you're a first-stringer. Three if you're white and can hustle up a couple of season tickets. But four is pushing it. Tim Williams—he could get four. Farnsworth, too. But Parks . . ." He shook his head. "He's defense, and that weighs against you in the glamor department." Foster took the cigarette from his mouth and sighted down it, aiming it at me like a dart. "If I may be so bold as to ask, why do you give a shit about an assault charge at this point? Parks is wanted for aggravated homicide. What the hell difference does it make if he beat up someone six months ago?"

"There was something wrong with the case," I said. "Something that might have had a bearing on yesterday's murder."

"What kind of bearing?" Foster said with interest.

"I was hoping you could tell me."

"Quit playing games, Harry," Al said irritably.

I handed him the folder and said, "Read the arrest report, the one on Candy Kane."

He reached over and pulled the folder to his side of the desk, dribbling some ashes on it in the process. He brushed the ashes off and read through the Xeroxes.

"So?" he said when he was done. "It seems pretty cut-and-dried."

"Except for the fact that Candy Kane was killed in a car accident on the night of the arrest. She's been dead for six months."

"Oh, that's bad," Foster said, flipping the folder shut. "That's bad when your star witness is dead."

"And I'll tell you something else. Your friend Clayton doesn't want me poking around in the murder case. He threatened me last night."

"He's a bad man, Clayton," Foster said seriously. "I already told you that. He made this case?"

I nodded. "He made both this case and the Parks drug arrest. What do you think?"

"No body, no crime. That's the law, isn't it?"

"That's the law."

"With the Candy Kane girl dead, you know as well as I do the DA wouldn't press a charge unless Bill had signed a confession. Since confessing to an assault rap is no day in the country, you gotta figure that Bill had some powerful motivation to stand for the charge. What would make a guy like him do that, especially since he'd weaseled out of the same thing three times before?"

I already knew the answer. I just wanted to see if Al came to the same conclusion. "Clayton had something else on him. And Parks confessed to the lesser charge to avoid prosecution on the big enchilada."

Al stubbed the cigarette out in the tin ashtray. "Sure he had something else on him. And we both know what that was. The drug bust. There was never going to be a trial on this assault thing. It was all arranged. Your boy would cop a plea in closed chambers and get a suspended sentence. In return he agreed to testify before the grand jury. That's probably why Clayton didn't want you nosing around. It's kind of embarrassing when you blackmail a guy into copping out on assault, and the guy goes out the next day and assaults someone to death."

"Especially when he murders the person who helped you make the drug case in the first place."

"And what does that mean?" Foster asked.

"Clayton had some help in setting Parks up for the drug bust. The girl Parks killed, C. W. O'Hara, was working for him. And the girl Parks allegedly assaulted was C.W.'s best friend."

Foster snickered. "That's sweet, isn't it? And right up Phil's alley. Looks like that son-of-a-bitch Parks got shafted royally. They must have all been in on it. They get him angry enough to attack the girlfriend. C.W. calls the cops. Phil shows up, and finds drugs on Bill—just like he knew he would. And busts him."

"It *does* look that way, doesn't it?"

"Tell you what, Harry," Al said. "You leave that rap sheet with me, and I'll see that it gets in the right hands. You might want to talk to George DeVries too. He's got access to the DEA files. And you know George."

I laughed. "I know George," I said.

* * *

Laurel and I spent the rest of the night in. I brought the pizza home, after I'd finished with Al, and she and I ate it out of the box on the living room floor. Around midnight, she started getting ready for bed. I'd already talked to Petrie by then, and Laurel had spoken to Stacey, who had leaped at the chance to go on a free vacation. Two first-class tickets to Hawaii and $2,250 in traveler's checks were to be waiting for them at the airport.

I could tell from the look in Laurel's eye that she expected me to make love to her before we went to sleep. Watching her strip down to her socks, I got the urge, all right. Moving sexily about the room, she reminded me a little of Nastassja Kinski, although Laurel wasn't quite that smashingly good-looking.

Even though I wanted to screw her and she was ready to screw me, I held back. The sheer rapacity with which she'd extorted the two thousand dollars from me had left a bad taste. Of course, I knew I was being a hypocrite— that I had painted her into a very tight and nasty corner and that she had responded instinctually to being trapped. I suppose it was the instinct itself—the naked greed—that had put me off, although I wasn't sure why, since she'd evinced it on just about every occasion I'd been around her. Moreover, what she had told me would prove useful. In fact, it already had, with Al. I just didn't like the price she'd made me pay to get her help.

It didn't take Laurel long to pick up on the change in my attitude. Her sensors were finely tuned to rejection. When I didn't respond to her advances, she sat down heavily on the edge of the bed, crossed her legs, put a hand under her chin, and stared at me with a melancholy smile.

"You ever been poor, Harry?" she said.

"I've been down and out a few times."

"It's no fun, is it?" she said. "To be afraid to open the mailbox, for fear you're going to find another bill in there that you can't pay. Or to be afraid to open the door at noon for fear that it's a certified letter from some collection agency that's about to take you to court. To be afraid to answer your phone in a normal tone of voice, for fear that the dun on the other end will recognize you and start jacking you around for dough. To be afraid to drive around the streets, 'cause there are warrants out on traffic tickets that you couldn't afford to pay. You ever been that poor?"

"No," I said softly.

"Well, I have," she said. "And I don't ever intend to be again. I've got to stand on my hind legs in this world, Harry, 'cause I've learned the hard way that no one else is going to be there to catch me when I fall."

I got up and walked over to the bed.

"No!" she said, holding up both hands to stop me. "I don't fuck anyone for charity. And I don't expect anyone to do that to me."

She lay back on the mattress, pulled the sheet over her, and curled up in a ball.

Late that night, I made love to her. It wasn't very good for either of us. There were too many different feelings being played out, feelings that had nothing to do with sex. But it made me feel better, and I think it soothed her pride.

The last thing she said to me, in the dark, as she turned away to fall back to sleep, was, "That's another hundred bucks you owe me."

XXI

I got up early the next morning, left Laurel a note saying that I'd be back at ten, and drove downtown to the courthouse to find George DeVries. It was barely eight thirty on a sultry Sunday, and the only thing moving on the streets, outside of me and a couple of patrol cars, was the blue morning haze, hanging like smoke above the tarmac. I parked the Pinto beside a meter on Main and walked over to the courthouse. It was two flights of hobbed brass stairs to the DA's offices.

The second floor hallway was full of that milky, morning half light that peeks in at southern exposures and puddles up on concrete. I splashed through it past the myriad offices of the DA's staff. A surprising number of doors were standing open for so early on a Sunday, and I could hear the drone of desk fans up and down the hall. The only door that mattered to me was the one to George DeVries's office, and it was shut tight. I knocked on the frosted glass insert, and to my satisfaction a lazy Southern voice called out, "Come in."

I opened the door, walked through a vacant anteroom and into DeVries's office. George, in white dress shirt and speckled bow tie, his shirt-sleeves rolled up, was sitting behind a cluttered desk, leaning back in his chair and gazing out an open window at the hazy Mount Adams hillside in the distance. He didn't turn around in the chair when I approached the desk, just let his head loll to the right.

"Hi ya, Harry-boy," he said in his Kentucky Colonel's voice. "How's tricks?"

"Tricks are good, George," I said, sitting across the desk from him.

He smiled familiarly, and his skin wrinkled up like crumpled butcher paper. George had aged since I'd seen him last. He'd developed a paunch that popped the buttons on his clean white shirt, and his face had grown even more weathered with the years. He'd always looked like a red-haired Carl Sandburg. If the trends continued, I thought, I'd have to change poets—to Auden, maybe.

"You're up mighty early, aren't you?" he said. "You got something on your mind?"

"Bill Parks," I said.

George shook his head sorrowfully and swung his chair around to face me. "I'm getting a little weary of hearing that name."

"Who else has been asking?"

"Who hasn't?" George said. "The papers, the TV guys —you name it."

"How about Phil Clayton. Has he been asking?"

"Phil don't ask, Harry," George said dryly. "He tells."

"He was in charge of Bill's case, wasn't he?"

"No comment," George said.

"I already know that he was, George."

"Then why are you asking, Harry?" he said with his wrinkled grin.

I'd played this game before with George, who was not famous for his scruples.

"George," I said. "You're not going to give me a hard time about this, are you?"

"I have to, Harry-boy," he said apologetically. "I'm sorry, but this one is top secret. I'm afraid I can't help you out at all."

George ducked his head and pretended to examine his manicure, but I could see that one little corner of his right eye was reserved for me.

I picked up my cue. "That's a damn shame, George, because I'm working for the Cougars now, and I know for a fact that they'd be mighty grateful for any help you might see fit to give me. Mighty grateful."

George stopped admiring his nails and looked up at me. "How grateful's that?"

"I think I can guarantee a couple of season tickets on the fifty yard line. And maybe a little something extra in the ticket envelope, to buy popcorn and beer with."

"Blue seats?" George said.

"Any color you want, George."

He smiled so broadly I could see the gold bridgework on his molars. "That's mighty white of you, Harry. I've said it before and I'll say it again. You're okay."

"Spare me, George."

He hunched forward in his chair, cribbed his hands in front of him, and put an earnest look on his face, like a car salesman closing a deal. "What do you need?"

"A couple of transcripts," I said. "I'd like to see the pretrials on Parks's busts. He has two of them that I know of, both in December. One on an assault charge and the one that the papers are writing about—the drug arrest."

"They're the same case," George said with a wink.

I'd figured as much the night before. "You're on top of this, are you?"

George shrugged. "You're not the only one giving away tickets, Harry. I got a family to feed."

"Tell me about the case."

George leaned back in the chair, cupping his hands behind his head. "All I know is what I hear. I haven't seen the actual transcript. The DEA's got it, and for some reason, Internal Affairs is looking at it too. I guess maybe Phil got a little carried away on this one."

"Carried away how?"

"I don't know that."

I gave him a look.

"Honest Injun," he said, holding up one hand. "All I can tell you is the scuttlebutt I've heard."

"Then shoot."

"The assault complaint was phoned in last New Year's Eve. It went straight to Clayton, just like it had been ticketed that way in advance. Phil busted Parks at the Caesar Apartments and just happened to find a shitload of cocaine on Parks's person. Parks was given a choice—plead guilty to the assault, testify against his suppliers, and get immunity on the drug charge; or do the whole nine yards on felony possession and the assault to boot."

"So he copped the plea."

"Uh-uh," George said. "Your buddy Bill is a stand-up guy."

I stared at him for a moment. "You're telling me he didn't plea-bargain?"

"That's what I hear. He confessed to the assault, all right. But he refused to plea-bargain on the drugs. He decided to do time on both charges."

That certainly blew Al Foster's theory out of the water. And surprised the hell out of me. "Then what's all this shit in the paper about grand juries?" I said. "What kind of crap is Clayton putting out?"

"From what I hear, Clayton gave Bill a chance to think things over. You know, fifteen-to-twenty can start to look mighty long to you if you brood about it. Apparently Parks came around at the last moment. Or that's what Clayton claims. He says the Cougars gave Parks a little push in the right direction."

I'd heard that story too. And according to Petrie it wasn't true. Which meant that if Parks had gotten a push, it had come from someone else. *"Did* Parks testify?"

George shook his head. "The docket says a mystery witness was scheduled to go in on Friday. You know what happened."

"He killed the girl instead."

"That's the way it looks."

"I'm told she set him up," I said.

"Somebody did," George said. "The assault bust was an obvious setup. They were after drugs from the start and they knew they were going to find them. All they needed was an excuse to make a search, and the assault was just the ticket. It must have been the O'Hara girl."

"It looks as if her friend was in on it too."

"I would think so, yeah, seeing that she was the one who took the beating."

"Can you do me one more favor, George?" I said to him.

He rubbed his grizzled jaw and gave me a look. "You sure they're going to be blue seats?"

"Absolutely."

"Well, for a pal . . ." he said.

"Find out why Internal Affairs is so interested in Clayton."

He grunted. "You're not asking much, you know."

"I don't need it right away. I can give you a day or two."

"A day or two, he says." George laughed. "I'll do my best, Harry. But there are no guarantees on that one."

"I trust you, George," I said.

* * *

I picked up an *Enquirer* in the courthouse lobby and read through the morning's news on Parks. The front-page headline read, MURDERED GIRL HELPED SET PARKS UP, and the article underneath it recapitulated most of what George DeVries had just told me. Apparently Clayton was still leaking news to the press—why I wasn't sure. There was a paragraph on Parks's career with the Cougars in which the allegation made in the *Post* on the previous day—that the Cougar management had helped Bill secure immunity on the drug charges—was repeated word for word. I could almost hear Petrie gnashing his teeth.

There was nothing in the paper about Barb Melcher, however. Which was an odd thing for Clayton to withhold. In a way, she was more directly involved in the drug bust than C.W. had been. The arrest had taken place in her apartment; she was the one who had taken the beating, which had been the cue for Clayton to arrive on the scene; and if I didn't miss my guess, she was the one who had taken the fall for her friend C.W. when the assault led to the drug arrest. It was pretty clear that Parks hadn't blamed C.W. for his legal problems. He would hardly have moved in with her after the arrest and set up house for better than five months if he *had* suspected that she'd betrayed him. Up until Friday he must have assumed that the Melcher girl was indirectly to blame for his troubles, or that the whole episode was just very bad luck.

I wasn't sure how C.W. had convinced her friend Barb to take part in what was apparently an elaborate and dangerous charade. Maybe she hadn't. It was possible that C.W. had only planned on provoking a loud argument with Bill—just enough of an excuse to justify Clayton showing up on the scene in response to a disorderly conduct call. It was possible that the assault itself had been an unplanned accident, the result of Parks losing his violent temper. Why Parks had attacked Barb rather than C.W. I didn't know. Perhaps he had taken his wrath out on Barb because C.W., his usual target, had just told him that she was pregnant. Maybe the announcement of the pregnancy itself had triggered the fight. Laurel had said that Parks was none too pleased by the news, and C.W. had probably known that it would make him angry, although she might not have figured that he'd get angry enough to start swinging. And maybe the Melcher girl had stepped in between Parks and C.W. in order to protect her friend—and had ended up with two black eyes.

Whatever the scenario, the fact that Barb and C.W. were on Donaldson Road, near the airport, when they crashed strongly suggested that Barb was trying to put as much distance between her and Bill as she could. I thought now that that was why she had looked so antsy in the evidentiary photos. It wasn't disgust that I'd seen in her face, it was fear. She must have thought that Parks would pin the blame on her for bringing the police down on his head, and she'd wanted to get out of town as quickly as she could. It was just her bad luck that they'd hit an ice slick on the way.

I wasn't at all sure how C.W. had justified jeopardizing Barb Melcher and betraying Parks in the first place, but Petrie's idea seemed as good as any. Maybe she *had* thought that getting Bill off drugs was worth the risk. She might have convinced herself—and Barb, too—that she was doing Parks a favor. Given her opportunistic nature, it was also possible that she'd used the occasion and the unexpected tragedy of Barb's death to worm herself more deeply into Parks's life.

Even if that hadn't been the plan, it seemed to have worked out that way. According to Laurel, Parks temporarily turned over a new leaf after the bust, giving up drugs, finding religion again, moving in with C.W., and contemplating marrying her. Of course, the honeymoon hadn't lasted very long. Their love affair had been falling apart practically from the moment it began. Beyond a doubt, it would have ended even if Parks hadn't found out that C.W. had betrayed him, although it might not have ended so violently.

It had been clear all along that Bill wasn't a very bright man. What I hadn't recognized before was that he was also a naive and crudely sentimental one. C.W. had seemed to have little trouble, at first, manipulating him, presumably using her pregnancy, her sex appeal, a little old-time religion, and what small guilt Parks himself must have felt for the death of Barb Melcher to bring him to hand. He had foolishly given her his loyalty. Nor was she the only person in whom Bill had placed a misbegotten confidence. By anyone's standards, he didn't owe Kaplan a thing following the bust—not after the financial screwing that the Professor had given him. And yet Parks had refused to testify against his agent or anyone else. At least, he had refused at first. Unlike Monroe, Calhoun, and Greene, he'd been ready to go to jail for the rest of his life to protect his so-called friends.

I didn't pretend to fully understand Bill's thinking, but from what I'd learned over the last few days, it seemed to me that he must have been a man guided chiefly, and stubbornly, by impulse. And whose instincts, in so far as they were governed, weren't governed by reason but by the myths of the clubhouse. Stick by your buddies no matter what and they'll stick by you. Although Bluerock was a much smarter man, I could see bits of the same psychology in him, just as I could see bits of C.W. and Barb in Laurel and her friend Stacey. I still had trouble seeing Parks as a victim—after what I'd found in that ranch house, I could never see him only as that. But it was becoming apparent that a lot of people had been jerking his lead, and that in the matter of the drug arrest at least, he had behaved more honorably than most of his friends.

XXII

I called Bluerock from a phone in the courthouse lobby and arranged to pick him up on my way back to the Delores. At ten sharp I pulled up in front of his house. Otto was sitting on a lawn chair in the shade of the front porch overhang, staring placidly at the quiet Sunday street, a case of beer lying at his feet like the family dog. Six or seven of the cans had been opened, and dead soldiers were scattered like cigarette butts on the porch slats.

"Nothing like a good breakfast," I said to him as I came up the walk.

Bluerock grunted, then belched. "Yep," he said. "Most important meal of the day." He reached down, pulled a can of beer out of the carton, and tossed it over to me. "You look a little beat."

I opened the beer and took a sip. It was warm and flat, but it was wet. "It's been a busy morning." I sat down on one of the porch steps and drank the rest of the beer.

"I've been doing some figuring, sport," Bluerock said,

as I drank his beer. "Whose idea was it to bring me in on this thing? Yours or Petrie's?"

"Mine," I said.

"And whose idea was it to dangle that carrot in front of my nose?"

"You mean the extra year of playing time?" I said.

He nodded.

"I came up with the idea," I said. "Petrie agreed to it."

"Just like that, huh?" Bluerock said.

"Just like that."

He stared at me with a disturbing smile. "I called Petrie this morning and told him his part of the deal was off. I don't take pay for being a friend—to Bill or anyone else."

It took me a second to realize that he was offended. *I'd* offended him, by arranging for a payoff. If I'd thought about it the day before, I would have known better.

"I didn't mean any insult, Blue," I said to him. "It's just that it's likely to be risky. I thought you deserved to be paid for that risk."

He took a deep, noisy breath through his nostrils. "I'm not going to get pissed at you, Harry," he said, although he sounded plenty pissed. "But I want you to understand something. And I'm only going to say it once. I never did anything in my life that mattered to me just for money. And football matters to me. So do my friends. Got it?"

"I got it," I said.

"All right then," he said, blowing all the air he'd taken in through his nostrils out through his mouth. "Let's get started."

He got to his feet and stepped out into the sunlight. He was wearing a Hawaiian shirt with gaudily painted parrots on it, khaki safari shorts, gym socks, and sneakers. As big as he was, he looked like a hood on holiday.

As soon as he stepped off the porch, his bulldog face turned mean. It wasn't a meanness that had a direct object, either. It was an all-purpose mean. His huge brow furrowed, his gray eyes closed down to slits, his mouth shut like a car door being slammed. He was wearing his game face, and it couldn't have been more impressive if he were holding a sign that said, Don't Mess With Me.

"Are we going to kick some ass?" he growled.

"Well, not right this minute."

He shot me a dark look. "You better get ready to kick ass, sport," he said ominously. "Because trouble is coming. Don't you think for a minute that Walt doesn't know what you're doing, 'cause he does. From what I read in the papers, he dodged a bullet with Bill. And he knows it. He doesn't want you stirring up the waters. He doesn't want you finding Bill. He wants Bill good and dead. And that guy, Clayton, you told me about last night, you gotta figure he'd be just as happy if Bill were out of the way. Less trouble. Less embarrassment. Easier to explain things."

"Blue," I said. "We're not on a rescue mission."

"Maybe you're not," he said. "But nobody's proved Bill's guilty of anything, yet—doing drugs *or* killing the girl."

It was true enough. Perhaps it was a testament to my prejudices, but the thought hadn't even entered my mind.

"I think you better accept the fact that he murdered her," I said.

"And you'd better accept the fact that if you want to find out the truth, sooner or later you're going to have to talk to Bill. He's the only one who knows, sport. Nobody else was there."

I nodded grudgingly. "What if he doesn't want to talk?"

"We'll cross that bridge when we come to it," Bluerock said. "There's still a lot of ground between us and it."

* * *

To my surprise, Laurel wasn't there when Bluerock and I stepped into the apartment at ten fifteen. She showed up about twenty minutes later, with a Pogue's shopping bag under her arm. She took one look at Bluerock—all six feet three inches, two hundred sixty pounds of him stuffed into that Hawaiian shirt and those khaki shorts—and her mouth fell open.

Bluerock gave her his cold, dismissive sneer. "Who's the chippy?" he said to me.

"You're a rude dude, aren't you?" Laurel said, dropping the shopping bag on the floor.

"Fuck you, lady," Bluerock answered, staring at her icily. "I don't have time for you."

Laurel put her hands on her hips. "Fuck you, too!" she snapped.

I stepped between them before they could come to blows.

"Laurel, this is Otto Bluerock. Otto, this is Laurel Jones. Laurel was a friend of C.W.'s."

"It figures," Bluerock said. "They travel in packs."

"At least my friends don't butcher pregnant women," Laurel said indignantly.

I told both of them to shut up. "You've got to get ready to leave," I said to Laurel. "And you . . ." I stared at Bluerock.

He glared back at me. "And me—what?" he growled.

"Just cool it," I said. "Okay?"

"Just don't forget to say please," Otto said.

Trying to keep two prima donnas in an apartment the size of mine was no easy task. And I spent the next thirty minutes guarding the space between them. Around eleven thirty Laurel came out of the bedroom, a valise in one hand, a straw beach hat in the other.

"I guess I'm ready," she said, fitting the hat on her pretty blond head.

I checked her over, like a mother examining her child on the first day of school. She'd put on her Waterhole makeup—bright red lipstick, black eyeliner, rouge on her cheeks—and she was wearing a thin linen jumper with no underwear underneath. That was going to get her noticed long before she stepped out on the beach at Waikiki.

She smiled at me nervously. "Am I presentable?"

"Just barely," I said.

"This could be the last time we see each other," she said, with a sudden pout.

"I'll survive, Laurel."

"So will I," she said blithely. "Maybe I'll find me one of them rich, good-lookin' Hawaiian boys. Get married and raise sugarcane. They gotta be an improvement over some of the football players that you meet." She said it loudly enough so that Otto could hear her in the living room. I heard him grunt.

"Take care of yourself, baby," she said, giving me a peck on the cheek. "Don't think badly of me when I'm gone."

"Laurel, about last night . . ."

She put a finger to my lips and shook her head. "Don't give it a second thought," she whispered. "That's just the way life goes. Like the song says—I gotta be me." She petted my cheek. "You look after yourself, hear?"

She picked up her suitcase and walked into the living room. Around twelve a taxi pulled up on Burnet outside the Delores. I helped Laurel take her bag down to the cab. Stacey was already sitting in the back seat, squirming with excitement.

"Stace!" Laurel squealed. "Can you believe it?"

Stacey bounced up and down. "No!" she shrieked. "Oh, God, it's just too much! Totally bosco!"

Laurel gave her a withering look. "You're going to have to watch your language when we get over there," she said as she got into the back seat beside Stacey. "You don't want those rich plantation owners thinking we're rubes, do you?"

I handed Laurel her bag and closed the door. She waved at me through the window. "Bye, Harry," she said. "I'll phone you when we get there!"

The last I saw of her, as the cab sped off, she was lecturing Stacey again on some fine point of etiquette.

XXIII

When I got back upstairs I found Otto reading through the Candy Kane arrest sheet that had been lying on the rolltop desk.

"Did you know her?" I said.

He nodded. "I met her a couple of times. She was a sweet kid. Not much upstairs, but reasonably honest. I could never fathom why she hung around with that bitch C.W." He put the sheet back down on the desk and asked, "What did Barb have to do with Bill?"

I explained to him about the assault arrest, and the bearing it had on Parks's troubles with the law. I also gave him my theories on what had actually happened that night in Barb's apartment.

When I'd finished, he said, "If Bill was set up, I don't think Barb knew about it. She wasn't the conspiratorial type, and she was too stupid to keep all the details straight anyway. I think it was C.W.'s show from the start. She knew what would happen when she sprang that pregnancy bullshit on Bill. She knew he'd come out swinging. And when he took a poke at her, Barb must have gotten in the way." He shook his head. "Looks like she got in the way in a big way. The poor, dumb cunt."

I sat back on the couch and stared at him for a moment. "You know, Clayton couldn't have brought the bust off if he hadn't known that Bill would be holding. Isn't it about time that you came clean with me about his drug habits?"

"What do you want me to say?" Bluerock said, slapping his knees. "Yeah, he did some cocaine. So did the whole defensive line. So did most of the offense. So what?"

"I'm not passing judgment," I said. "I'm just checking the facts."

"Well, check this out, then," Bluerock said. "There are all sorts of reasons why guys do coke. And one of them is that it gives you an edge on the field. It doesn't make you *think* you perform better, you *do* perform better—at least, physically. Of course, the shit also distorts your judgment. But when you play nose guard, judgment isn't what counts. Reaction is what counts. I'm not saying Bill didn't also get high on the stuff. I'm just saying that when he started taking it it was to improve his game. Anyway, coke wasn't Bill's drug of choice."

"What was?" I said.

"The shit he got from Walt," Bluerock said bitterly.

"I thought he got his cocaine from Walt," I said.

"He did, but you can get that anywhere. From carpenters and bankers and deejays. From just about every other guy you run into at the Waterhole. Hell, they have a special room upstairs to get high in. What I'm saying is that you don't have to go to Kaplan's club to get flake. But you do have to go there if you want to get juice. At least, you do if you want to get it without a 'scrip."

"What's juice?" I said.

"To a guy like Bill," Otto said with a grim look, "it was life itself."

"And what does that mean?"

"Juice is the musclebuilders' name for anabolic steroids, sport. For Dianabol and half a dozen other brands of injectable testosterone. It's what you take to get that ripped look. It's what you take to get superstrong."

"Bill took steroids on top of cocaine?" I said.

"Bill took steroids *before* he took cocaine. He's been doing them as long as I've known him."

Of course, I'd heard about anabolic steroids. There had been a number of recent articles on their abuse in amateur and professional sports. I knew they were an artificial form of male hormone, and I knew that athletes took them to build muscle. Most of the articles I'd read seemed to agree that they were effective, that a bodybuilder couldn't put on the same kind of bulk without using them. But you paid a hell of a price for getting big. At the very least, they screwed up your endocrine system, and at worst, they could outright kill you.

"I don't get it," I said to Bluerock. "Why would a guy as big and strong as Parks jeopardize his health just to add a few more pounds of muscle?"

"For the same reason he snorted coke," Otto said. "To improve his game." Bluerock gave me a cagey look. "You remember Fred, the guy we saw at the bowling alley?"

I nodded.

"Well, he does Dianabol, too. All of Dr. Walt's boychiks do. It's their little secret. It's what makes them a group—that and the bullshit philosophies of their guru, which are mostly centered around steroids, anyway. Only Freddy and most of the others like him take the shit because they were born weak, because without the drugs they'd just be ordinary oversize guys, pushing cargo around on some loading dock. They aren't true athletes —they're little guys in big guys' bodies. They got no heart, and they know it. They feel it in their muscles, like a lack of strength."

"And Parks?"

"He's the genuine article," Bluerock said. "He's got all the natural gifts and the fiercest heart of any man I've ever met. Bill would die to protect a friend."

"It sounds like he was doing his best to die all by himself."

"Maybe so," Bluerock conceded. "But consider this. They polled a bunch of Olympic athletes—world-class competitors—before the Games. They asked them whether they would be willing to take a toxic drug, a drug that was guaranteed to kill them in a couple of years, if they knew that taking the drug would guarantee them a gold medal. You know how many of the athletes said they'd take it?" He didn't wait for me to answer. "Almost every goddamn one. That's Bill, sport. That's the way he thought about it."

I went over to the desk and took out the capsule I'd found in Parks's desk. "Is this Dianabol?" I said, handing it to Bluerock.

He shook his head. "No. They've got an oral dose, but this isn't it." He gave the pill back to me. "I don't know what that is."

"Well, Bill was taking a shitload of it before he freaked out," I said. "There were about a hundred of these in the desk in his room, alongside a picture of his mom and a couple of pamphlets announcing the end of the world and how to cope with it."

For the first time since I'd met him, Otto Bluerock looked genuinely pained. "The poor son-of-a-bitch," he said sadly. "He didn't say a thing to me."

He hadn't said a thing to anyone, I said to myself. That was the problem. Of course, I hadn't talked to Jewel yet. Or to the Reverend Dice. I'd get around to talking to both of them later that day. At the moment, however, I was thinking about Bill himself.

Something that Bluerock said had struck a chord. Not the steroid business, which I didn't think was connected up to anything except Bill's potential for self-destruction, but the part about his fierceness of heart—his tendency to sacrifice for his friends. I'd recognized that side of him too. It was what had kept him loyal to Kaplan and to C.W. It was what had kept him from testifying before a grand jury. It was what made his decision to cop out at the last moment, to play ball with Clayton after refusing to compromise for better than five months, so damn strange. Clayton had claimed that the Cougars had pushed Parks into the decision, and if I didn't know that they hadn't I might have bought the story. After all, a man like Parks would have felt a certain amount of loyalty to his team. But if you took the Cougars out of the picture, Bill's sudden change of heart was completely out of character, and damn suspicious. Or so it seemed to me. Just as suspicious as the fact that he'd supposedly been prevented from appearing before the grand jury because he'd discovered C.W.'s treachery.

I asked Bluerock what he thought of Clayton's story, and he came to the same conclusion.

"Bill wouldn't have sold anybody out to protect himself."

"Not even if it meant giving up football?" I said.

Otto shook his head with disgust. "He wouldn't have been giving up football, man, he'd have been giving up playing a game on Sundays. That's all. I told you before, to a guy like Bill it was all football. You don't stop being yourself just 'cause you're not dressed in pads and standing on Astroturf."

"That's too pure, Blue," I said. "We're not talking about a saint here."

"Then look at it like this, Harry. What would testifying

have gotten him? A suspended sentence? Hell, he probably would have gotten a suspended sentence anyway. Or been shocked out in six months. It's the first-string rule, man. Cops are fans too. So are DA's."

"They put Mercury Morris away," I said.

"He was a dealer, for chrissake. Bill was caught with some flake. The point is, whether he got a suspended sentence or six months or five years, he wouldn't have been worth shit to himself if he sold out his friends."

"Kaplan was no friend," I said.

Bluerock grunted. "You know that, and I know that. But Bill didn't know that. He's been training with the guy for the last three years. Kaplan's his agent, for chrissake! He's got the deposit on his fucking brains! And he's got the keys to the juice dispenser. Sure, Bill knows that he won't go to jail if he makes a deal with Clayton. So what? The league suspends him automatically, whether he cops out or not. He has to go through mandatory rehabilitation after the suspension. And at the end of it, the Cougars are going to trade him away or release him on waivers, or if he's lucky, sign him for peanuts. Wherever he lands in the league, he's going to wind up with a drug rep. And Walt Kaplan's going to break his legs, or hire somebody to do it. You know Walt's reputation, Harry. You don't screw him and come away laughing. And if all that isn't enough, what about Bill, sport? His sense of himself? What happens to it? To his fucking life's work that Petrie's always talking about?"

"He messed that up a long time ago, Blue," I said.

"Look, what's the point of arguing about it?" he said angrily. His face turned red and bunched up like a fist. For just a moment I thought he was going to lose control the way he had in that Bloomington bar. But he caught himself, and with a visible effort, pulled back.

"We gotta work together, sport," he said after a moment. "Otherwise, we're going nowhere."

"We've also got to be honest, Blue," I said.

"Christ, you're relentless," he said. "You ever do any coaching?" He laughed wearily. "Okay, sport. You've got the ball. Run with it."

XXIV

The first person I wanted to talk to was the Reverend Carl Dice, C.W.'s father confessor. If Bill had changed his mind about testifying before the grand jury, I figured Dice would have heard why. And if, as Bluerock and I suspected, Bill hadn't changed his mind at the last moment, Dice might be able to supply us with a reason for Clayton's lies. Clayton's motives were really at the heart of the case—at least, as far as the Cougars were concerned. But until I heard something definitive from George about the in-house investigation, I'd have to settle for what I could piece together from other sources.

I found Dice's address in the phone book and talked Bluerock into paying him a visit. But not before arguing again with Otto, who had handed me the ball but hadn't quite let go. It was his idea that we should pay Walt Kaplan a visit first. According to Otto, Bill himself was the person we needed to talk to. And since Walt had a vested interest in keeping tabs on him, Bluerock figured that the Professor would know where Bill was hiding, or have a good idea where he could be run to ground. When I asked Blue how he planned on getting Kaplan to cooperate with us, he had a simple solution.

"Beat the shit out of him," he said.

I eyed Otto for a long moment, hoping he was joking. But there was no humor in his voice, or in his look. He jerked at the lobster-bib lapels of his Hawaiian shirt, made his bulldog face into an expectant mask, and tapped his left foot impatiently, as if he were awaiting a response to a reasonable suggestion.

"Let me get this straight," I said. "You think we should march into that club—all two of us—and take on Walt, Mickey, and the rest of the gang."

"Yeah, that's about it," Bluerock said cheerfully, as if he'd liked the way I'd put it. "Take 'em by surprise."

"Christ, where'd you learn tactics, Otto—the playing fields of Warner Bros.? This isn't *Little Caesar.* This is real life."

"In other words, you're going to pussy out," he said.

"Yeah," I said, and immediately started to feel like a sixteen-year-old kid again. "For the time being," I added defensively.

"Okay. You're the detective."

"I *am* the detective," I said.

"Sure," Otto agreed.

But as we walked out the door of the apartment, I heard him whisper, "Pussy," under his breath.

Carl Dice lived on a pleasant, sunlit street in Delhi, a fashionable neighborhood on the west side of town. The street, Bradford Avenue, ran west off Rapid Run, curling up to the great forested ridge above the Ohio and plateauing in a long stretch of four-bedroom ranch houses overlooking the river. Dice's house was located at the cul-de-sac at the end of Bradford. As I pulled up in the Reverend's driveway, a springer spaniel came bounding through a railed fence to the right of the house, nose down, tongue lolling as if he were chasing a rabbit. He stopped cold beside my car door and sat down on the tarmac, a happy look on his long, sloppy face.

"Maybe I'd better stay by the car," Otto said. "Guard it, in case he attacks."

"Fuck you," I said.

We got out, and the spaniel leapt back to its feet, gamboling beside us as we walked up to Dice's front door.

It was a large, immaculately kept ranch house, with several waxy green magnolias in the yard and a cement carport to the side. There was a silver Audi 5000S sitting in the port, with a bumper sticker, "Honk If You Love Jesus", plastered on its Teutonic rear end. I went up to the door, with Bluerock and the spaniel trailing behind me, and knocked. A short, extremely clean-cut man in his mid-thirties answered. One glance at him and I knew he had to be Reverend Dice. Like most evangelists, he looked as if he'd been dressed by his mother, and he had an air of beatitude about him, as if he *were* his mother. He was wearing a plaid shirt that still held the folds it had had on the store shelf and spotless tan slacks with a crease running down each leg that could give you a paper cut. He had a child's small white teeth and wide round eyes. There was even something childlike about his expression. Nobody over eight ever looked that happy just to answer the door.

"Yay-yass?" he said, like a cartoon granny.

"Reverend Dice?" I said.

"Yay-yass," he said again, as if all were forgiven.

I could feel Bluerock bristling behind me. Even the spaniel took a step back, as if he'd come upon something too sweet for his palate.

I dug a business card out of my wallet and handed it to

Dice. "I'd like to talk to you about one of your parishioners."

"I've no parish, friend," Dice said in a mellifluous voice that was scented slightly with the garlic he'd had for lunch, and with the mouth spray that he'd used to cover it up. "The Lord's work requires no church. No, nor license, either." He raised a scriptural finger. *"Although,* it would be a blessing to have a permanent sanctuary, a place of prayer and retreat. And if the Lord sees fit to grant me that gift, I would not say nay."

From the look of him, I had the feeling he wouldn't say nay to anything that turned a buck. He had a couple of gold rings the size of brass apples on his fingers, and it was clear from what I could see of the house that the price of his furniture had come out of the collection plate before the money for his place of prayer and retreat.

"Would you mind giving me a few minutes of your time?" I asked.

"Well," he said, glancing at his Rolex, "I do have a prayer meeting in half an hour."

"I'm sure the Cougars would appreciate it."

"The Cougars?" he said with curiosity. "You are working for the Cougars?"

I nodded.

"Then perhaps I can spare a moment. Come right in," he said, waving his arm. *"Mi casa es su casa,* as our friends south of the border like to say."

As I started through the door, Bluerock caught me by the arm.

"I think I'll skip this one, sport," he said. "I gotta weak stomach."

"All right," I said. "I shouldn't be too long."

I walked into Dice's plush home, and Bluerock went back to the car, the dog wandering after him.

"Your friend has something wrong with his stomach?" Dice said.

"Too much for lunch," I said.

"He is a Cougar, is he not?"

"He is," I said.

"I thought I recognized him. You know, I am a close personal friend of many of the players on the team."

From what I'd heard he was a closer friend to the wives of the players. His wimpy, childish manner wouldn't have gone over well with most of the athletes I'd known. In fact, I could hardly believe that a man like Parks would have given him the time of day.

Dice led me down a short hall to his living room. There was a long picture window on the far wall, looking out on a magnificent view of the river and of the Kentucky shore. A squared off, buff-white conversation pit was situated in front of the picture window, with teak bookshelves on either side of it and an ivory Oriental carpet on the floor. There were no books on the shelves. They were filled instead with religious artifacts—statuettes, manger scenes, pamphlets. Dice plucked one of the pamphlets from the shelves as we passed the bookcases and handed it to me. It was the same pamphlet I'd found in Parks's desk, the one announcing the end of the world.

"It's coming, friend," he said, holding up an admonitory finger. "Believe it."

Dice sat down on the sofa, crossed his legs, and folded his hands on his knee. "Now, how can I help the Cougars?"

I sat down across from him. "You can tell me about C. W. O'Hara and Bill Parks," I said.

He nodded his head, but his eyes didn't move, as if they were weighted in their sockets like the eyes of a doll. "Carol was a close friend," he said. "We all mourn her passing."

"Would you mind answering a few questions about her and Bill?"

Dice smiled tolerantly. "Being a minister is a little like

being a psychiatrist, Mr. Stoner. My friends come to me with many problems, and I listen to them and try to give them sound advice. But they would not tell me the things that they do if they thought I would discuss them with other people."

"I understand the need for confidentiality," I said. "But seeing that the girl is dead and that Bill Parks is in a great deal of trouble, couldn't you see your way to making an exception?"

Dice made a troubled face. "What is your interest in this matter?" he said.

"I'm trying to clear up the confusion surrounding the girl's death."

"For the Cougars?"

"Yes," I said.

Dice leaned back, planting his hands at his sides and examining me with a critical eye. "Aren't the police looking into the murder?"

"Of course."

"Then I fail to see why the Cougars would want to finance an investigation of their own."

"They have been implicated in Bill's problems with the law," I said. "They want to clear their reputation."

"Ah, their reputation!" Dice said, with irony in his voice. He clasped his knee and pulled himself forward again. "I don't think I'm going to be able to help you, Mr. Stoner. Not without some assurance that what I say won't be made public."

I studied his face. For some reason, he was beginning to remind me of George DeVries. "What would it take to reassure you?" I said.

He pursed his lips and put a finger beside his nose. I thought he was about to click the heels of his patent leather shoes and vanish. Instead, he said, "A contribution would be appreciated."

It seemed as if an awful lot of people were trying to get

rich off of Bill Parks's troubles. But then, I supposed, there was nothing new about that. "How much of a contribution?" I said warily.

Dice shrugged. "Under the circumstances, I'm sure the Cougars would want to be generous," he said sweetly. "In fact, I think it would be a very nice gesture on their part to contribute to the funding of a team chapel. Of course, it wouldn't make up for the way they've fucked Bill and their other employees over. But it would be a start."

I stared at him for a moment. I'd been wrong about the Reverend. He looked like a Milquetoast, but he had the soul of an agent.

"You don't approve of the way the Cougars deal with their personnel?"

"*That* is putting it mildly," he said with his slick smile. "I do not intend to help them clean up their messes without making them pay."

What could I say? I needed his help, and he knew it. "I think I might be able to arrange a contribution," I told him.

"Fine." Dice got up and went to the bookshelves. He pulled what looked like another pamphlet from the shelves and brought it over to me. "Would you mind calling your friend in to witness the transaction?" he said, handing me the paper.

I glanced at it. It was a boilerplate contract—what amounted to a personal promissory note. I wondered how many of the Cougar wives and players had signed them. Dice certainly had an ample supply on the shelves.

"Just leave the amount blank," he said as he handed me a plastic pen with *Reverend Carl Dice* embossed on it. "You may keep the pen, to make your neighbors jealous."

"Jealousy is a sin, isn't it?"

"One of the worst. But human—all too human."

I looked up at him. "You weren't always in the religion business, were you, Reverend?"

"I sold cars, Mr. Stoner," he said coolly.

XXV

I called Bluerock in to witness the extortion. He signed on the witness line, I signed for the Cougars.

"You know," I said to Dice. "This won't stand up in court unless it's notarized."

"*I* am a notary," he said, and pulled a seal down from one of the shelves. He smiled at me after he stamped the document. "I went through many lives before I found my true calling, Mr. Stoner."

"How big a bite are you going to take?" I asked.

He rubbed his lower lip. "Enough to make it hurt," he said.

"Isn't greed a sin too?"

"A terrible vice. One that I suggest that you consult your employers about. They are such experts." He sat down opposite Bluerock and me. "You must think I'm a terrible devil. And I am a bit of that, when I have right on my side.

"Carol O'Hara should never have died," he said with something like real feeling in his mellifluous voice. "She was a good soul, and she was trying to do the right thing for herself and for her man. If it hadn't been for your employers, I think she would still be alive."

"What does that mean?" Bluerock said.

"You read the papers, Mr. Bluerock," he said. "If the Cougars had shown the slightest interest in Bill as a person, this whole tragic business would never have happened. But the Cougars didn't show an interest. They never do. What an odd attitude the NFL ownership has about its players. They are expected to exhibit loyalty, spirit, and self-sacrifice in the service of management. They are expected to go out on the field and risk what are all too often permanent disabilities, in order to win. And how does management reward their warriors? With negotiations that break the heart of even the most dedicated veteran. Or with instant waivers, if the man has been too badly hurt to suit up. Or with a trade to faraway places, if he gives them trouble at the bargaining table. Or with callous indifference, as is the case with Bill, if he has problems that don't jibe with the all-American image that the NFL is so eager to ascribe to its personnel.

"So I'm not going to feel too bad about whatever figure I write on this note," he said. "This isn't greed, Mr. Stoner. It's justice."

"Justice for whom?" I said.

"For her," he said.

I looked around the room—at the teak bookshelves, loaded with promissory notes, at the plump white sofas from Closson's, at the beautiful Orientals on the floors—and shook my head. "You know, I have the feeling that this isn't going to be your last job, Reverend—protecting the poor. I have the feeling that you have another calling in store, something less free-form, more institutional."

"Tut-tut, Mr. Stoner," Dice said, wagging his finger. "You must learn to lose gracefully in negotiations, just as the players do." He folded up the promissory note and stuck it in his pocket. "Now you may ask whatever questions you deem fit."

"Before you went into your Independence Day speech, you said something about C.W. trying to do the right thing for herself and for Bill. What did that mean?"

"Just what it sounded like," Dice said. "Before she came to me, Carol was a lost soul. She had no purpose, no values, no sense of direction. All she had was a racking sense of guilt, which was nothing more than her soul crying out for the truth. I helped show her the way to that truth."

"Did she have to sign one of those things first?" I said, pointing to the shelf full of contracts.

"Everyone has to pay his way, Mr. Stoner. That is the first law of life. Certainly, Carol made donations."

"And what did she get in return?"

"Counseling. Advice. Instruction."

"Instruction about what?" I said.

Dice gave me a cautious smile. "You must know about the problem she had created for herself."

"You mean Bill's drug arrest?"

He nodded. "She had betrayed her lover, and there was another person involved. A person for whom she felt responsible and who was accidentally killed."

He was trying to be tactful. But I already knew that he was talking about Barb Melcher.

"Did C.W. tell you about her part in the drug bust?" I asked.

"She talked around it, the way people feeling an overwhelming guilt will do. But I got the message."

"Did Bill know what she had done?"

"No," he said. "Certainly not. It would have destroyed her if he'd found out. She lived in constant fear of that possibility. And of course, they were having so many other problems—with money and with each other. Which is what made her final decision so brave."

"What decision?"

"To testify before the grand jury," he said.

For a moment I was too surprised to speak. And Blue-rock looked just as stunned as I was.

"C.W. was going to testify to the grand jury?" Otto finally said.

Dice nodded. "Frankly, I tried to talk her out of it. I thought it was much too dangerous, especially since they had been having such terrible fights about the baby. But she seemed to feel as if she had no choice, as if she owed it to Bill and to her friend, for whom she had never stopped mourning. And to her unborn child most of all." Dice had an odd look on his face. "You know I speak of Christ to many people. I say the words and they listen. But they seldom listen with their hearts. Carol did," he said with a touch of amazement. "She truly believed that she had to atone for her sins. She truly believed that amends must be made."

Even a charlatan must have his successes. And the fact that C. W. O'Hara's change of heart struck even Dice as something of a miracle didn't make it any less real.

"When did she make her decision to testify?" I said.

"Last Sunday," Dice said.

"Did Bill know?" Bluerock asked.

"No," Dice said. "But he might have been told. The papers say that he himself changed his mind about testifying. Perhaps that was the reason why. Perhaps she finally shamed him into doing the right thing. If so, it was a last minute decision, because he was absolutely adamant about refusing to go to court."

"So C.W. decided to go in his stead," I said. "Do you know whom she was going to testify against?"

"The same people that Bill would have testified against. After all, she was with Bill constantly. She knew who had been supplying him with those dreadful drugs.

That's the only reason that she agreed to help the federal agent in the first place when he approached her—to help Bill regain his balance."

"Bill was doing that much cocaine?" I said.

"No," Dice said, "although the cocaine was what the agent was primarily interested in. It was the other substances that she wanted to wean him of."

"The steroids?" Bluerock said, glancing at me.

Dice nodded. "They were changing him so drastically, his mind and his body. And he simply couldn't give them up. And then of course Carol's baby had been affected."

"How?" I said.

"I'm not sure how," Dice said. "Carol had a series of tests done several weeks ago at Deaconess. She was supposed to get the results on Friday."

That was the same day that Clayton claimed Parks had found out about C.W.'s betrayal. If Bill had gotten bad news from the doctor, too, the combination could have been lethal. I made a mental note to check with Deaconess and get the results of C.W.'s tests. I also decided to pay Walt Kaplan a visit.

I hated to admit it, but it looked as if Bluerock had been right—we should have gone to see Walt in the first place. He was not only Bill's cocaine supplier, he was his source for steroids, too. And if C.W.'s baby had indeed been damaged by the drugs Bill had been taking, that would have given C.W. a very personal reason to want to see Walt put away, to see him punished. It also would have given Walt a good reason to eliminate C.W. And I had the feeling that that was exactly what he had done. Someone had told Bill all of C.W.'s secrets, and no one had a better reason to betray her than Walt did. Of course, that also meant that Walt himself had somehow found out about C.W.'s role in the bust and her decision to testify in Bill's stead. I didn't know where he'd gotten that information, but I intended to ask him—even if I had to use the method that Bluerock had proposed.

I looked up at Dice, wondering if he had traded C.W.'s secrets to Kaplan in exchange for one of those promissory notes. He was one of the few people who had known the whole truth—he and Clayton and C.W. herself. One of them must have given the truth away, deliberately or by accident. According to Laurel, Dice had a reputation as a gossip, although in this instance the seriousness of the situation must have given him pause. Moreover, his affection for the dead girl seemed genuine enough. Still, he was a greedy, fundamentally dishonest man. And if he had a loose mouth to boot, the facts might have gotten back to Walt, via one of the other players or one of the players' wives.

"You haven't told anyone else about C.W.'s problems, have you, Reverend?" I asked.

Dice gave me a hurt look, as if I'd truly wounded him. "Of course not," he said. "I would have been killing her myself if I had. I loved that child. I tried my best to give her good advice. But the situation was so unpredictable —Bill was so unpredictable."

His eyes went blank, as if he were no longer looking out at the world but looking somewhere within himself. His cupid's bow mouth twisted into a revulsed frown, as if what he saw inside had made him physically ill. "He'll go to hell, you know," he said in a spiteful, vicious voice. "He knew what he was doing. He'll go to hell because he knew that he was wrong. He had a conscience, and he turned away from it. He felt guilt over what he had done to himself and to Carol through his drug abuse, and he denied it. It was such an unmistakable judgment on his sins; but he blamed her instead of looking inside himself. He thought it was a kind of weakness to feel guilt. His mother did that to him. A terrible woman."

"His mother seemed to be on his mind last week," I said.

Dice nodded. "She was hounding poor Carol—calling her constantly, vilifying her to Bill."

"Why?" I said.

"Because of me, because of my influence on the girl and her influence on Bill. Carol finally had to tell her she was pregnant, thinking that the woman would relent once she knew that they were common-law man and wife. But that only intensified her fury. She threatened Carol. She threatened me."

Dice looked up at us with an eerie and disturbing light in his eyes. "I tried to get him to take Jesus back in his heart. But he wouldn't do it. He thought Jesus would make him weak. He thought the girl and I would make him weak. He believed that his physical strength was his salvation. And he would not give up his faith in his body, even at the cost of his soul. He had made his muscles into a god, because at his very heart he knew that he was a weak and cowardly man. He will pay for his vicious arrogance. He will pay with his immortal soul. He will pay for all time in deepest hell."

"That's bullshit," Bluerock said suddenly.

The visionary light in Dice's eyes went out like a snuffed candle. He looked up at Otto as if he were seeing him for the first time. "It's the way I saw it, friend," he said.

"Well, the way you saw it is fucked. You're fucked."

Otto leaned forward on the couch and put a chilling scowl on his face. "Look at you," Bluerock said contemptuously. "You puny little puke. You haven't got the slightest idea what it feels like to be strong. You make your living preying on people's weakness—praising them for admitting it, encouraging them to revel in it, twisting them so they think that their bodies are evil, that true salvation can only be bought at the cost of this." He pinched his bicep. "Well, I got news for you, shithead. It's a blessing to be strong. It's a blessing to feel rage and to be able to express it. It's a blessing not to be afraid to act on your impulses, to react spontaneously to the gross fucking insults and insufferable stupidities that people like you foist off on the world. People like you were Bill's problem, fucker. Not Jesus and not sin. People like you, who took his money and told him how to live his life and fed him on drugs and betrayal and utter bullshit. You and Jewel and Walt and Clayton and Petrie and that cunt C.W., who gets religion after she dicks him over royally and then puts him in a spot that no man could get out of whole. You're the ones who turned what was good in him into weakness and insanity. You're the ones who belong in hell. I ought to break your fucking neck!"

Bluerock leapt to his feet. He was so mad that he'd begun to spit. His forehead bulged as if it were horned, his face was a livid mask of fury. There was no way I was going to be able to stop him if he went for Dice, and Dice knew it. The preacher turned white down to his fingertips, drew his knees up on the couch, and stared at Otto in terror.

"Blue," I said softly. "Save it for Walt and Clayton. You're not going to do Bill any good from jail."

He looked at me, then looked back at Dice, who was cowering on the sofa. Without saying another word, he stalked out of the room. Dice looked so relieved I thought he was going to pass out.

As soon as he was sure that Otto had left his house, he got up and walked over to the phone. "I'm going to call the police," he said. "That man is a menace."

"You better quit while you're ahead," I said icily. "You call the police and I'll swear out a warrant of my own, for extortion."

"I've extorted nothing from you," Dice said. "You

gave of your own free will. I am a nonprofit corporation."

"You're an asshole," I said. "And if you want to remain among the living, you'll get away from that phone."

He thought about it a second and saw the light. Dice went back to the couch and sat down heavily, a petulant look on his little-boy face.

"And as for that promissory note, keep it under five hundred. Or I'll send Bluerock back tomorrow."

When I got outside, I found Bluerock standing by the car—a lively grin on his face.

"Pretty good, wasn't I?"

"That was an *act?*" I said.

"Nope." He got into the Pinto. "It was practice," he said. "I like to work out before a game. I hit harder that way."

XXVI

As we drove down Anderson Ferry to River Road I explained my thinking to Bluerock about Walt Kaplan's probable part in betraying C.W.

"Why not take it a step further?" Otto said when I'd finished. "If you're willing to grant that Walt set C.W. up, who's to say he didn't set Bill up too?"

"What do you mean?"

"I mean Kaplan wanted the girl silenced, right? So what makes you think he didn't kill her himself and make it look like Bill had done it? Two birds with one stone."

"It's possible," I admitted. Only I didn't believe it. There was something too terribly personal about the savagery of the murder—something that related to Parks alone.

"Walt'll tell us," Bluerock said confidently. "He'll tell us everything. You'll see."

"You're that anxious to confront him?" I asked.

But he didn't answer me. He had a peculiar light in *his* eye, although I knew that it had nothing to do with sin or salvation. I'd seen that light before—in the war, in the jungle. It worried me.

"We need a plan," I said.

Bluerock looked at me out of the corner of his eye. "We *got* a plan, buddy," he said fiercely.

It was half past three when we pulled up in front of Kaplan's club on Winton Road. Bluerock didn't even wait until the car had stopped before hopping out onto the pavement. He was through the front door of the gym before I'd turned the engine off, the tail of his Hawaiian shirt flapping behind him.

"Christ!" I said out loud.

I flipped open the glove compartment, pulled out the Gold Cup, and shoved the pistol into my belt. It only took me about twenty seconds to make it into the club, but by then all hell had broken loose.

"I told him Walt wasn't here!" the acne-faced kid behind the front desk said frantically as I walked in. His ghetto blaster was lying in two pieces on the desk in front of him, its wire guts sprouting willy-nilly out of each end. A can of Pepsi sat on its side beside the radio, draining slowly over the desk and onto the concrete floor.

"Where's Bluerock?" I said.

The kid raised one trembling arm and pointed to the gym. His face had gone pale to the roots of his red hair.

I walked through the entryway into the gym. There were only half a dozen hard-core musclemen working out in the late afternoon heat, and all six of them were staring in wide-eyed wonder at the wake of Bluerock's progress—overturned dumbbell racks, exercise bikes, curling stands. The bodybuilders stood frozen astride the Universal machines, like cast-iron lawn animals.

I walked to the far end of the gym, picking my way through the wreckage. The door to Kaplan's office had been kicked open, the jamb splintered at the lock. Bluerock was standing inside, hands on his hips, face beet red, a dark scowl playing on his face like a spotlight.

"He's gone!" he said incredulously. "The fucker's gone!"

"Where?"

Bluerock shook his head savagely. "Out of town. Him, Mickey, and Habib. At least, that's what the little faggot at the desk said."

"Let's go, then," I said.

Bluerock didn't move. He stared at the desk furiously and then looked around the little white-walled office, until his eyes settled on a wooden folding chair. Without a word, he yanked the chair off the floor, lifted it above his head, and brought it down hard on Kaplan's desk. The chair shattered like glass, wood chips flying everywhere.

"Feel better?" I said.

He glared at me, the back of the chair still clutched in his hands. "Don't fuck with me, Harry!" he said in a voice trembling with anger. He threw the broken chair against the far wall and pushed past me back into the gym.

I stopped at the front desk on my way out. The kid had just gotten another glimpse of Otto blowing by him out the door, and his face looked windburned.

"Where'd Kaplan go?" I said to him.

He didn't answer me. He was still thinking about Bluerock. I slapped my palm on the desktop, and he snapped to attention.

"What?" he squeaked.

"Where did Kaplan go?"

"Out of town. I don't know. He don't tell me everywhere he goes."

"You want me to call that guy back in here?" I said to the kid.

His face collapsed. "No!" he shouted. "God, no."

"Then tell me where Kaplan went."

"I don't know," the kid said in a pleading voice. "Honest to Christ, mister. He just took off, around one. Him, Mickey, and Habib. He said he'd be out of town for a few days."

"Did he have a bag with him. A suitcase?"

"Yeah. A carry-on thing."

"So he was headed for the airport?"

"Yeah. He had some tickets in a folder. I guess he was headed for the airport."

"Which airline?"

"I don't know," the kid said.

"What color was the folder with the tickets?"

"Blue," the kid said. "Blue and white."

That sounded like Delta or People Express.

"You better not be lying to me, son," I said, glaring at him.

"I'm not lying," the kid said almost hysterically. He stared pathetically at the desk. "Look what he did to my radio."

I caught up with Bluerock in the parking lot.

"If we'd gotten here an hour or so earlier, we might have nailed him," he said, giving me an ugly look.

"He may be back tomorrow," I said. "We don't know where he went."

"He went after Bill," Otto said with so much certainty in his voice he almost convinced me. "He wants him dead, and tomorrow could be too late."

"We don't know that," I said.

"Yes, we do," Bluerock said. "That guy, Habib. He's Walt's strong-arm man. When Habib gets called in, somebody disappears."

"Who is he?"

"He runs a karate school out in Blue Ash. Does a lot of weird drugs. He's built like a refrigerator and he likes to hurt people. I mean really hurt them."

"Great," I said under my breath.

"We gotta find out where they went."

I nodded at him. "We will."

When we got back to the Delores, I set Bluerock the task of tracking Kaplan down.

"Just keep phoning the airlines. Start with Delta. Then People Express. If you don't have any luck with those two, try the other major carriers. We know he left within the last hour or so, so concentrate on outgoing flights between two and four."

"What am I supposed to say?"

"Tell them it's an emergency. Tell them that you work with Kaplan and that you have to get an urgent message to him. Tell them that he left on vacation this afternoon, but you're not sure where he went. They'll take it from there."

"What if he used a phony name?"

"Then we're cooked," I said. "At least, for the time being."

He eyed me coldly. "Next time, maybe you'll listen to me."

"Look at it this way," I said. "If we'd gotten there before he left, we might never have known what he was up to."

"We'd have known," Bluerock said bitterly. "He'd have told us—where he was going, when he was leaving, and how much the goddamn tickets cost."

I started for the front door.

"Where are you going?" Otto said.

"To Deaconess," I told him. "I want to know what those test reports said."

"Just don't take too long," Bluerock said. "We may have a plane to catch."

XXVII

Deaconess Hospital is located on Clifton Avenue—just about a mile and a half from the Delores. It only took me a couple of minutes to drive there and a couple more to park in their lot on Straight Street.

I walked from the lot to the lobby and over to the reception desk, a long chrome counter with colorful graphics painted on the wall behind it. The cheerful trim didn't disguise the hospital smells of disinfectant and alcohol, or improve the melancholy looks of the people sitting on the benches in the waiting area. The receptionist, a pretty little Chinese girl in a white nurse's uniform, smiled fulsomely as I walked up to her.

"How can I help you?" she said.

"I need to speak to a doctor in your obstetrics department."

"What is his name?"

"I don't know his name," I said. "I just know that it starts with *A* or *P.*"

The receptionist gave me an odd look, which wasn't

surprising. I figured I could smooth matters over by making the inquiry look official. I pulled out my trusty Special Assistant's badge and showed it to her.

"I'm investigating Carol O'Hara's murder," I said.

"The football player's girlfriend?" the girl said.

"Yes. She had a series of tests run here a couple of weeks ago. Prenatal tests. I'd like to talk to the doctor who ran them."

The girl consulted a Rolodex on her desk. "It was probably Dr. Ashram. He's in charge of prenatal testing at our clinic."

"Is he here now?"

"I think so. He may be in the lab. I'll page him for you."

While the girl was paging Dr. Ashram, I went over to a bank of pay phones opposite the reception desk and phoned George DeVries. It wasn't quite five o'clock, and there was an outside chance that he was still sitting at his desk, staring out the window at Mount Adams. I let the phone ring ten times and hung up. When I turned back to the receptionist there was a dark-haired, bespectacled man in a white doctor's tunic standing beside her.

"Are you Dr. Ashram?" I said as I walked over to him.

He nodded. "Yes, I am Dr. Ashram. And what would your name be, sir?"

"Stoner."

"Ah, Mr. Stoner," he said, almost joyfully. "How may I be of help to you?"

Dr. Ashram was a Pakistani gentleman and he spoke English with a merry, singsong lilt. His face was acne-scarred and almost as deeply pitted as George DeVries's. His jet-black eyes sparkled as if he'd just heard a joke or told one.

"I'd like to talk to you about one of your patients," I said, showing him the badge.

"This is what Miss Chang has been telling me," he said. "Would you like to come to my office, then?"

"If you wouldn't mind."

"No problem," he said, and smiled a toothy smile, as if in the face of his own insistent courtesy he'd found mine rather funny.

We took an elevator up to the fourth floor. I followed Ashram down a corridor lined with deserted offices on the west wall and with plate glass windows on the east. The windows were in shadows and the fluorescent lights overhead hadn't taken hold yet, so the hall had the dim, crepuscular look of library stacks. When we got to an office door with Ashram's name on it, the doctor dug through a pocket of his loose gabardine trousers and fished out a huge key ring loaded with keys. He found the one he wanted almost immediately, unlocked the door, and waved me through it, flicking on the light as I went in.

His office was neat and modern-looking—a steel secretary's desk and several tall files in the antechamber and a larger wooden desk and a half dozen more files in the main room. Several X-ray viewers were posted on the walls, and one of them had been left on. There was an X ray clipped to it. I glanced at the X ray—it looked like a negative of a summer thunderstorm.

"I never could figure out how you can read those things," I said, sitting on a hobbed leather captain's chair across the desk from Ashram.

"It is an art and a science," he said in his fine, cheerful voice.

Ashram opened the top drawer of his desk and pulled out a wrinkled pack of Camels.

"It is a terrible vice," he said apologetically, "but one that I cannot seem to rid myself of." He shook a cigarette from the pack and fit it into his mouth as if he were screwing in a light bulb.

"So, what do you wish to know, Mr. Stoner?" he said as he lit the cigarette.

"Carol O'Hara came to you a couple of weeks ago for a series of tests."

"Yes," he said. "She did."

"Why did she need the tests?" I said.

"She had been referred to me by another doctor," Ashram said. "Doctor Anthony Phillips."

"He was her obstetrician?"

Ashram shook his head, scaring away the smoke that was hanging in front of his face. "Not at all," he said. "He was the doctor of her husband. I mean, of course, the doctor of the football player."

"Bill Parks?"

"Yes."

"Why was Parks seeing a doctor?" I asked.

"This you would have to ask Dr. Anthony Phillips," Ashram said. "I believe the man, Parks, had a liver ailment. I'm not sure of the exact diagnosis, but there was concern that the unborn child might have been infected. I was asked to do some tests."

"And the results?"

"My tests showed that the child was mongoloid. There were other complications, as well. Deformities."

"What caused these problems?" I said. "The liver ailment?"

"It is possible, of course, although deformities of such an extent are usually genetic in origin. This is what I told Miss O'Hara."

"When did you give her the diagnosis?"

"On Thursday afternoon of last week."

"Was Parks with her at the time?"

"No."

"And how did she react?"

Ashram shooed the smoke from his eyes. "She was heartbroken, of course, even though she had been ex-

pecting the worst. It is always difficult for a mother to
face such a calamity, you know. Indeed, she was so distraught that her friend had to help her out of the office."

"I thought you said she was alone?"

"No," Ashram said. "I merely said that her husband—
that Parks was not with her. She did bring a friend along,
a girlfriend."

"Do you remember her friend's name?"

He shook his head. "She was a young blond girl. From
Kentucky, I think. I do not recall her name."

Unfortunately, I was very much afraid that I did.

Of course, there was no way to get in touch with Laurel
until she arrived in Hawaii. And she didn't *have* to be the
blond girlfriend who had accompanied C. W. O'Hara to
Dr. Ashram's clinic on Thursday. Nevertheless, I was
feeling pretty badly used as I rode the elevator back to
the hospital lobby. It wasn't as if she hadn't demonstrated that she was untrustworthy. In fact, she'd told me
outright that she'd do whatever she had to do to look
after her own interests. Moreover, most of the information she'd given me was sound. I'd confirmed it through
Bluerock and other sources. It was what she hadn't told
me that worried me. And why she hadn't told me. Knowing Laurel, I figured that withholding information had
probably turned her a buck. The question was, from
whom?

I walked over to the phone stands opposite the reception desk and called George DeVries again. When he
didn't answer a second time, I called information and got
the number of Dr. Anthony Phillips. His answering service said he was in surgery at Jewish Hospital. I decided
to try to catch him before I went back to the Delores. But
first I called Bluerock at home, to see if he'd found out
anything about Walt Kaplan's plane trip.

"No!" he said. "Not a fucking thing!"

"They must have used aliases," I said.

"That's not too good, is it?"

"No," I said. "That's not good."

"Look, Bill was talking about his mother all week," Bluerock said. "Maybe I should call her. Maybe she knows where he is."

"It's worth a shot," I said.

"Oh, by the way," Bluerock said. "Some bitch has been calling you up for the last couple of hours."

"Was it Laurel Jones?" I asked, probably because she was on my mind.

"She was the one in your apartment today?"

"Yeah."

"No, it wasn't her. I would have recognized her voice. I don't know who this one was, and she wouldn't leave her name or a message. She said she had to talk to you."

"Well if she calls again, tell her I'll be back around six thirty."

"You know, I didn't hire on to be your fucking answering service," Bluerock said as he hung up.

XXVIII

I drove across Clifton from Deaconess to Jewish. Dr. Anthony Phillips was still in surgery, according to the Emergency Room candy striper I spoke with. When I asked her what kind of surgery, she said, "Cancer, I guess. That's his specialty."

I didn't know what to make of that.

I told the girl I was with the DA's office, showed her my badge, and asked her to tell Dr. Phillips that I would be waiting to talk to him after he finished his operation. She said she'd give him the message.

I wandered over to the waiting area and sat down across from an enormously fat woman in a striped knit shirt and red rayon slacks. A very thin man, her husband I thought, sat beside her, resting his head in one gaunt hand and saying nothing.

A little past six, a slender mustached man wearing a blue surgical cap and gown walked up to the reception desk. He said a few words to the candy striper and she pointed in my direction. He came over to me, a weary, skeptical look on his face. Given the nature of the job he had just done, I figured that he probably didn't have a lot of patience left for strangers.

"Are you the cop?" he said acidly.

The fat woman pushed herself up with alacrity, and her husband lowered his hand and leaned forward in his chair.

"I'm the cop," I said. "How'd the operation go?"

"I don't know," Phillips said, sitting down on the chair beside mine. "Ask me in five years."

"You're a cancer specialist?"

He nodded. "That's one way of putting it."

"You had a patient I'm interested in. Bill Parks."

The surgeon looked at me for a moment. "You know I'm not supposed to talk about my patients. That's the law."

His by-the-book attitude surprised me and ticked me off. "You're not a psychiatrist," I said. "Whatever you were treating him for isn't going to be used in his defense."

"Now, how do you know that?" he said.

"And what does that mean?" I said.

Phillips looked over at the fat woman, who was watching us with naked curiosity.

"Let's go down the hall," he said, getting to his feet.

I followed him down a corridor to the surgeon's lounge—a drywall cubicle furnished with a couple of chairs, a sofa, and a table with a coffee machine on it. Phillips boosted himself to a cup of coffee, then sat down on the sofa.

"I guess it really doesn't make a difference if I talk to you about Bill," he said, stirring the coffee with a forefinger. "He's a dead man, anyway."

"What's he got?"

"What hasn't he got is a better question. Hepatic disorders. An endocrine system that is not of this world.

Mammogenesis. Testicular atrophy. Enlargement of the skull and jaw. You name it, he's got it. Plus, he's still growing."

"What do you mean, he's still growing?"

"You know—growing. Getting taller."

"He's twenty-nine years old," I said. "How could he be getting taller?"

"Therein lies the problem," Phillips said. He swallowed the coffee in a gulp, crumpled up the styrofoam cup, and tossed it into a brimming wastebasket in a corner of the room. "The Cougars' trainer sent Parks to me about six months ago. Bill had been developing tumorous breast tissue, and the trainer knew enough about steroids and growth hormones to realize that they were the culprits."

"He was growing breast tissue?" I said.

Phillips nodded. "What do you know about steroids?"

"Not a lot."

"Well, let me explain a few things," he said. "An anabolic steroid is an artificial form of testosterone. Testosterone stimulates the development of male sexual characteristics like chest hair, large muscles, deep voice. The artificial form is generally given to people who don't produce sufficient amounts on their own—children who aren't growing properly or older men who have had prostate surgery or testicular cancer. Unfortunately, it's also taken by athletes to stimulate muscular growth. And it does do that, undeniably. But it also has some peculiar side effects. For one thing, when you take unnaturally large doses of artificial hormone, the body stops developing hormones of its own. As a result, the testicles may atrophy if the dose is continued over a long period of time. To avoid that problem and other organic complications, athletes 'stack' the drugs. That is, they take anabolic steroids in combination with androgenic hormones designed to counteract the side effects of the anabolics.

Of course, those androgens also have side effects. They stimulate the development of female sexual characteristics. Males produce small quantities of androgens naturally. But when they are taken in artificially large doses, you start to see the kind of problems that Parks was experiencing—growth of breast tissue, changes in the timber of the voice, loss of sexual potency."

"Steroids can affect potency?" I said.

"Good Lord, yes. The sexual ups and downs that these drugs induce are easily as drastic as the physical changes. The effects range from virilism to impotence—sometimes both. And when the athletes go off the drugs, as they must do to guard against liver damage, there is a period in which the natural hormonal levels are very low, while the body readjusts to producing its own chemicals. During that period depressions, sometimes violent depressions, are commonplace."

"Parks was arrested several times for assaulting women. Do you think those assaults might have been induced by the drugs? By frustration over impotence."

"It's entirely possible," Phillips said. "Or he might have been experiencing a virile reaction and simply gotten carried away. That's what I meant about this problem constituting a legal defense. This man hasn't been in complete control of his mind or his body for many years."

I asked the obvious question. "Could the drugs have driven him to murder?"

"They certainly had some bearing," Phillips said. "I didn't do a psychological work-up on him. His physical problems were so extensive that they occupied all our time. But there was no question that he was unstable. His reaction to my diagnosis was so violent that I thought I was going to have to call some of you people in to subdue him. Luckily, his girlfriend was with him, and she managed to calm him down."

"What was your diagnosis?"

"Precancerous lesions of the chest. A suspicious spot on the liver. Testicular tumors. I recommended a biopsy on both the liver and the testes. And I also recommended that the girl go to a specialist and have their baby tested immediately. The possibility of chromosomal damage in a case like Parks's was extremely high. Good Lord, he'd been playing with one of the fundamental fluids of life."

"Did he have the biopsy done?"

Phillips shook his head. "His reaction to my diagnosis was complete denial. To him it was inconceivable that his body could let him down. I suppose it was also impossible for him to accept the fact that he'd brought this trouble on himself."

"When did you see him last?" I said.

"Ten days ago today," Phillips said. "He agreed to stop taking steroids for a few months. He also talked about taking a few days off from training camp and visiting his mother in Montana. I think he still thought that a little rest and some chicken soup would make the tumors go away, like a cold. I gave him some capsules to take— antidepressants to help him through the drying-out period. And he agreed to come back for some follow-up blood tests in six weeks."

"So he hadn't taken any steroids for several days prior to the murder?"

"If he kept his word, yes."

"And during that time he would have been experiencing a deep depression—possibly a violent one."

"The way a man reacts when he kicks any powerful drug," Phillips said. "He certainly would have been reflecting on his mistakes. From what I've heard the girl did go to the obstetrician I recommended, and the baby was severely deformed. Parks was convinced that there would be nothing wrong with the child, just as convinced as he was about the health of his own body. In fact, I think he looked on the baby as a test case—proof that I was an alarmist and that his girlfriend was behaving like a fool."

"How did she react to your diagnosis?"

"She was very frightened and very concerned for Parks and for her unborn child."

I got up to go. "Thanks," I said. "You've been a help."

"I hope so," Phillips said dismally. "In some cases, it's hard to know."

XXIX

I thought about Parks all the way back to the Delores. If it was all so sad, I wondered why I felt like laughing. And yet that was exactly what I felt like doing. All he'd wanted was to be the best football player he could be, and he'd ended up murdering C.W. and his child, giving himself cancer, and growing breasts. Everyone that he'd believed in, everyone except for Bluerock, had betrayed him. Even his own body had betrayed him. And at the end, he hadn't even been able to turn to the girl, to C.W., whom I now thought had really loved him, and who had tried to make up for the way she, too, had betrayed his trust. In his mind, she was part of the problem—she and the child she was carrying—even before Walt told him the ugly truth. Just two more reminders of the impotence and disease that were ravaging his own body.

He had never been much of a thinker. He'd relied on his instincts, on what his body told him to do. But on those last few nights, even that circuit had sputtered and failed. At the end, there had been no thought at all. Just

Bill and those antidepressant pills and the reflection of his body and the dark, hot space in between. Maybe he just sat there waiting for someone to fill that space—another face, another body, someone to blame. Dr. Ashram had told C.W. about the baby on Thursday. I assumed that she'd told Bill the same day. So by Friday, the truth had become undeniable, and this pathetic, put-upon, self-created Frankenstein had had no defense left against it, except the all too ready violence that had been brewing inside him in the heat. The news that C.W. had betrayed him to the police and was going to betray him again in front of the grand jury must have been the spur that had let that violence loose, that had sent it hurtling outward against the symbols of the larger betrayal he had visited on his own body. He hadn't just killed the child, he'd killed himself—the part of himself in her that was disease and madness incarnate.

What was left of him after that bloody act wasn't worth saving. I even knew where to look for him, now. Phillips had told me where he was headed—back home, back to Mom, back out of it all. He wasn't going to make it back. Perhaps he'd kill himself on Mom's embroidered rug, a final reproach to the woman he'd obviously never been able to please. Or maybe the diseases themselves would kill him. Most likely, Walt Kaplan would do him that favor. I was sure that was where Walt and Mickey and the hired gun, Habib, were headed—to tuck Bill safely away in some Montana woods, where he would never come back to haunt them in the jury box. Why Walt had decided to go to that extreme, I wasn't sure. Something had him scared. Maybe it was the murder itself, or the savagery of it. Bill Parks was clearly a madman, and madmen are unpredictable.

As I pulled into the parking lot behind the Delores, I tried to think of a way to explain it to Bluerock—to explain what a dreadful, farcical mess his friend Parks had made of his life. But the truth was, I didn't want to explain it, didn't want to listen to Otto's inevitable rationalizations, his gripes and protests. I was weary of Bill Parks, and I didn't want to hear Otto extol the pristine ideals of athleticism again. There was nothing wrong with his ideals. It was the man he was defending who'd gone indefensibly bad.

I trudged upstairs, unlocked the door, and opened it, to my surprise, not on Bluerock but on Laurel's friend, Stacey. I must have done a double take, because it took me a good moment to realize that Bluerock was sitting there too.

"Hello, sport," Otto said with a disturbing note of solicitude in his voice.

I glanced at him then took a closer look at Stacey. She was sitting in the desk chair, a straw purse in her lap, her hands on her purse, her head slightly bowed. She was still dressed for vacation in a light summer dress. Only all of the high spirits had gone out of her face. She looked the way Bluerock had sounded—as if someone had died.

"What are you doing here, Stacey?" I said uneasily. "You're supposed to be on your way to Hawaii."

She raised her head slowly. It was obvious that she'd been crying. Her punky makeup had been scrubbed off, probably because the tears she'd been shedding had made a mess of her face. Her eyes were red and puffy, and there were marks on her cheeks that she'd missed when she was washing up, little black crow's-feet where the mascara had bled down.

"Where's Laurel?" I said.

Stacey bit her lip. "She's gone," she said in a trembling voice, and began to cry. She put her hand over her face and sobbed out loud.

"Somebody better tell me what's going on here," I said nervously.

"Take it easy, sport," Bluerock said. "The kid's had a tough day."

"How did she get here?" I asked him.

"I told her to come over the last time she called. She's the one who's been calling you all afternoon. She'd been sitting alone at the airport for about five hours."

"Alone?" I said. "What happened to Laurel?"

Bluerock gave me a grim look. "She says Laurel met three guys at the airport. The meeting had apparently been prearranged. Laurel told Stacey that she was going to go to her house and talk to these guys, and that she'd be back at the airport in an hour. If they missed their flight, they'd catch another, later this afternoon." He glanced at Stacey, who was still sobbing loudly in her chair. "Laurel never came back."

I walked over to the girl and pulled her hands from her face. She gasped as if I'd torn her clothes off.

"Why'd she go with them?" I said, pressing my face into hers. "She must have given you a reason."

"She knew them," the girl said helplessly. "She said she'd done business with one of them—a great big guy with a beard."

"What kind of business?" I said angrily.

"I don't know!" Stacey said, staring fearfully into my face. "She was friends with them. She didn't act scared. She went off on her own. And she never came back."

"Christ!" I said furiously. I felt like slapping Stacey's stupid, frightened face.

"Take it easy, Harry," Bluerock said.

" 'Take it easy,' " I repeated sarcastically.

"C'mon," I said, hauling Stacey to her feet.

"Where are we going?"

"To her house," I said.

"I don't want to go there," Stacey said, trying to pull away from me. "I don't want to get in any trouble."

I stared at her for a moment, hearing those words

again. The same ones Laurel had used about her friend
C.W.

"Just get the fuck out of here, then," I said, between
my teeth. "Go on. Get out!" I shoved her toward the
door.

She turned back to me from the doorway, her face
tearstained and terrified. "Don't I get to go to Hawaii?"
she whined.

If Bluerock hadn't jumped to his feet and grabbed me
by the arms, I think I would have slugged her. She took a
quick look at my face and ran down the hall.

"C'mon, sport," Bluerock said. "Let's go."

"I've got to call the cops first," I said with real dread in
my heart.

"I'll do it," Bluerock said, picking up the phone. "I
won't give my name. Otherwise it could be a long night."

The Newport cops had responded to the anonymous
tip and were camped at Laurel's apartment by the time
Bluerock and I showed up on the scene. I met one of
them, a patrolman, coming down the apartment house
stairs to the courtyard. From the ashen look on his face, I
could tell that the worst had happened.

"Somebody must have really hated her," the cop said,
looking sick.

Bluerock eyed me with concern. "You sure you wanna
go up there, sport?" he asked.

I pushed past the cop and walked up the six flights to
Laurel's apartment. There was a knot of plainclothesmen
at the top of the stairs. I recognized one of them, a
lieutenant of detectives named Driscoll.

"Hi ya, Harry," he said. "What're you doing here?"

"I knew the girl," I said.

"Yeah?" He gave me a sympathetic look. "Maybe you
better not go in there now."

"I think I have to," I said.

Driscoll shrugged. "It's up to you."

I followed a short uncarpeted hallway decorated with posters of Dan Marino and Joe Montana into a small living room, furnished sparely in bright primary colors. A cherry-red sofa. A yellow beanbag chair. An electric-blue plastic parsons table between them. Some wicker-work hanging from the ceilings. An asparagus fern on the window sill. Another set of posters—John Travolta and Kris Kristofferson—on the walls.

A second group of cops—forensic men, judging from the pop of flashcubes—were gathered in the bedroom. I walked over to the doorway and looked in. Then I went over to the couch and sat down heavily on the cushions. Bluerock came over to me. So did Driscoll.

"The lab thinks it was Parks again," Driscoll said, after a time.

"That's what they were meant to think," I said, feeling the dullness, the lassitude of shock, spreading through me. Each part of me slowly falling asleep.

"You all right, sport?" Bluerock said.

I nodded, although I wasn't all right.

"It's the same MO," Driscoll went on. "And they found some physical evidence that ties Parks into it. It was Parks, all right. The crazy bastard."

I looked up at Bluerock. "You think it was Parks?"

"You know what I think," he said.

"I'm going to need a drink," I said to him.

He raised me to my feet as if I were a child. "Can you make it downstairs?"

"Yeah," I said.

But halfway down the stairs my legs gave way, and I had to lean on him until we got to the car.

 XXX

We went to the Busy Bee.

I had three double Scotches in the space of a half hour, and I didn't even feel drunk. Just dead inside. About halfway through the fourth Scotch, I did start to feel the liquor. Around the fifth, I got violently ill.

I managed to make it to the john, but I didn't make it to the stall. I threw up in one of the washbasins, banging my head on the porcelain sink and sliding to the floor. I sat there on the tiles until Bluerock came in and picked me up again.

"This is getting to be a habit with you," he said with a grimace. "Let's go back to your place. Get some rest."

I shook my head. "We gotta go after them," I said to him. "They killed her."

"I know it," Bluerock said. "We'll take care of them in the morning."

"Gotta go," I said stupidly.

Bluerock hauled me out of the john.

Hank Greenburg, the bartender, took a look at me and made a face. "Christ, Harry, are you all right?"

"He's fine," Bluerock said, as he guided me toward the door. "Just had a little too much to drink."

I woke up around seven the next morning, feeling nothing but a cold, vicious rage that covered every inch of me like a rank sweat. I didn't even try *not* to think about Laurel, about the way she had looked when they'd finished with her. In fact, I fed myself on the image, turning it over in my mind again and again, until I was angry enough to butcher them the way they had butchered her. She'd been a greedy fool, greedier and more foolish than I had imagined. But for a few days I'd thought of her as mine.

I wandered into the living room and found Bluerock sleeping on the couch. He woke up with a start as I passed by him, as if he had been singed by my shadow.

We didn't say a word to each other until I'd fixed some coffee.

"Do you feel up to talking about her?" he said as we sat down across from each other in the living room.

I nodded. "I feel up to more than that."

"You've got the look, all right," he said with a nod. "Why do you think they did it?"

"She knew something," I said. "Something Kaplan was afraid of. She knew about the drugs. Maybe that was it."

"But why would he wait until now to shut her up?"

"Why would he wait until now to go after Parks?" I said. "Obviously, C.W.'s murder changed something. What it was, I don't know yet."

"She'd apparently been doing business with Walt, your friend Laurel," Bluerock said.

I'd been thinking about that, too, while I was making the coffee, thinking about what it was she could have sold to Walt that he couldn't have gotten from anyone else. And I'd come up with one disturbing possibility.

"I found out yesterday that she'd been lying to me about how much she knew," I said. "She went with C.W. to the obstetrician. So she'd heard about what was wrong with the baby, and about what was wrong with Parks."

"What was wrong with Bill?" Otto said.

It took me a second to realize that I hadn't told him about Dr. Ashram or Dr. Phillips.

"The steroids Bill had been taking had ruined C.W.'s baby. And they were killing Bill."

"Killing him?" Blue said, shocked.

"Literally. His whole body was riddled with disease. And his mind had been affected too. He was pure madness, Blue, by the time of the murder. When Kaplan told him how C.W. had betrayed him back in December and what she was planning to do in court this week, it pushed him over the edge."

"What makes you so sure Walt didn't kill her himself," he said predictably, "and make it look like Bill had done it—just like he did with Laurel?"

"You're not listening to me, Blue," I said. "The man was out of control. His life was out of control. Kaplan might have loaded the gun for him, but Bill pulled the trigger."

"Maybe so," he said, although he didn't sound convinced. In spite of all the evidence to the contrary, he hadn't accepted the possibility that Bill Parks was a murderer. Otto was a brutal man, but like Bill, he had a sentimental streak, especially when it came to his friends. But then the two went together, as someone once said— brutality and sentiment.

While he was mulling about Parks I went back to what I'd been saying about Laurel. "Kaplan had to have a source for his information about C.W.—someone to tell him her secrets. I thought at first that the source was

Dice, but I'm beginning to think that it might have been Laurel."

Bluerock frowned. "She sold her friend out for money?" he said in a contemptuous voice.

I nodded. "It's ugly, I admit. But it wouldn't have been out of character. And she was apparently a lot more privy to what was going on in that ranch house than she'd let on to me."

"Say that's true," Bluerock said. "That's still not a good enough reason for Walt to kill her."

I didn't think it was, either. I really didn't know what to think about the second murder—until George DeVries called at eight thirty with the final piece of the puzzle.

I had a feeling it was George when the phone rang. I snatched the receiver up eagerly, as if it were a call from home.

"I think I got that information you wanted on Clayton, Harry-boy," George said, after he'd said hello.

"Tell me," I said with appetite.

"You won't forget about the tickets? Or the popcorn-and-beer money?"

"I won't forget," I said.

"All right," George said. "I don't have the whole picture yet, but what it looks like is that Philly was playing a little dirty pool. He busted Parks just like we thought, with the help of Parks's girlfriend. Only Parks wouldn't play ball. No matter how hard Phil leaned on him, he wouldn't agree to testify in court. So it shouldn't be a total loss, Phil approaches this guy Kaplan on his own. He tells him he's got Billy-boy in the bag, and that he's going to send him away forever unless Kaplan agrees to cop a plea. Now, Parks was this guy Kaplan's meal ticket, so he doesn't want to see him put away. But he's not about to cop a plea to save him, either. Instead, he and Philly came to an arrangement."

"What kind of arrangement?" I said.

"Well CID isn't exactly saying, but if you read between the lines it looks like Phil got paid off—and I mean big money—in return for sitting on the Parks drug indictment and leaving Kaplan alone. Of course, now Philly's claiming that it was all part of a plan, that he was taking Kaplan's dough as evidence in a conspiracy to obstruct. But I don't think CID is going for it. See, there was a fly in the ointment."

"C. W. O'Hara," I said.

"Right," George said. "How'd you know? The girl gets a case of the guilts, goes down to the DA on her own, and offers to testify against Kaplan if they drop the drug charges against her man. Now the DA's never heard of Kaplan or the Parks case. Philly hasn't told him. As far as the DA knows, all he's got on Parks is the New Year's Eve assault. He starts to get curious, and notifies CID. Phil gets wind of the investigation, and things start happening. He knows he can't play footsie with Kaplan anymore. That's all over with. Instead, he approaches the girl, and *he* agrees to arrange immunity for Bill on both charges, if she promises to help him out."

"Help him out how?" I said.

"She's got to testify to the fact that Phil was the one who convinced her to go to the DA—that she'd been working with him all along. In other words, she's going to help him cover his tracks. I guess the girl made the deal, because she was the one scheduled to testify on Friday. But Kaplan must have gotten wind of the fact that Philly was planning to sell him out. Nobody seems to know how Kaplan managed it, but you know what happened. The girl ended up dead."

I knew how he'd managed it, but I didn't say anything. Instead, I played dumb, and asked George if there was any possibility that Kaplan himself had killed C.W.

"No. Parks killed her. Forensic is certain of that. But

it's pretty obvious that Kaplan was an accessory before the fact. The question is, how did he get Parks to do it?"

"What about all the stories Clayton fed to the papers about the Cougars helping make a deal for Parks, and about Parks being scheduled to testify?"

"That was all a smoke screen," DeVries said. "I mean, Phil had to come up with something reasonable-sounding to tell the press. And nobody at CID was sure enough of the facts to contest what he was saying. Now he says that he was just trying to buy time to throw Kaplan off the track, while he tried to put the case back together in a different way."

"How was he planning to do that?" I asked.

"He says he had another witness lined up, someone who could testify against Kaplan. Some chippy who was a good friend of O'Hara's and who knew Parks, too. But he was having trouble bringing the witness to hand. He claims he had her on a drug charge, but when he talked to her on Sunday morning she wouldn't play ball. Apparently she wanted to be paid off in exchange for testifying. And now Phil claims she's disappeared."

She hadn't disappeared. She'd been murdered in a Newport apartment house, murdered in the act of attempting one last piece of extortion.

I was almost astonished by how deftly she'd managed it. Laurel *hadn't* been at the apartment when I'd come home with Bluerock on Sunday morning. I thought she'd been out shopping. I guess she had been, in a perverse way. Shopping for the highest bidder for her services. That was undoubtedly why she'd rendezvoused with Kaplan at the airport—to see how much he was willing to pay to keep her quiet. If so, it had been a mistaken piece of daring, and she'd paid for that mistake more horribly than she could have guessed. But Laurel had never lacked chutzpah. Nor had she ever disguised her greed.

"I guess Phil's only hope now is to find Bill and bring

him back alive," George said with a laugh. "He's gone off after him, I know that. But even if he does make the case, he's still going to have to explain all those deposits to his savings account. You know, the funny part is that the money probably came from Parks himself, from Kaplan's cut of the contract. In fact, the theory is that that's why Kaplan had talked Bill into renegotiating—to get a bigger nut to pay Philly off with. What a dumb fucker this Parks was, huh?"

"Pretty damn dumb," I said.

"Well, I guess you can call the Cougars up and tell them not to worry now. There'll be a retraction in the papers, as soon as Phil comes back to face the music. While you're talking to them, you might mention the tickets."

I told him I would.

"I guess that's it," George said. "Case closed."

Only it wasn't quite closed—not for me.

XXXI

I called Petrie up after I finished with George. Bluerock listened in on the conversation so I wouldn't have to explain it a second time.

When I was done, Hugh breathed a sigh of relief. "So it's all settled now."

"All settled," I said.

"And things can get back to normal. Call me in a couple of days, Harry. I'm going to arrange a bonus for you—you've earned it. And tell Bluerock that the deal we made is still on, if he changes his mind. I guess we owe him something too."

It wasn't until I'd hung up the phone that I realized that he hadn't even mentioned Parks. That the Grand Guignol fate Bill had inflicted on himself hadn't even moved him to comment.

Maybe he was just relieved to be out from under. Laurel's murder had made the morning papers—with its tie-in to Bill. So that had probably been on his mind, too.

I stared at Bluerock for a moment, and he stared back at me.

"We've been fired," I said.

"Have we, now?"

"And you've been invited back to training camp."

He nodded noncommittally. "But we're not really done, yet, are we?"

I shook my head. "No."

"I called his mother in Missoula last night. She made a big point of telling me she didn't know where he was. I didn't even have to ask. She also had a few unkind words for C.W., who according to her had gotten just what she deserved."

"I'll bet," I said. "Dr. Phillips told me that Bill had planned to visit Jewel last week. Bill seemed to think that going home would solve all his problems. Of course, that was before he found out about the baby and about C.W."

We looked at each other again. "Well . . ." he said.

"You know what you're getting into?"

He nodded.

"I know why I'm doing this," I told him, as I started for the bedroom to pack a bag. "I can't say I understand why you are. You know, he did do it, Blue. He did kill her. There's no question about it anymore."

"Does it make a difference to you that the girl lied to you?" he said, giving me a sharp look.

"That's a different situation," I said.

"Why? 'Cause you fucked her a few times? A friend's a friend, Harry. You take them the way they are. And you don't sell them out because they disappoint you. They're going to kill Bill. You know it and I know it."

"They're probably doing him a favor."

He sighed. "Probably. But that's beside the point. Maybe he took the big dive. But he had somebody behind him all the way, pushing or prodding or selling a ticket."

He had a point. "Like you said, he was the football."

"He still is," Otto said with feeling. "*Somebody* owes him a break, even if it's just the chance to die in his own way."

"He may not get that chance, Blue," I said. "If I find him, I'm turning him in. And you know what Walt has in mind."

He looked at me for a second. "Like I told you, we'll cross that bridge when we come to it."

By midafternoon we were jetting high over the Rockies. Bluerock had bought a pile of comic books at an airport newsstand and kept his nose buried in them throughout the flight. He'd managed to change clothes before we left, so he didn't look quite as conspicuous as he had in the Hawaiian shirt. But there was no way that he wasn't going to stick out, no matter what he had on.

I tried to get some sleep during the flight, but I was too keyed up to relax. And then, every time I closed my eyes I saw Laurel lying on that bloody bed, and I'd go cold with rage again.

I knew that she'd invited disaster, that she had been toying with Kaplan the way she had toyed with Phil Clayton. The way she had toyed with me. She'd wanted to make a big score—that's what she'd told me. But she hadn't been quite pretty enough or lucky enough to do it the way that her friend C.W. had. So she'd made a place for herself on the fringe of the scene, eking out a living in the creases of that hard little world. She probably hadn't thought that she was doing C.W. any harm, by keeping loose tabs on her for Kaplan. And unlike Stacey, she had done the right thing on Friday night, when everything had fallen apart. She had tried to help her friend, unaware that she herself had played a pivotal role in the tragedy. And when she'd come to on Saturday morning, with Clayton breathing down her neck and Kaplan on her trail and me painting her into a corner, I supposed that she'd decided she had to look out for herself. All I was offering her was a ticket out, and she had wanted more than that.

Around seven we landed in Missoula. We'd transferred to a two-engine plane in Casper, and the last leg of the trip had left Bluerock looking as green as the shirt he was wearing.

"Christ," he said as we stepped out of the plane. "That was the worst flight I've ever been on."

"Any flight that doesn't go down is a good flight," I said to him, and patted the ground with my palm.

We called a cab from the airport and had him drive us to a TraveLodge on Missoula's main drag, Broadway. It wasn't much of a street—or much of a town, from what I could see through the cab window. It was all drab, weatherbeaten brick and peeling aluminum siding—a brutally ugly, utilitarian place, like a mill town without the mill. It stretched out on a mountain valley floor, flat, fading, and brittle. All around it, in sharp contrast to the ugliness of the town itself, were lovely timbered foothills and blue mountain peaks. The Rattlesnake Mountains, the desk clerk at the motel told me.

"Snow Bowl's to the north—the way you came," the man said affably, as if he figured us for summer skiers. He was a thin old man with a frail, friendly face, gold-rimmed glasses and a billowing white shirt that he'd once filled out fully, but which now hung around his withered torso like a lamp shade.

"We're not here for skiing," I said to him.

"We're hunters," Bluerock said over my shoulder.

"Not the game season," the old man said. "You might do you some fishing, though. Good trout fishing on Clark Fork."

"We'll check it out," I said.

The motel room was clean and comfortable—better

than I'd expected. While I took a shower, Bluerock arranged with the desk clerk to rent a car. By the time I'd finished showering, Otto had the car, a red Dodge Colt, waiting in the lot. Otto came back up to the room while I got dressed. It was close to nine, Cincinnati time, but we'd gained two hours on the flight, so the sun was still playing brightly on the worn brick buildings outside the motel window.

Bluerock reached into his shirt pocket and pulled out a jagged page that he'd torn from a phone book. "Bill's folks live out on Route Ninety-three. The clerk gave me instructions on how to get there."

"We've got a stop to make first," I said.

"Where?"

"Sporting goods store," I said to him. "There's one open until nine on Brooks. At least, that's what the Yellow Pages said." I stared into his bulldog face. "You ever handled a weapon, Blue?"

"I've done some deer hunting," he said. "I'm no crack shot, if that's what you mean."

"Well, at least one of *them* is."

"So what do we do about it?"

"We try to get to Bill before they do," I said.

"And if we don't? If they try to stop us?"

It was a question I wasn't prepared to answer—at least, not at that moment and not at Bluerock's behest. Around Otto it was just too easy to act rashly and to think about it later, to follow the impulse wherever it led, whatever the consequences. I'd already found myself doing it—playing up to him, trying to fulfill the demands he made on himself and on his friends, acting the macho in spite of myself and enjoying it. But the time for recklessness, even Bluerock's vaguely principled brand of recklessness, was past. Kaplan, Mickey, and Habib weren't playing a scrimmage. Neither was Clayton. Or Parks.

I put it to him bluntly. "Are you prepared to get your-self killed over Bill?"

"Are you prepared to forget about what they did to the girl?" he replied.

I didn't have to think about that one. "No," I said.

"Then what are we going to do?" he said, giving me a sidelong, slit-eyed look. "Why the hell are we talking about guns, if we're not planning on using them?"

"I'm hoping we won't have to use them," I said.

He shrugged and sat down heavily in a chair by the motel room window. "If you say so, sport," he said. "But you know as well as I do what it's going to come down to."

Bluerock stared out the window at the street. The brick shops were ablaze in the sunset, a white shimmer of light like sun on chrome. He closed his eyes against the glare and put his head back against the seat cushion. I pulled a fresh shirt from my duffel and put it on.

Bluerock laughed suddenly, a single bark of contented amusement.

"What's so funny?" I said over my shoulder, thinking vaguely that he was laughing at me, at my scruples.

He opened his eyes and looked up at me. "I was think-ing about something that happened to me a few years back. It just popped into my head. Christ knows why."

"What was it?" I said, sitting down across from him on the edge of the bed.

"We were playing in Phoenix," he said. "It was a late fall day, and the sun was setting over the rim of the stadium like it is out there now, just a big white glare like a spotlight. We'd gotten our asses kicked for three quar-ters, and the game was out of hand. Everybody knew it. We were just running out the clock, trying to hold the humiliation level down to a minimum. But one of our guys fumbled on our own thirty and out came the Stars again, with a good nine minutes left to play. They were already up by twenty points. With any less time on the clock they probably would have run it out. But nine minutes—hell, that's an eternity. They had to go for it. And they did. They moved the ball down to our three, then we stopped them for two downs for no gain. And it was third and one. We figured they'd throw one into the end zone and settle for a field goal if they missed connections. So Coach called a blitz. I was lined up on the weak side, playing down, like a lineman. Instead of passing, they ran a sweep to the strong side, their guards and tackles pulling. It was just one of those lucky plays. The blocking back was supposed to cut me, but he got tangled up with Bill instead, and I came in clean on the quarterback. I got to him just as he was handing the ball off. In fact he practically handed it to me. I hit him square in the numbers and managed to corral the running back too. Both of them went down hard, and the ball just skittered around in the backfield like a puck on ice."

Bluerock laughed again at the memory. "It was just right," he said with satisfaction. "My old lady was in the stands. Her fucking family was from Phoenix. My Dad was still alive then, and he'd come down from Milwaukee. All day long I'd wanted to show them something. And there it was. When I got up at the end of that play, I felt like life couldn't get any better. I tell you, sport, at that moment my bags were packed and I was ready to board the train."

I smiled at him, enjoying his enjoyment of the moment. "Who recovered the fumble?" I said.

Bluerock grinned lazily. "They did," he said. "One of our linemen kicked it into the end zone and one of their linemen fell on it in for a TD."

He laughed, and I laughed too.

"Hey," he said, holding out his hands in apology. "It's never perfect. It just gets close. And sometimes it gets closer than other times. You keep lining up and making contact."

He got up from the chair.

"You ready?" he said.

I got up from the bed and tucked the shirt into my pants. "I guess so."

Bluerock started for the door. "Let's go get 'em, then," he said.

XXXII

It wasn't until after we'd bought shotguns, ammunition, and a pistol at the sporting goods store that I got a full sense of the absurdity of the situation. Driving along a twilit Montana highway with purpling mountains on either side of us and a back seat full of death. And for what? For Frankenstein and his bride? For a girl whom I'd liked but hadn't loved?

If you think too deeply about your loyalties, you can think yourself out of them. It was Bluerock's kind of logic; but it was shaping up as a Bluerock kind of night—like the night we'd spent a few days before, drinking and carousing and making thin, adolescent fun while we searched for Bill Parks. That fun had landed me in jail and sent Bluerock to the hospital. This time, I knew full well that Otto's kind of fun could get both of us killed. It could end in madness, what we were doing—boyish, spirited, high-minded madness, like the honorable dares of adolescence or the reflex heroics of the playing field. Only this time we could end up dead.

I tried to size up the situation reasonably, to tote odds like a paramutual, to be sane and cautious and professional about what we were doing. And all the while, I could hear Bluerock beside me, saying, "Odds are for losers. For pussies. For wimps. Real men do what they have to do—and the hell with odds." To Bluerock, we were in it for the glory, for the sheer principle of the thing. It was third and goal all over again. The game was already lost, but his friend was in trouble and my friend had been killed. Never mind that his friend was a madman and that Laurel had been a charming but treacherous tramp. We owed it to both of them to make things right, to shed justice like paladins or to die trying. To make contact. It could end in madness, all right. And in spite of my toting up, I could feel a part of me warm to the silly, dangerous notion. We hadn't become friends for nothing, Bluerock and I. And we *were* friends. There was that, if there was nothing else unequivocal about the whole crazy enterprise.

So I didn't do any more thinking about the reasons, good or bad, for what I was doing there. I thought only about what lay ahead. About how to get to Parks, if I could. About how to survive Kaplan and his pals, if I couldn't. About how to keep Bluerock from getting his ass blown off, trying to redeem himself and his wacky, murderous friend.

We got to the Parkses' ranch just as the sun was setting. An access road veered off from the main highway, cutting through a dark stand of pines and ending in a dirt yard, in front of a small white house that was crumbling at the corners, like stale cake left out on a plate.

A tall, stocky man was sitting on the porch steps. He eyed us hostilely as we got out of the car. He looked to be in his early fifties, with a rugged, florid, deeply lined face, a bull neck, and a heavy gut that filled up his flannel shirt and spilled over a wide, buckleless belt tied like a rope at his hips. His brilliantined gray hair was combed straight back from the forehead, hanging in stiff, arrow-shaped tufts above his shirt collar. The thick coat of Vitalis almost made his hair look barbered, but the tufts in back gave him away, like wild curls sneaking out beneath a shower cap.

Behind him, from the porch of the house, a woman was looking through the black mesh of a screen door—not staring at us but watching the man, watching his back. I couldn't see her face clearly in the lamplight, but there was a purpose in the way she stood, as if she were monitoring his movements.

"Mr. Parks?" I said as I walked up to him.

He grunted at me. "I'm Lew Parks. Who are you two, and what do you want?"

Bluerock came around the side of the car and walked up to him. "Don't you remember me, Mr. Parks? I'm Otto Bluerock. I'm a friend of Bill's. You met me once in Cincinnati."

The man nodded abruptly. "I think I do remember you. How you been, son?"

"Okay," Otto said. "You think we could talk to you for a few minutes? About Bill?"

The man looked back at the door of the house where the woman was standing. "I guess so. You looking for him, too, are you?"

I glanced at Otto. "Who else is looking for him, Mr. Parks?"

He stuck his hands in his trouser pockets. "Some guy come by this afternoon. A cop name of Clayton. I sent him on his way." He laughed. "Dumb bastard thought he could get by me for a few lousy dollars."

I hadn't counted on Clayton showing up, although I suppose I should have. He had to do something dramatic to get back in the department's good graces, and bring-

ing Bill in might turn the trick for him. If we didn't get to
Bill quickly, Phil'd have to be dealt with, just like the
other three.

"You boys come on in," Lew Parks said.

We followed him up the porch steps. As soon as the
woman saw us approaching, she turned away from the
door and disappeared into the house.

There was a small foyer behind the screen door,
papered in yellow stripes.

"You can wipe your shoes on that mat by the door,"
Parks said, disguising an order as an afterthought. "Jewel
don't like anyone tracking dirt through the house."

Bluerock and I wiped our shoes on a cocoa fiber mat in
the hallway.

Up close, Parks smelled strongly of bourbon. It could
have been an aftereffect of the murders, but the tremor
in his hands made me think differently. He had the kind
of parched-lipped, sallow-eyed face that measures time
by the pint. But then with Jewel as a helpmate, it was
probably inevitable.

Parks paused before going farther into the house,
searching the hallway as if he wanted to avoid running
into his wife. While he did his reconnaissance, I took my
own look around. Given the decrepitude of the farm, I
was surprised at how well kept everything was inside.
What I could see of the place was like a page from the
Sunday supplement.

"Let's go to the study," Parks said, when he'd satisfied
himself that Jewel wasn't lurking around a corner. "It's
more private there."

We followed him down the hall to the study. I glanced
through a couple of open doors along the way. Every
room was the same—plump, pillowed contemporary
American furniture in floral designs, papered walls, shuttered windows, deep-pile carpeting on the floors. All of it
immaculately clean. Picture perfect.

The study was leaner and more masculine than the rest —an oak desk, with a ladder-back chair behind it and a captain's chair across from it, an oak sideboard with a pile of trophies on it, a few framed newspaper articles and photographs on the walls, and a couple of bookshelves full of Reader's Digest Condensed Books. Parks fit into the ladder-back chair like a tongue into a groove, planting both hands on his knees, straightening his neck and staring at the sideboard. Amid the trophies stood one lone fifth of whiskey. He glanced at it furtively, as if it were a pretty girl passing by.

"You boys want a drink?" he asked, when his thirst got the better of him. I could tell from his tone of voice that he didn't really want to pay our tab.

Otto shook his head.

I said, "No, but you go ahead."

Parks wet his lower lip and replied, "Well, maybe just the one."

He got up and went over to the sideboard, tipping the fifth back and studying its contents like a man studying the label of a wine. "Just let me get a glass," he said over his shoulder and walked out of the room, taking the bottle with him.

While he was gone, I walked over to the table full of trophies. They were arranged in tiers on the sideboard, like the layers of a wedding cake. The ones on the lowest level were for state wrestling championships, next higher up were weight-lifting trophies, and sitting on top was a silver punch bowl. I took a look at the inscription on its side: "Big Eight Lineman of the Year, William Parks, 1977."

"He should have won the Outland in seventy-eight," Parks said as he came back into the room. "He would have, too, if he hadn't torn his knee up halfway into the season. He missed six games and still made all–Big Eight. But it cost him." He dashed the whiskey bottle into a jelly glass he was holding in his right hand. "Christ, did it cost him."

Parks took his glass and bottle back to the desk and sat down again in the ladder-back chair. I sat down across from him and watched him drink. Bluerock leaned against the sideboard. Almost at once the whiskey took effect, reddening Parks's face and clearing his eyes. His hands stopped shaking too. He poured another ounce into the jelly glass and drank it in one swallow.

"Did you ever see Billy play?" he said to me. "On TV, maybe?"

I nodded. "Many times. He was good."

"He was better than that," Lew Parks said. "He was going to be one of the great ones. *If* he could've gotten his mind right. I don't know how many times I've told him that you play the game up here." Parks touched the glass to his forehead. "Ask any coach worth his salt— football's fifty, sixty percent mental. Of course, you gotta have the build for it, and God knows Billy's got the strength and size. But concentration, that's the key. You concentrate, you don't get hurt. Billy thinks it's all down here." He pinched his right bicep through the shirt sleeve. "That's why he popped his knee. That's why he didn't get drafted until the eighth round. Have any idea how much money that meant, getting drafted eighth round instead of first?"

"A goodly amount," I said.

"Hell, yes. A goodly amount." Parks began to cry. Just like that. Without any warning. Crying for what might have been. Crying a little bit, I thought, for all that money his son would never make. Although that might have been unfair.

I glanced at Bluerock. He was staring, shamefaced, at the carpet.

"Do you have any idea where he is, Mr. Parks," Bluerock said huskily. "It's important that we talk to him."

Parks looked up at us, tears streaming down his cheeks. He started to say something, when a voice from the hall said, "No!"

All three of us glanced at the doorway. Jewel Parks was standing there, scowling at her husband. She was a large woman, rawboned and running to fat. But unlike Parks, she wore the weight well. On him it looked sloppy; on her it added sensual appeal. A big-breasted, big-hipped woman with bobbed brown hair, a bee-stung mouth, and a fair-skinned, pretty, careworn face. She was wearing a white linen dress that crossed at her bosom and swept in thick folds around her belly. It was clear from the way she carried herself that she was used to being looked at by men, and that she liked it. She must have been something fifteen years before, I thought.

The surprising sensuousness of his wife made me reevaluate Parks. I hadn't really thought about it because of his gruffness and his booze, but he must have been a handsome, athletic kid himself, fifteen or twenty years before. He still had an athlete's frame—big shoulders and arms. But the flesh had sagged on the hanger, like an old suit with change left in the pockets. He looked ten years older than his wife and ready for middle age. He also looked as if he was aware of the difference and slightly cowed by it.

As soon as his wife came through the door he scrubbed his cheeks with his fists, as if she'd caught him doing something shameful.

"You might have offered these men a drink, Lew," she said as she swept into the room. Her voice was low and melodious, an odd complement to her husband's barking bass. "Seeing that they're whiskey drinkers like yourself."

"I did offer them a drink," Parks replied testily. "I'll offer them one again, if it suits you."

She didn't answer him. Instead, she stared directly at

Bluerock. "I know you," she said, giving him a fierce, reproachful look. "I know what you want, and you won't find it here."

"I can handle this, Jewel," Parks said feebly.

"No, you can't, Lew. You can't handle anything with a bottle in your hand."

Parks rattled in his chair, exactly as if she had laid her hands on his shoulders and shaken him violently. "Watch your mouth, Jewel," he said hoarsely. "I said I could handle it."

"Just like you handled Bill," she said. "Just like you handle everything else."

"Watch your mouth, Jewel," Parks said again. "I'm warning you."

The woman glared at him. "You're warning me," she said contemptuously. "Just take your bottle, Lew, and go outside and play with the animals."

For a moment I thought he was going to hit her. But, of course, he didn't. It was a scene they must have played out time and again, although the urgency of the situation made it seem particularly ugly. Giving his wife a vicious look, he snatched the whiskey bottle up by the neck and stalked out of the room.

Once Parks was gone, Jewel sat down on the corner of the desk and eyed each of us, in turn—malevolently, as if we were minions of Satan.

"Why did you come here?" she said. "What did you expect to find?"

"We want to help him, Mrs. Parks," Bluerock said.

"He's in danger," I said.

She laughed. "Danger?" She sucked her breath in sharply, as if the sight of us gave her pain. "*You* are the danger that my son is in. You and that awful woman who seduced him. You are the ones who led him astray. Who taught him evil habits."

"Try to understand this," I said. "Some men are coming to kill him. We have to find him, or else they *will* kill him."

"Lies!" she said stoutly. "He is God's perfect child, and Jesus will protect him."

"Not unless Jesus has a gun," Bluerock said under his breath.

The woman stood up suddenly and walked over to the sideboard. Bluerock leaped out of her way.

"I want you to see something," she said and pulled a framed picture off the wall. She stared at it for a second, then handed it to me.

It was a faded color picture of her and her husband taken in a prosperous year. They were standing in front of the farmhouse, which in the photo looked as solid as a castle. The woman was young and smiling, dressed in gingham, her sunlit hair blowing about her face. Lew Parks was grinning, too. He looked lean and handsome. A cap, tilted at a jaunty angle, sat on his head like a crown. Behind them the fields were tall with grass, turned yellow in the photo by age. Between them, a good-looking boy of about five or six stood smiling.

"Jesus will protect my son," she said. She pulled the picture from my hands and hugged it to her breasts. "My son," she said heavily. Her face bunched up, but she held back the tears by sheer force of will.

"Get out!" she shouted angrily. "Get out. And leave him alone. For God's sake, leave him alone. You've done enough to him, you and your kind. You've ruined his life. At least have the mercy to let him die in peace."

XXXIII

We left Jewel Parks alone in the study, clutching that sad memory to her chest. Lew Parks was sitting outside on the stoop, head bowed, the bottle of whiskey held loosely in one hand.

He didn't look up as we walked by him to the car. But as we started to drive away, he came running across the yard, waving his hands at us wildly.

"Slow down," I said to Bluerock.

Parks leaned in at my window, panting and sobbing. "He's in terrible trouble, isn't he?" he said. "My boy?"

I nodded. "The worst kind of trouble."

"You've got to help him," he said, looking desperately around him as if he were afraid *she* was listening in.

"We have to find him first," Bluerock said.

"He's at Mary Reno's house," he whispered. "On Big Flat." His lips trembled into a smile. "She used to be his girlfriend in high school. She's looking after him now."

"Where is Big Flat?" Bluerock said.

"Take Ninety-three back east, then turn north at Blue

Mountain. Sixty-six Big Flat. It's a nice house. She's a nice girl."

Bluerock gunned the motor, leaving the man standing there in the dust of the tires.

It was completely dark by the time we got to Big Flat Road—a two-lane highway running north along the base of Blue Mountain. To our left the mountain blocked the night sky. To our right the Missoula valley stretched out beneath us—a sprinkling of white lights in the far distance. The road was tree-lined, the oaks arching over the roadway from either embankment like a canopy. About three miles north of the 93 cutoff, we started to see houses to our right, perched on the ridge overlooking the valley. They were modern-looking ranches and A-frames—a hell of a lot more elaborate and more expensive than anything I'd seen in the town. Whoever Mary Reno was, she had some money.

The houses were clustered relatively close together, a little monied enclave dotted with spruce trees and pines. The first one in the group was number 60. It was set back a dozen yards from the roadway, with a cement driveway leading up to it. There were no lights on in the house. Sixty-one and two also looked deserted. But as we got closer to sixty-six, I could see a porch light twinkling in the darkness. There was a man standing on the front stoop of Mary Reno's small redwood A-frame. There were also two cars parked in the driveway leading to the carport.

"Goddamn it," I said, half to myself, knowing already that it was them. Knowing, as well, what that meant for Parks, and for Bluerock and me.

Bluerock started to slow down as we neared the Reno house.

"Keep going!" I shouted at him.

He glanced at me nervously and pressed the accelerator.

By the time we passed sixty-six we were going at a pretty good clip. The man on the stoop watched us as we whizzed by. I could see his face clearly in the headlights. It was Mickey—big, dumb Mickey. He was holding something in his right hand. He tried to hide it as we came near him, but I got a glimpse of the rectangular barrel and the long cylindrical grip extending beneath it.

"Christ," I said. "He's got a Mac-Ten."

"What's a Mac-10?" Bluerock said.

"A machine pistol."

"Shit," Bluerock said grimly. "A machine gun."

We kept driving for a half mile beyond Mary Reno's home. We came to a roadside turnaround, and I told Bluerock to pull over.

"This is all wrong," I said to him when we stopped. "We have no idea who's in that house or what they're packing."

"Bill's in that house," he said with anguish in his voice. "We've got to go back."

The sane part of me was saying, Wait them out. Wait until they've finished with Bill. But the sane part also knew that if Parks was in there, the girlfriend was in there too. Mary Reno. And I knew perfectly well what they would do to her, how they would arrange it to make it look as if Bill had butchered her and then killed himself. Another dead girl, like C.W. Like Laurel. I thought about that for a minute more and went cold inside. I simply couldn't let it happen again. I couldn't sit back and wait for them to finish.

I stared into Bluerock's anguished face. "I'll go back there alone," he said to me, "if I have to."

"You will, will you?" I said, smiling at his bravado.

"Yes," he said fiercely.

I took a deep breath and felt it all melt away—all logic,

all constraint, all sanity. "Fuck it," I said to him. "I guess it's as good a day as any to die."

"That's the spirit," Otto said with a laugh, and pounded me on the shoulder.

We were both out of control by then. Two good buddies out on a little hunt in the big dark woods. It was suicidal madness, and yet I couldn't have stopped it if I'd wanted to. And I didn't want to.

"Are we going to kick some ass?" Bluerock said, putting on his game face.

"I guess we are," I said, putting on mine.

I reached into the back seat and got the shotguns. They were Winchester pumps. I loaded five shells in each. Took a handful of shells and stuffed them in my pants pocket. Bluerock took an ammunition box in his mitt and shoved it inside his shirt. I had one extra loaded clip for the .45. I stuck it in my other pants pocket. I pumped one of the shotguns, flipped the safety off, and laid it on the seat beside Bluerock. Then I cocked the other one and flipped the safety off.

"The best way to do it is to go straight through the front door," I said, fighting like hell to think straight. "If we dick around trying to find some tricky way in there, we're probably going to get killed before we get inside."

"Straight in," Bluerock said, and swallowed hard.

I took a big deep breath. "Pull up in the driveway and park behind the last car. We have to take Mickey out first. Get out of the car and shoot him. Aim low. Try to hit him in the middle of the body. You've got five shots, so don't waste any. And reload as quickly as you can. You do know how to load that thing?"

He nodded.

"Once we knock Mickey down, we go straight through the door. Blow the damn thing off its hinges and go straight in, like a narcotics bust. For chrissake, don't waste time. Straight through the door. Shoot anything that shoots back."

"Anything?"

"We don't have time to ask questions, Blue."

"What about Bill? And the girl?"

"They'll have to take their chances. They've got a better shot at surviving us than they do of surviving what Walt has planned for them."

"Who goes in first?" he said.

"Whoever gets to the door first."

"Okay," he said. "Let's do it."

XXXIV

Bluerock started up the engine, put the car in gear, then turned in his seat to face me.

"It's been good knowing you, sport," he said with his bulldog look. "I owe you a drink or two after this is over."

"We'll get drunk as hell," I told him.

He turned back to the steering wheel, put one hand on it, and grabbed the shotgun in the other.

Blue eased the car out on the highway, backed into the turnaround, and headed south toward Mary Reno's house.

In less than a minute I could see the light on the porch, glimmering through the pine trees. Then I could see the porch itself, and Mickey standing there. He lowered his arms when he saw our headlights—to hide the machine gun. The door behind him was situated in the middle of the A-frame window. The window was heavily draped, but there were lights on inside, filtering through the muslin folds of the curtains.

Bluerock slowed down as he got close to the driveway. I clutched the shotgun in one hand and grabbed the door handle in the other. As we turned into the driveway, Mickey took a step off the porch. He peered at us quizzically, squinting through the headlights.

My heart was pounding so hard I could feel it in my throat. Bluerock pulled to a stop and I shouted, "Go!"

As soon as he opened the car door, Bluerock dived to the ground, rolling across the grass yard to his left. Mickey raised the machine pistol to his hip and trained it on Blue. By then I was out of the car with the shotgun at my shoulder. I fired as soon as the shotgun barrel cleared the roof of the car. The butt of the shotgun slammed back into my shoulder and the muzzle flash looked as if it extended all the way to where Mickey was standing. The roar of the piece was incredible—like a thunderclap.

I'd aimed low—too low. The pellets hit Mickey below the knees, taking a bite out of the pavement that he was standing on and raising a cloud of cement dust and shrapnel, as if a grenade had gone off at his feet. Mickey fell backward, firing the machine gun as he went down. The gun made a vicious rattling *brrapp!*, spewing fire like the shotgun. The bullets flapped through the pine trees with a sound like a flock of birds taking flight.

I saw Bluerock leap to his feet. Then I was around the car and heading for the front door. I almost tripped over Mickey as I ran to the stoop. It didn't register at that moment, but one of his feet had been blown off at the ankle and was still standing, in its shoe, on the cement walk. There was blood everywhere on the walk and the grass.

As he came up to the door Bluerock fired the shotgun from his hip. The wood exploded as if it had been hit by a wrecking ball, leaving a gaping hole in its center. Shoulder down, Blue crashed through the hole, firing as he went. I was right behind him.

The blast of his shotgun had smashed a table lamp on the far wall. It was sparking like a firecracker on its broken base. One of the drapes had begun to smolder, and there was already a good deal of smoke in the room. I fired one blast to my left as I came through the door, tearing a hole in an overstuffed sofa. And another blast straight in front of me. I didn't see Walt or Habib but I knew they were firing back at us. I could hear the *brrapp* of a machine pistol and the whizz and pop of the bullets as they shattered furnishings and windows and tattooed the plaster walls. I dived to the floor behind the sofa. I could see Bluerock crawling behind a table a couple of yards to the right of me. I shoved a few more rounds in the shotgun. Pumped it and came up, firing.

I hit someone on the far side of the room. I heard him groan and cry out, "I'm hit!"

I pumped again and kept firing in the direction of the cries. There was so much noise and so much smoke in the room that there was no way to pick a target. I fired at the sound of the guns and at the shifting shapes in the smoke. I fired five times, dived back down behind the sofa to reload, and felt my right arm go numb. I didn't know how many times I'd been hit—I didn't even know, until then that I had been hit. But when I looked down at my body, I saw that the right half of my shirt, from shoulder to wrist, was soaked with blood. I sat behind the sofa, breathing hard and listening to the machine pistol go off again and a shotgun roar. I pulled the Colt out of my belt with my left hand and stood up, firing at the muzzle flash of the machine pistol. I fired seven times, flipped out the empty clip and slammed in the fresh one with my bad hand, firing seven more times into the smoke and wreckage. It wasn't until I'd squeezed off the last shot that I realized that I was the only one still firing.

I threw the pistol to the floor, scooped up the shotgun, braced it against my left leg, and pumped it with one hand. I started across the room, but my legs wouldn't hold me, and I went down heavily on my knees.

I must have sat there for a full minute, listening to the dead silence of the room, watching the smoke swirling and sliding along the floor. There was a police siren wailing in the distance. It was another minute before I realized that they were headed our way.

I tried to get up again, but I couldn't stand. I'd lost too much blood. I crawled back toward the door, using the butt of the shotgun to pull me along. Somewhere in the chaos of the room something made a thud. If it was Walt or Habib, there was no way I could protect myself any longer, so I didn't worry about it. I kept crawling, back to the spot where I'd last seen Bluerock.

He was still there, lying faceup behind the table, the shotgun in his hands. I couldn't tell if he was alive or not, but he'd been hit full in the chest. There was blood pulsing out of his shirt. There was blood everywhere— on his face and on the floor around him.

I stared at him sadly and wondered what had happened to his friend Parks in all that smoke and madness —to the man for whom he had given his life. Something made a noise to my right. I looked up, dizzily, expecting to see a gun barrel pointed at me. Instead, I saw a cop, pistol in hand, staring into the room with a look of shock on his face. He was the last thing I saw before I passed out.

XXXV

They took me to a hospital in Missoula. I'd been hit three times. Once in the right shoulder. Once in the right hand. And once in the side. I should have died, the doctor told me. Like Bluerock.

He had been declared dead on the scene. Him, Mickey, Walt, and Habib. And Clayton, too. Phil Clayton. Nobody seemed to know what he'd been doing there. Whether he was negotiating with Walt or trying to entrap him. The Cincinnati Police finally decided the matter by choosing to make a hero out of him. And out of me too.

They sent Al Foster up personally to tell me the good news. By then I'd been in the hospital for two weeks, and my wounds had healed sufficiently to allow me to be wheeled around by a pretty, no-nonsense nurse named Flo.

Al found me in the hospital cafeteria, sitting in my wheelchair.

"How ya doing, Harry?" he said, sitting down across from me at the table.

I did a double take and smiled at him. "I've been better."

"I hear you lost a foot of intestine," he said.

"And a piece of my palm." I waved my bandaged hand at him.

"That's tough." He looked at me for a moment and shook his head. "You're crazy, you know that?"

I nodded at him.

"You here to take me back?" I said.

"I'm here to decorate you," he said.

"You're kidding."

"Nope. You've got some friends in high places. Even old George stuck his neck out on this one. And your friend Petrie at the Cougars too. George is going to testify that he swore you in as a special deputy before you left town—you and that guy, Bluerock. And Petrie is going to pick up the tab for your medical expenses. You're a lucky guy."

"A lucky guy," I said with a laugh.

"The bad news is that Clayton's getting a medal, too. His last one, thank God. Six, two, and even, he was up here planning to sell Parks out. After that, I don't know what he had in mind. Some double cross, probably, that would have snared Walt Kaplan and made Phil look like a hero." Al pulled a cigarette out of his shirt pocket. "And now he is a hero. The way we're going to tell it, he was with you when you busted Kaplan. He was on your side and got killed in the shoot-out."

"That stinks," I said angrily. "For all I know, he shot me. Or Bluerock."

"I know, Harry," Al said soothingly. "But it's just too ugly the other way."

I stared at him for a moment. "I'm not going to go for it, Al. When I get home, I'm telling the truth. I owe it to Bluerock."

He sighed. "Think about it, Harry. You're not going to

do Bluerock any good now. And you're going to make bad trouble for yourself."

"I can stand a little trouble," I said.

He laughed. "So it would appear."

We sat there for a while, talking. When Al got up to leave, I asked him what had happened to Parks. No one at the hospital had been willing to tell me, although I'd questioned a dozen people.

"He's right here," Foster said. "Up on the third floor in the psychiatric ward. He's got nothing left upstairs, according to the doctors. And he's got terminal cancer to boot. They can't ship him back to Cincinnati to stand trial unless he goes into remission. And the chances are that that's not going to happen."

"How long's he been here?" I said.

"Since the day you got shot. Apparently he got sick that morning and some friend of his, some woman, brought him into the Emergency Room." Foster smiled. "Bill gotta break there—or, at least, his girlfriend did. Because from what we can piece together Walt and Phil showed up at the woman's home right after she and Parks left. They didn't know he'd been hospitalized. They'd figured he'd gone out and that he'd be back later in the night."

"Instead, we showed up," I said, savoring the blackness of the joke. "We did it all for nothing."

"Sorry, but that's the way it figures," Al said with a mordant grin. He got to his feet. "So long, Harry." He raised his hand. "See you in the papers."

"So long, Al," I said.

Later that afternoon, when Flo was busy tending another ward, I worked my way out of bed, got into the wheelchair, and wheeled myself out to the elevators. The ugly little irony that Al had left on my plate had begun to stink. We'd done it for nothing. For sport. For the sake of a stupid locker room code. And Blue had ended up dead. And Clayton had ended up a hero. And Parks . . . I just wanted to see him—once. To let him know how much his friend had sacrificed to keep him alive. Only they wouldn't let me talk to him when I got to the psychiatric ward. Just stare at him from a distance, as if I were still a spectator in the stands. I could see him from the nurses' station at the far end of the ward. He was in a steel frame bed beneath a big barred window. The sun was shining through the window, lighting up a patch of floor and the sheet on the bed. His mother was sitting in the shadow beside his bed, reading from a book in her lap. She looked at Parks now and again. He looked at nothing. He was staring at the wall across from his bed, out the far window, at the blue sunlit sky. His face looked ravaged, thin and sunken. His eyes said nothing. They just stared out at the distant mountains beyond the barred hospital window.

XXXVI

It was almost fall by the time I was released from the hospital. The first person I called when I got back to Cincinnati was Mike Sabatto at the *Post*. Somebody needed to know the truth, although I wasn't sure he'd print it. But somebody needed to know.

He agreed to meet me at the Busy Bee. I showed up about a half hour early and went over to the bar to say hello to Hank Greenburg.

He smiled affectionately at me as I sat down at the bar.

"Long time no see," he said, pouring me a Scotch and pouring one for himself. "I'm glad you're back, Harry. I'm glad you're okay."

I smiled at him.

He raised his glass in a toast. "Who we drinking to?"

"To Otto Bluerock," I said, picking up my glass.

"He used to play football, didn't he?"

"Yeah."

"I think I read where he got killed."

"Yeah," I said. "He got killed."

"To Otto Bluerock, then," Hank said, downing the Scotch in a gulp and smacking the glass down on the bar. "Hail and farewell."

L